Niles Public
Library District

6960 Oakton Street
Niles, Illinois 60648

STEVE PERRY

ACE BOOKS, NEW YORK

This book is an Ace original edition,
and has never been previously published.

BLACK STEEL

An Ace Book / published by arrangement with
the author

PRINTING HISTORY
Ace edition / February 1992

ISBN: 0-441-06698-4

Ace Books are published by The Berkley Publishing Group,
200 Madison Avenue, New York, New York 10016.
The name "ACE" and the "A" logo
are trademarks belonging to Charter Communications, Inc.

PRINTED IN THE UNITED STATES OF AMERICA

10 9 8 7 6 5 4 3 2 1

For Dianne;
And for Allen Kijek, who
showed us how a brave man dies.
Thanks for the salmon, Al,
and for the lesson.

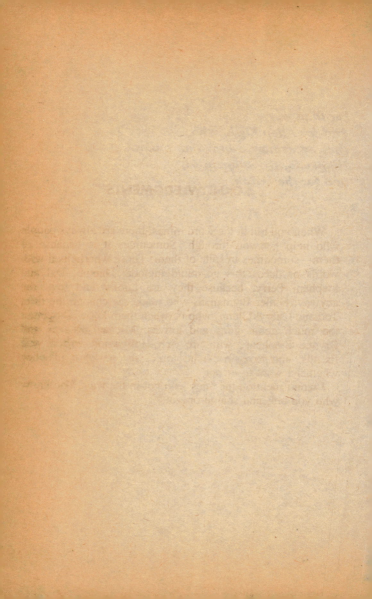

ACKNOWLEDGMENTS

When you toil in the word mines, there are always people who help get you through. Sometimes it is because of them—sometimes in spite of them. Those who helped with words or deeds this go-round include: Dianne, Dal and Stephani Perry, because they are family and love me anyway; Ginjer Buchanan, who made me change the title; Tod and Cheryl Glenn, who between them know altogether too much about guns and knives; Michael Reaves and Brynne Stephens, who are rich Hollywood writers and friends; and Roxanne, who forces me to learn patience whether I want to or not.

I won't mention the ones who got in the way. You know who you are, and shame on you. . . .

"Once swords are crossed the gun becomes useless."

—*Miyamoto Musashi*

"Anyone who does not fear death himself can inflict it."

—*Niccolo Machiavelli*

Part One
Black Steel

ONE

DEATH CAME FOR him by mistake.

Sleel had left the commercial hopper and was walking in the shade under the protective gamp toward the airport terminal when a woman with a sword stepped out of a darker shadow. There were other people moving under the billowy canopy, but Sleel knew immediately that the swordswoman had come for him.

"Stupid," Sleel said, shaking his head. He was wearing the matador uniform, dark gray orthoskins, spun dotic boots, and bilateral spetsdöds. The would-be assassin was a good eight meters away. She wasn't a big woman, but size didn't mean much when it came to this kind of thing; it was ability that counted. Still, even if he suddenly went blind, Sleel could hit her before she moved a meter. She wasn't flashing a projectile weapon around; she'd have to get close to use that blade, and that was just plain foolish. And because it was so suicidal, it made Sleel think again. Maybe she had a partner? Since she didn't have a prayer of getting to Sleel before she ate a load of shocktox, something was definitely wrong with this picture.

Sleel scanned the people around him, extended his perception to its fullest, searching for another enemy. Overhead the neosilk gamp fluttered in the tropical afternoon breeze, making tent noises. Some of the other passengers on the flight had taken notice of the fem with the sword and were viewing her with alarm. The smell of hot plastcrete rose and mingled with the hopper's fuel exhaust residue and machine lube from the luggage carrier that rolled past in the Hawaiian sunshine. The air was heavy with humidity and warm even under the canopy. Just another day in paradise, right?

If there were others lining up to attack him, Sleel couldn't spot them. Could it be just the one woman? Was she really that stupid, to think she could just stroll over and carve one of the galaxy's best bodyguards, just like that? Somebody who outgunned her with two fully loaded spetsdöds to her sword?

Apparently so. The swordswoman smiled, a thin-lipped and tight expression. She had chocolate skin and very white teeth, with red-brown hair curled tightly into a cap over her skull. She wore freight handler's coveralls with the sleeves rolled up, and there was a tattoo on her left upper arm a couple of centimeters above her elbow. The sword was about a meter long, slightly curved, thicker than a foil but thinner than a saber. Some kind of shiny handguard protected the grip. The blade was black. Maybe it was stacked carbon or squashed plastic to be that color. Maybe she was wearing body armor under the coverall; maybe she thought that would protect her.

Lotta maybes here. The fem wanted him to see her coming, that was obvious. Otherwise she could have just waited until Sleel passed and skewered him from behind. The swordswoman couldn't miss seeing the spetsdöds, and yet she was willing to go up against them with nothing more than what was essentially a real long knife, its use limited to arm's-length range. She had to have a reason to believe she had a chance of making it. What?

Sleel took it all in as he stopped and stood, waiting.

The assassin started to move toward Sleel. She managed half a step before Sleel snapped up his left hand and fired his spetsdöd. The little back-of-the-hand dartgun gave a dry cough and spat a missile loaded with shocktox. The tiny dart hit the swordplayer on the forehead directly above the bridge of her nose. Right between the eyes.

So much for that.

The swordplayer blinked but kept coming.

Sleel frowned.

The bodyguard fired thrice more, one dart for each of the assassin's hands, one for the tattoo.

Nothing. The woman kept coming. She was almost close enough to swing the sword. She was laughing soundlessly now.

Well, *shit*! Should have gone for the eyes—

Sleel dodged, letting his body flow into the Ninety-seven Steps, his feet describing the last dance of Bamboo Pond, his hand lifting for the natural flow into Arc of Air, reacting with the proper patterns to the shape of the attack. It was almost a reflex after so many years of practice.

The assassin twisted, altered her cut, and tried to follow Sleel. She was pretty good with that blade. Sleel ducked as the sword slashed the air over his head. The matador skipped into Neon Chain, and drove his fist into the woman's left kidney with more force than he'd intended. Fear did that to a man, and anger at being made afraid added power to the strike.

The swordswoman staggered, and Sleel finished the dance by shifting to Helicopter, spinning and hammering the woman's temple with the edge of his knotted hand.

The assassin fell, the sword clattering onto the plastcrete. The blade rang like metal when it hit.

A man yelled something hoarsely, and a woman cursed.

Sleel spun, looking for more attackers. There were none.

He came up from his defensive crouch. There was a sharp gingery smell in the air, some local pollen, probably, that reminded him of his childhood. All of a moment, he felt like he was nine years old. He shook the feeling. He had other things to worry about. Like:

What the fuck was this all about?

The port cools were apologetic as to how the would-be assassin had gotten past them. Sleel showed them his ID cube and his permit for his weapons, but they were more interested in the their own loss of face. How'd a fem with a fucking unsecured *sword* get into the passenger area?

Sleel on the other hand wanted to know why the woman had come at him. And how the still-unconscious woman had taken four shocktox darts and kept coming. That was why the fem had been smiling before she'd moved; she'd known the spetsdöds wouldn't stop her. Maybe she hadn't known that matadors were as adept with their bodies as their handguns. Or maybe she'd thought the sword made up for it. Whatever, it made for a nasty surprise. Sleel remembered Dirisha saying something once about some world where people worked with poison fish and had developed a kind of immunity to certain spetsdöd chems. Maybe that was it.

Fucking *lot* of maybes here, Sleel. Best you clear some of them up before they get you killed.

"You Sleel?" came a small voice.

Sleel looked down to see a little girl of about eight standing there. A port rat. He restrained himself from pointing one of his spetsdöds at her. "Yeah. So?"

"Got a message for you. Jersey Reason is waiting outside."

Jersey Reason? Here on the Big Island? And how did he know Sleel was here?

Questions, more questions. It was like being back in primary edcom, with the holographic teacher yammering at you. Sleel flipped the little girl a five-stad coin. She snatched it from the air, grinned, and took off.

Outside Sleel spotted the flitter, an armored rig with protected fans. Whoever had built the thing had done a good job of it; somebody less adept than Steel probably wouldn't have immediately spotted the spidersilk plate and denscris windows.

Sleel also recognized Jersey Reason, though he'd only met the man once and that almost a year past. The old geep had suckered them with his defenses, though at the end Sleel had seen through the holoproj. He looked pretty much the same as Sleel remembered, short, almost tiny, with thick white hair and a short beard, also white. Too much light from various suns had damaged his skin and he was wrinkled and tanned, crinkled smile lines framing his pale blue eyes. Reason stood next to the armored flitter, alone.

"Sleel," he said. As it had before, the deepness of his voice came as a surprise.

"Reason."

"You had some trouble inside." Not a question.

"Nothing to speak of. Not a test of yours, was it? You like to play games, I remember right."

"No, she wasn't mine," Reason allowed. "Although I'm

surely responsible. She probably thought you were coming to help me and wanted to make a point by killing you."

"Now why would she want to do that?"

Reason smiled, showing perfect teeth. "Want to take a little ride?"

"Sure."

Inside the flitter, Reason said, "Got a place to stay?"

"Not yet. I thought I'd surprise myself."

The flitter lifted in a blast of wind and tilted forward on its cushion of air, moving smoothly out into the traffic.

"I have a house in Old Kona," Reason said. "You can stay there. Plenty of room."

Steel shook his head. "Hey, this is a great song and shuffle routine and all, but why don't you fill in the gaps here?"

"Ever direct, aren't you? When we met the first thing you did was shoot me with a spetsdöd."

"No, I shot a holoproj *image* of you to prove it was a fake."

"That's why I'm here. Your ability to cut through what was an almost perfect illusion intrigued me then and it still does now. I need your help."

"Keep talking."

"Somebody wants to kill me. I'd like for you to keep them from doing it."

Sleel nodded. Well. He was a matador; that's what he did. "I don't work cheap."

"I know. Money is not a problem."

"All right."

"Just like that? No questions?"

"Oh, I got lots of questions, but they'll keep. Pull over at that intersection, next to the used flitter lot."

"Why?"

"Since money isn't a problem, we're gonna buy another vehicle."

"What on Earth for?"

"Because I haven't had time to check this one out. The thing with hiring me is, you do what I say when it comes to security; that's the only way I can shade the odds our way."

Reason nodded. He guided the flitter to a stop.

"I get out first, you don't until I say it's okay."

Reason nodded again.

Sleel stepped out and looked around. Nobody obvious was following them. The sunshine was warm, the smell of local flora thick, mixed with the more acrid stinks of civilization. He waited for thirty seconds, scanning the surroundings. Nothing. "Okay, let's go," he said.

As the two of them moved into the used flitter lot, Sleel felt an urge to smile. He hadn't worked for almost six months and still had enough stads to go another half a year before he had to find a job, but this was the right thing to do. Reason had helped them when they needed it; fair was fair. Things had been slow since Sleel and the others had helped Emile kill Marcus Wall—again.

"Pick something in a nice color," Sleel said, gesturing at the flitters and ground carts parked around them. "And tell me about the woman with the sword."

Reason drove, Sleel watched for danger. The flitter was a couple of seasons old, low klickage, and while not armored, unlikely to be rigged for a bomb or any electronic listening devices. Somebody could retrieve the other flitter later when Sleel had time to check it out.

"This is the third attacker with a sword," Reason said. "The first one showed up on my island in Puget Sound three weeks ago. He somehow got past all my perimeter defenses and into my house. He didn't see through my holoproj like you did—I've improved the image, by the way—and I had him immobilized for questioning when he came to. I used a mild form of sleeptox, but he didn't wake up, he died."

"Unusual," Sleel said.

"It certainly surprised me. Not as much as the failure of my wards to keep him out. I figured that if one man could get that far it might be a good idea to move until I found the problem in my security systems."

"Good thinking."

"I have several houses on this planet. One of them is in Australia, almost in the middle of nowhere. Nearest neighbor is ten klicks away. I didn't tell anybody I was going there. One afternoon a week after I arrived, another swordsman showed up. He had bypassed my outer security devices and was busy kicking my door in when I triggered a zap field."

"Real interesting. Lemme guess. This one didn't wake up either."

"Correct."

"Hmm. Can they do a brain squeeze on an unconscious person?"

"The woman?"

"Yeah."

Reason nodded. "I don't know. But I have some . . . influence with the local authorities. I'll see what can be done." He reached for the flitter's com and waved it on. After a few moments, they were linked with Reason's "influence" in the neighborhood coolshop.

"Ah, M. Reason," the female voice said. The voice was deep, throaty, and had a nice tone to it. Although the flitter was equipped with full com gear, the transmission was nopix from the other end. "I was just about to call you."

"Officer Bligh. You were going to call for . . . ?"

"The woman who tried the matador at the port. It's the strangest thing. She's dead."

Reason glanced at Sleel. He said, "A pity. Find out what you can about her, would you? I would much appreciate it."

"Surely."

The contact was broken.

"Well, well," Sleel said. Then, "This cool on your payroll?"

"No. I did her a favor once and she is grateful."

Sleel didn't pursue that.

"This is your area of expertise," Reason said. They were floating along past a riot of plant life, thick tropical greenery splashed with bright orange and red and blue flowers. To their right lay the ocean, and a thin line of breakers washed up on the rocky shore below the road. "What do we do now?"

"We go to your house, check it out, and wait until your friend the cool gives us something to go on. You have any enemies you want to tell me about?"

Reason laughed. "I was a thief for more than half a century before I got out of the biz," he finally managed. "After the

Confed fell, it wasn't as much fun as it had been. If all the people mad at me for what I took were to line up, they'd probably reach to the horizon. And those are just the ones who suspect I had something to do with it. I expect that the ones who are certain, men, women and mues, wouldn't lose a second of sleep if I shuffled off into the final chill."

Sleel nodded. "Okay. So we have to narrow that down a little. It probably isn't a conspiracy of all of them; we just need to find the right ones."

Reason laughed some more. "You're an optimist, Sleel."

"Yeah, well, dead bosses don't pay real well. You have to look on the positive side."

Sleel grinned. So this one might be hard. That was good. No point in doing easy stuff. He always liked it better when the odds were against him. You couldn't show anything if a job was going to be a walk in the country.

What was the point in being the best unless people could see it?

TWO _____

RIFT, IN THE Delta System, lies dozens of light years away from Earth, normally a six-day trip by Bender drive. It is one of three planets in the system, the other two being Lee and Thompson's Gazelle. Rift is also the least civilized of the trio, exports mainly certain technologies involved in waste recycling, and has upon it three major land masses, unoriginally called the Greater, the Middle and the Lesser Continents. Upon the Lesser Continent is the old Romantic Enclave, and deep therein a fair-sized hereditary estate known as *La Casa del Acero Negro*.

The House of Black Steel.

In the main gymnasium Hoja Cierto dodged the simulacrum's cut and V-stepped to his left with his return strike. The lac's parry blocked Cierto's blade with a convincing ring of steel on steel, and the vibration might be ersatz but in the boosted *sturz* field, Cierto felt it nonetheless. He spun away as the lac stabbed at him with its cutlass. The computer's gain was rigged to illegal standards and turned up to full; should the lac's weapon get through his guard, the pain would be as real as that of an actual sword. A fatal strike would be just as deadly to Cierto, who wore no protection, and who was in fact naked save for his sword and a groin strap. He danced away from the lac's stab and follow-up four-step attack: head cut, heart stab, back and forth slash, and lunge for the groin. The lac was programmed to the ability of an expert human in superb condition, and would be considered a worthy opponent for a top player in most styles of fencing. The lac used most of the power of a mainframe viral matrix for its moves, and could be adjusted to the rules of classical foil, épée or saber, kendo, the Indo hard-knife, *keras pisau*, or *wojanaz*, the Polay war-blade, among others. On open-program as it now was, it was allowed use of any of these techniques. The only requirement was that it alter its appearance if it changed modes, offering a half-second or so of warning.

The lac T-stepped in and shimmered, changing colors, and suddenly it held *two* blades, one in each hand.

Such was not cheating, since Chinese split-sword was within its programming, but to go from facing an opponent with a cutlass to one with twice the armament was certainly apt to give a man pause. Perhaps fatally so.

Not Cierto. Instantly he dropped to his left side under the lac's whirling figure-eight slicings and whipped his own weapon out in a flat arc ten centimeters above the floor. He felt the muscles of his lat and shoulder burn with the effort. Everything he had went into the cut. So sharp was the *zhaverfrayshtol* sword's edge that the blade sheared completely through the lac's left ankle. Before the surprised lac could finish its crippled fall, Cierto rolled, came up, and drove the point of his sword up under the lac's sternum, skewering its heart. There was a convincing spurt of blood as the man jerked his weapon free and the lac crumpled to the floor. Were it a man, it would be dead.

The lac shimmered and vanished as Cierto stood. He saluted the fading simulacrum by bringing the flat of his sword to his forehead before snapping the weapon down in the ritual slinging of blood. This was hardly necessary, since the blood disappeared along with the lac, but it was part of the technique. Then he turned to face the fifteen students gathered around the perimeter of the fighting ring. Perspiration rolled down Cierto's muscular body and his heart beat rapidly, but he smiled at his students. The smell of his own sweat was high, and he was tight, especially in the shoulders and arms from swinging the sword, but he was alive.

"Miguel. What have I demonstrated?"

"That you are without peer, Patrón."

"This is true, but not the answer I seek. Juanita?"

"You have demonstrated that you can defeat even a man who cheats."

"Also true, señorita, but the wrong answer. Josito?"

"Once the sword is drawn there are no rules."

Cierto nodded. "Ah, at last the correct response. None of the classical styles offer the ankle as a target for the sword; nearly all of the sport styles limit attacks to the upper body. In sport you play by the rules. In combat to the death, there are no rules. Opponents without feet can hardly chase you around and once down, become lesser threats. They might still kill you if they are adept in ground attacks or defenses, but you will have an advantage if you know how to take it."

He wiped sweat from his eyes. "When I was much younger and less skilled, my own left foot had to be regrown due to this very same strike when I dueled with another who also walked the Masashi Flex. I was fortunate to survive. It was not a lesson to be forgotten."

Josito said, "What of this opponent, Patrón?"

Cierto's smile thinned. "I was defeated, but my opponent was weak and so allowed me to live. This was a mistake—someday there will be another match."

Cierto's smile returned to full brightness. "Josito, since you have understood the lesson, you have therefore earned the right to be next misionero. You are now *Proyectil Sacro*."

The young man flushed with sudden joy and pride. "Patrón! You honor me!"

"Sí. Do not dishonor our house by failure. As the Holy Missile, you have a great responsibility. Other projectiles before you have failed to reach their target and since we have not heard from Karenita, we must assume that she, too, has been unsuccessful."

"I will not fail, Patrón!"

"Such is my hope."

When the students had filed out, Cierto wiped the perspiration from his body with a towel, cleaned the oils of his hand from the grip of the sword, and wiped the blade with a small square of cotton victoria cloth. Again, this was unnecessary, since the blood upon the blade had been but imaginary, a computer-generated falsity without substance. Plus the ebony metal of the sword itself, the unique *zhaverfrayshtol*, was virtually immune to staining. The blade had been folded over and hand-hammered in a manner similar to the old Damascus and Japanese styles of hot forging; the secret formula for the black steel thus worked had been handed down from Patrón to Patrón for centuries, not too long after mankind had first left the Earth. The body of the slightly curved blade would bend almost seventy degrees without breaking, it was as the finest spring steel, while the edge was tempered by the use of special ceramic clays that made it hard enough once it had been sharpened to score virtually anything less than diamond. The secret had belonged to Cierto's house for two hundred and forty-five years.

A wave of emotion as black as the sword he cleaned came over Cierto. No longer was the formula the secret of the House of Black Steel. Fifty-five years earlier the method had been stolen, in the time of Cierto's grandfather. The old man had been only a few years away from his death, and it had fallen to his son, Cierto's father, to find and punish the thieves. He had begun the task but had died before it had been accomplished. It had taken Cierto nearly a decade to finish the search. A score of men and women had been killed to uncover the names of the thieves who had dared trespass upon the House of Black Steel. There had been five of them. Only one remained alive, and he was resourceful; but with luck, he would soon join the others.

Oddly enough, there had been no mention of any usage of this particular kind of black steel anywhere in the known galaxy. There were many ways to make metal dark, of course, from dyes to heat treating to the addition of certain minerals, but no other that produced the weapon-grade material used in the casa's swords. Cierto had a computerfax firm searching, and while the material was best suited for the making of perfect swords or knives, there were certainly other uses for such a substance. The reward he offered for information pertaining to this subject was quite large. As far as he had been able to find out, the secret had never come to light elsewhere. That was good. When the last thief met his end, perhaps the secret would once again belong to none other than the House of Black Steel.

He looked at the weapon he held. The metal was indeed black, but not a flat black. There were lighter and darker streaks, wavy lines, where the folding that made the many hammered layers showed. It seemed to make the blade glow in rich, dark shades from point to guard. The hilt was a broad curved band of nickel-stainless steel, mirror bright to contrast with the blade, and the handle was of curlnose tusk, burnished smooth, the ivory gone a buttery yellow with age and use, fastened to the full tang with chrome-blued bolts. The sword had belonged originally to his father's father's father, had cost a month in the life of a master craftsman to produce, and was priceless. Certain wealthy collectors of such weaponry would give nearly everything they owned for such a piece as this, hundreds of thousands of standards, without a moment's hesitation. And unlike a museum item, this was still an active blade, bathed in the flesh and blood of more than a hundred men and women. A score of those killed had been by Cierto's own hand, weaving a shroud of fatal thickness. Cierto did not think the sword of his great-grandfather had an equal anywhere in the galaxy.

And if he could help it, it never would.

In a small Place of the Way, a *dojo* on Koji, the Holy World, a woman sat *seiza* in the middle of a large room. Save for herself, the room was empty of other life; empty too, was the woman's mind as she meditated upon the Void. The floor upon which she knelt was of highly polished zebrawood, the planking chosen and laid in such a way as to create large zigzag patterns. The woman wore *hakima*, a long split skirt of white silk, and a *gi*-style black silk shirt with three-quarter sleeves. Next to her on the floor, handle nearly touching her left knee, was a *katana*-patterned sword, edge outward, point to the rear, nestled inside a wooden sheath with twenty-three coats of white lacquer upon it. The blade of the curved sword was of black steel, hand-hammered in the old method; the handle was of pebbled ray hide, crisscrossed in the traditional manner with the diamond-wrap turnings of black silk cord, enclosed at the butt with a plain cap of stainless steel; the guard, too, was a circle of solid stainless steel the diameter of a small teacup, bearing a simple etching on one side. The weapon was four hundred years old; it had seen much use and it had dealt in both life and death, sparing more often than it had slain. It had come to the woman from her older sister, who had died during the overthrow of the Confed six years past. Before that, it had belonged to their mother, received as a wedding gift from her mother.

The woman meditated upon the Void. Next to her the sword lay waiting. In a moment she would pick up the sheathed weapon and it would be freed in an eyeblink to move through the intricate motions of *Kaji-te*, the *kata* called "Fire Hand." In a moment. But for now, the sword waited as its mistress meditated upon her entrance into the Void—a sword which had been made with such precision and care it had hardly an equal in all the galaxy.

Sleel looked around the house owned by Jersey Reason with grudging approval. He'd seen better private security, but not much better and not at many places. The house sat in the middle of a large lot—that had to be very expensive, given real estate prices on Hawaii—with clear views to the property lines in all directions. To the west lay the sea, to the east the road, and other houses bordered the north and south edges of the lot. A line of banana trees and other tropical foliage partially hid an electric come-see-me fence, but there were no trees close enough to offer a way over the three-meter-tall mesh. A locked gate to the front and one to the rear were the only ways through the fence.

"Here's the security console," Reason said.

Sleel nodded and looked at the setup. Overlapping sensor fields from permanent units buried under the ground covered every centimeter of the property, and any one could be disabled without losing a full scan. Zap fields could be triggered to cover the doors and windows; the house itself was hardwired to note circuit interruptions, motion, infrared or high-speed projectiles, any of which detectors could be combined with the others. On full alert, the house would be hard to sneak up on, Sleel knew. Armored photomutable gel cameras mounted in fifteen locations gave views of the house and all approaches to it, including from straight overhead, and the computer was smart enough to know what it was seeing.

"You got missiles on the roof?"

"Yes. Doppler-guided Peel one-oh-threes. Anybody who flies over my house at less than half Republic aircraft minimums is in for a big surprise."

Sleel nodded. He ran through the computer system's other armaments. His checks were permitted only after the security reader had identified Reason's voice, retinal patterns and a code phrase before allowing access. There were robot guns hidden about the grounds, gasbombs, and the house itself was sheathed in armor sufficient to stop small arms fire outright and probably slow down most bigger stuff. Not a cheap job, and one Sleel ordinarily would give passing marks to—except that the Puget Sound house and the one in Australia had similar protections. Whoever had come for Reason before knew some stuff.

Not good.

On the other hand, Sleel was fairly certain that should anybody swinging a big blade come knocking upon the front door, he could handle that. The first thing he'd done when he'd failed to stop the attacker at the airport with shocktox darts was change the loads on his spetsdöds to a formulation designed to knock down large wild animals. It hit harder than shocktox, did the animal trank, but that was too bad. People trying to chop him into soypro patties didn't rate real high on Sleel's popularity poll. If it took them two hours to wake up from the chem's effect, or if they didn't wake up at all, well, *that* was too bad, too. They should think about the risks before they pointed a sharp thing at him, that was how Sleel figured it. And if that didn't do the trick, he had some black-market Asp loads tucked away in his ammo case. Emile probably wouldn't approve such things, but he had higher principles than did Sleel. Where Khadaji had knocked down a big chunk of an army with Spasm so they could recover after six months in tetany, Sleel would probably have killed 'em outright. He'd never been much of a big-picture man himself. Dead attackers hardly ever bothered you again, Sleel figured, if you didn't

count Marcus Wall, and when they tried to kill you, they lost
their rights to keep wasting the communal oxygen.

"Okay," Sleel said. "I want to do a tour of the place on foot
to check out things myself. To do this right we probably should
have three or four other people rotating duty, but for now, we'll
wait and see what your friends in the local cool shop have to
say. If we get something, we'll check it out."

"I defer to your expertise."

Sleel shook his head. Funny old geep. Hard to look at him
and realize he'd been the best thief in the galaxy for longer than
Sleel had been alive. Well. That didn't matter. What mattered
was that he was now Sleel's client, and he couldn't have
anybody killing him. That would make Sleel look bad, and that
was the worst sin of all.

The com chimed and announced a call. Sleel took it. The
woman on the other end of the call gave him visual, and she
was quite attractive in a dark sort of way. She had brown hair
chopped short in a military buzz, even features, and from what
he could see, wore some kind of uniform. He kept his own
transmission pictureless.

"I'm looking for M. Reason."

"He's not available. I'll take a message."

"I have some information for him."

Sleel recognized the voice from the call in the car earlier. It
was the local cool; what was her name? Bley? Bligh? "I'll
download it, you like."

"I'd rather deliver it in person."

"At your convenience, fem."

"I'll be by in an hour."

Fifty-nine minutes later a small flitter arrived at the front
gate. Sleel was watching it on the monitors, and the resolution
on the holoproj was good enough to show him that Officer
Bligh or her double was at the controls. He touched a control
and the gate slid open. He watched the gate until it closed
behind the car. The cool parked the vehicle near the front door.
Sleel had one of the cameras zoom in on the flitter's interior
tightly enough to show that it was empty save for the woman.

"Company," Sleel called out. "Stay out of sight until I check her in."

Sleel took a couple of deep breaths and shook his shoulders and arms, loosening them. The cool wore street sheets, tight-weave orthoskin pants and tunic, probably with spidersilk armor under them, he would guess, proof against the most common handguns. She carried a military-grade hand wand on her belt in an appendix holster, and a shockstik baton dangling from a crowpatch on her left hip. She also had a dispenser of plastic cufftape anchored to her belt next to the shockstik. Standard police issue all, it looked like. Still, you never knew for sure. Things weren't always what they seemed.

"V. Bligh," the woman said into the doorcom.

Sleel watched as the computer checked the voiceprint with the one Reason had on file. "Match," the computer said. "Vicki Bligh, Kona Police."

"Admit her," Sleel said.

Bligh entered the house and the door slid shut behind her. Sleel stepped into view, watching her.

"You're the guy at the port," she said. "The matador. You working for M. Reason now?"

"Yep. And I know you're a cool and all, but would you mind putting the hardware there on the table?"

Bligh nodded. She put her wand, the shockstik, and a single-charge backup hand wand she'd had tucked into a calf pocket on her left boot onto the table.

Sleel said, "Hard object scan, subject Bligh."

The computer said, "Keycard, left tunic breast pocket. Cosmetic tube, right tunic pocket. ID cube, left pants pocket, infoball, ID cube, three stad and two demistad coins, right pants pocket."

"If you would," Sleel said, waving at the woman.

"M. Reason is being very careful these days."

"A sad necessity," Sleel said.

She put the other items onto the table.

"Poison scan, table," Sleel said.

"Negative known poisons," the computer said.

"Okay. This way, please fem. You can collect your gear."

"Aren't you worried about this?" She hefted the wand.

"No. I can shoot you before you could use it."

"You have a high opinion of your skill."

"Yeah, well, that's how it is."

She holstered the wand and stik, and pocketed the other items.

"Okay, Jersey," Sleel called out.

In the library, Bligh slotted the infoball and extra ID cube into the holoproj's reader. The air lit with an image. It was the face of the woman with the sword, from her ID.

"The name given is Karenita Thompson," Bligh said. "That may be false, given that all the other information seems to be bogus."

Sleel and Reason watched as the image turned in the air. A young woman, attractive enough, hair dyed a pale blue. Dead now.

Sleel had the comp enhance and enlarge the tattoo. It was odd-looking, a solid black design about the size of stad coin. "What's that?"

"Looks like a silhouette of a little house," Bligh said. "Not in our files. We're running it through Republic Security."

To Reason, Sleel said, "Any of the others wearing one?"

"I didn't notice. The first one is at the bottom of Puget Sound, the second probably feeding the dingoes. I should have kept them, but I didn't realize they were part of a parade at the time."

"She died from a systemic toxic shock," Bligh said. "She had a chemical nanoimplant in her brain. The ME says it was triggered by a specific combination of delta and theta waves that come only in very deep sleep or unconsciousness."

"Yeah? What did she do at bedtime every night?"

"A manual override."

"Be nasty if you forgot to turn it off," Sleel said. So. The assassin wore a failsafe. Get knocked out and you died. Forget to turn it off, you died. Nobody would get it out of you unless they happened to pick it up on a scan before it triggered. And since you were put into a deep sleep for brainscan, that would pretty much stop anybody poking around in your skull for answers. Cautious.

"Here's the recording of the attack."

Bligh waved at the comp. The air shimmered and a high angle of the underside of the gamp at the port appeared. There he was, Sleel saw, and there was the woman who had called herself Thompson, stepping out with her sword. Sleel watched with a professional eye as the downscaled woman in the recording went for the smaller image of himself. Damn, he looked jerky when he fired that first round. Sloppy.

"Anything on her of any help?"

"The lab is working on the clothes and sword. We found where she was staying, at one of the big hotels in New Kona. Nothing so far. The sword is interesting."

Sleel saw himself shoot the woman coming at him again without apparent effect. Damned if he didn't dance back a step when that happened! Fuck. You look like you were scared shitless there, Sleel. Bet you thought you had me then, didn't you, lady?

"Why is the sword interesting?"

"The steel in it is unique. Not quite like anything the lab has seen before. Doesn't match any known commercial grade. Got stuff in it they didn't expect, the way it's lined up."

The past-tense Sleel dodged the attack and began the dance of sumito. Looked pretty good . . . well, okay, his foot was off a little there during Air, and maybe he was bent too far during Neon Chain, but that punch was all right. Too hard, maybe.

"So the sword is funny. Does that help?"

"Not that we can determine. Her ID says she is from Thompson's Gazelle, and the cube has a Delta imprint, but the White Radio squirt from Thompson's Gazelle comes up no record."

"Maybe she lived a long way from town."

The assassin was down, and Sleel was scanning for more trouble. That looked okay.

"Maybe," Bligh said. "You want to tell me what this is all about, M. Reason?"

"Would that I knew," Reason said. "Somebody is sending people with swords after me; other than that, I cannot say."

"Well, if you figure it out, do let us know. A body in the port is bad for the tourist business." To Sleel she said, "I've never seen anybody move like that." She nodded at the final freeze-frame of the holoproj. "Like lube on glass. I don't know anybody who could be that smooth and cool with an assassin coming at them."

Sleel shrugged. Yeah, well, it looked like shit to him, but he didn't say it.

Bligh collected the cube and infoball and headed for the door. There would be a record of both in the security computer, though there didn't seem to be anything useful there. The swordswoman was a pro; she wouldn't have left any obvious clues as to who had sent her, not if she was willing to die if they caught her.

Sleel had the computer open the door. An alarm went off, a keening *whoop-whoop* at the same instant Bligh stepped into the doorway. Sleel yelled "Down! On the floor!" as he snapped his hands up, looking for targets. But instead of dropping, Bligh went for her hand wand. She was pretty fast, but not fast enough. The wand cleared the holster but before she could level it, the edge of a black sword cut into her neck from her left side, slicing all the way to the spine. Blood sprayed from the chopped artery and she fell back and away from the weapon. Sleel saw in slow motion the fan of hot crimson from the black steel as it was jerked from the woman's half-severed neck. Red painted a Pollock-spatter pattern on the wall and ceiling. As Bligh dropped, a man leaped into the hallway, screaming. He raised the weapon over his head and charged toward Sleel.

THREE _____

ON THE HOLY world of Koji:

The woman came up from *seiza*, the sword in her right hand as much a part of her as her arm. The ebon blade blurred and fanned horizonally through the air, bisecting the first of her imaginary opponents at the waist.

The flashing dark blade continued its loop, circling behind the woman outward and upward, then down to split the invisible skull of the next ghostly attacker. She stepped to her left and pulled the weapon back, locking her left hand on the hilt behind her right hand, point aimed at the throat of the third attacker. Her thumbs and forefingers were slack, middle fingers neutral, ring and little fingers tight against the silk cord and ray skin. It was not a thing of mind but of feel, it was either correct or it was not, and when it was correct, the sword was as the hand. When it was right, the woman lived in the steel as much as she did her own flesh. Now it was right.

The spectre lunged and was impaled upon the blade's tip, the woman's left hand driving the strike, heel against the stainless steel cap, right hand twisting and turning the weapon so that the cut became a blood-letting gouge, spearing and tearing asunder the unfortunate heart.

The imaginary attacker fell away, and the woman spun, slashing at the fourth and fifth and sixth opponents, driving them back. She leaped, cut, stabbed, ducked, and dodged, the sound of her bare feet squeaking on the wooden floor mingling with the *whish* of the blade whipping through the cool air of the *dojo*. She was sharpness itself, dividing upon her razored edges the layers of imagined reality around her.

The *Kaji-te* burned, covering the Five Attitudes, Upper, Middle, Lower, Left Side and Right, and the dancer danced among the attackers of her mind's eye, twirling, whirling, blocking death and striking it down until, all of a timeless moment, she was done.

She looked around the empty room, and her imagination covered the floor with bodies. She exhaled a short breath, inhaled again, and gave the vanquished a short nod of respect. She spun the sword in a circle, all wrist action, and snapped the point at the floor, slinging the blood. She moved to where the white wooden sheath lay. She kneeled next to the sheath, sat on her heels *seiza* again and picked up the sheath without looking at it, turning it so that the convex curve was away from her hip. She brought the sword's spine across her belly and touched the metal just above the guard to the mouth of the sheath and slid the back edge of the blade along the opening, left thumb and forefinger pinching the steel lightly to remove any remaining traces of imaginary blood. When the point reached the opening, she pivoted the sword on it and slowly pushed the weapon home, until the catch on the hilt locked it into place. The mating of steel and wood accomplished, she replaced the sheathed sword on the floor, inclined her head in a bow, and was done.

Kildee Wu blinked, as if coming from a trance. She had danced the dance flawlessly, but she did not consciously recall any of the moves. Of a moment, she had reached for her weapon; the next thing she knew, she was back in *seiza*, finished. That was how it should be. Thought was too slow when it came to the *iai*; moves had to be nearly as automatic as reflex. As a meditation it could be no less. *Iai* was the sword, *do* the way, and it had been her life for twenty of her thirty-five T.S. years.

She picked up the sword and went to the shower.

With the sword placed carefully into its rack, Wu stripped and tossed her silks into the washer. She padded toward the shower, stopping briefly in front of the mirror. She smiled at her image, a smile that seemed a bit crooked to her. She was hardly an imposing figure. Her black hair was cut short, her features more or less Oriental, and she was barely a hundred and fifty-two centimeters tall. Fifty kilos, tight, hips a bit wider than she would like, breasts small and mostly formed from underlying pectoral muscle. Her arms were developed enough so that the veins showed in her biceps, and she figured her body fat was maybe nine or ten percent. "Sthenic," that's what her ex-lover the medic had called her. He said it meant "healthy-looking," and she could live with that.

Yep, and a good, healthy, sweaty body it was now. Her own smell overcame the barn-straw scent of the dressing room. Best she get cleaned up and into fresh silks before her first kendo class arrived. *Sensei* Wu needed to look neat for the paying customers. During the dance, she was *other*, but now, she was simply Kildee Wu, a woman who needed a shower.

Bligh fell and the swordsman dashed past her toward Sleel. At the port, he hadn't been working; here, he had a job to do, a client to protect, and he didn't fuck around this time. He pointed his left spetsdöd at the running man—better angle on that side—and snapped off two shots.

One dart for each eye.

The guy could have been wearing lenses; that was possible, given how prepared the woman at the port had been. But even so, he'd damn well have to blink when the darts got there; that was reflexive, and it would take a hell of a lot of specific training to get around that one. At the very least it was going to slow him down considerably.

The swordsman screamed. He jerked his arms up over his face, still maintaining his grip on the black sword, then collapsed as the trank took him. He slid two meters to an unconscious halt.

Well. Not wearing lenses, Sleel saw.

They could grow him new eyes, assuming he lived that long. Probably not gonna happen, given how the other sword players had been rigged to self-destruct. Too bad.

Sleel moved toward the door, alert for another attacker, but saw none. Somehow that figured.

The matador squatted next to the fallen cool. The floor was

awash in blood, the big artery still spewing it out, but slowing
the flow as the heart finished the last of it. A few liters of it
went a long way when spilled on the floor like that.

"Com the medics," Sleel said to Reason.

Sleel used first aid, putting direct pressure on the throbbing
wound, but it was gonna take more than he had to bring her
back. If the medical team got here fast enough, they could
revive her and stave off the brain damage.

Abruptly the bleeding stopped. Shit. There went the pump.

"And call your vouch," Reason said.

A box the size and shape of a squashed suitcase appeared in
the hallway and rolled quickly to where the wounded police-
woman lay. The vouch extruded needles and lines and plugged
itself into the woman, piercing her armor easily. It began
humming loudly as it diagnosed the condition—massive blood
loss and shock and cutting trauma to the neck—and began
pumping oxygenated plasmoids and coagulants into Bligh.
Another line stabbed into the windpipe and began ventilation,
while a small pump cycled the administered fluids through the
circulatory system. A jointed arm with a surgical stapler began
working on the sword damage, first rejoining the cut carotid
artery portions and some of the other larger vessels with biostat
glue.

Nice toy, the vouch. Expensive, but handy. Sleel moved
back and allowed the machine to work. If the assassin were still
alive when the vouch got done with the woman, it would plug
him and see could it stop the effects of his suicide device, but
Sleel didn't give that much hope. These people were careful,
whoever they were, and it didn't seem likely they'd leave
somebody around to question. That was too bad, too.

"Let's go," Sleel said.

"Go? Where?" Reason asked.

"Away from here. A medical team is gonna be fanning in
shortly and a lot of people will be running around. Be easy
to sneak somebody who didn't belong in with them. Put
spraywhites on somebody, he looks like a medic."

"But—but—"

"We'll leave the gate open. There's nothing here worth
dying for, is there?"

"Hardly."

Sleel paused long enough to check the swordsman, who was still breathing. The man wore a handsized electronic device on his belt, and a smaller one stuck to his right boot top. Sleel didn't recognize the models, but he knew what the things were: confounders, electronic scramblers, and unless he were very much mistaken, real good ones. Sleel would bet a year's salary that the guy had come in hidden somewhere in Bligh's flitter. The luggage compartment, maybe, or wedged under it somehow, between the fans. The security comp had spotted him, sure enough, but not until he'd gotten to the front door—which Sleel had opened to let Bligh leave. Must have tapped into the com when Bligh had called and figured she would be allowed past the gate without too much trouble. Not bad.

The matador picked up the sword. Nice weapon, good balance to it. He touched the edge with one thumb, rubbing lightly across the edge and not lengthways, the way you were supposed to so you didn't cut yourself. The sword was sharp enough, though he knew little about such things. They weren't something you came up against very often in a high-tech society. Maybe in the Musashi Flex, where honor counted big, but not on the street where survival was more important. He nodded at Reason. "Let's move." He kept the sword as he led his client out toward the flitter.

Getting old, Sleel. You almost blew it. What would the other matadors say? They'd never let you live it down, they heard about this. Sloppy, real sloppy.

For a moment, as he and Reason lifted in their flitter, he thought about calling his old comrades. Bork would be through with his honeymoon by now, he and Veate. Dirisha and Geneva were probably looking for something interesting to do and this was sure as shit *interesting*.

But—no. He didn't want to run crying for help every time he stubbed his toe a little. Best if he figured out what was what first. No point in calling in the troops if it was something he could take care of on his own, was there? A few geeps with swords, how would that look? Man, he could almost hear Dirisha telling Geneva: Hey, brat, poor decrepit senile old Sleel needs somebody to help him cross the street so he don't

get run over by some kid in his daddy's flitter. We'd better go
and hold his hand, you think?

No, definitely not. Emile had taken on a planet's army by
himself, and the matadors had knocked the entire *Confed* on its
ass. Sleel could surely keep one old thief alive, couldn't he?

Damned right he could.

Hoja Cierto was most unhappy when Carlotta reported
Pedro's failure. Four of his students had died trying to erase the
final blot on the family name. True, they had done so with
honor, but failure was failure, and now the old thief had but
that much more to answer for.

Lying naked upon his bed, Cierto considered the ceiling of
his room. He would spend all of his students if need be, but it
seemed such a waste of his training to have them stopped. And
according to Carlotta's report, the condemned man had gotten
himself a bodyguard, one of the matadors of whom so much
had been spoken. Cierto had never dealt with these matadors
directly, but he knew that some of them had walked the Flex
before they learned sumito, taught by the Siblings of the
Shroud. Some of them had been ranked quite high, if the
stories could be believed, and the fighting art of shrouded
priests was second to none when it came to bare hands. Two of
the projectiles Cierto had fired had been stopped by this
matador, and so he was responsible for their deaths, even
though it had been the brainchoke that had actually killed them.

Cierto grinned. In the Old Language, "matador" did not
mean "bodyguard." It meant "killer." On Earth, these men had
faced beasts in the ring and slain them with swords.

He sat up, the muscles of his belly tightening as he swung
his legs over the edge of the bed. Well. We shall see how this
matador fares against a beast who also carries a sword. One
who is without peer using his weapon.

The thought of such a battle aroused him. He touched a
button on the bedside com.

"Juanita?"

"Si, Patrón?"

"Come to my room. I have something for you."

The young woman's voice trembled slightly. "At once, Patrón."

Cierto smiled, hearing the touch of fear in her. There were swords, then there were swords, and a man must be adept in using both kinds, no? Cierto usually preferred his sheath to be the tightest of the three a woman had to offer, but this time he felt potent enough want to use them all when Juanita arrived. And he certainly intended to do so.

FOUR

ABOARD THE STARLINER *Pachelbel*, Sleel and Jersey Reason enjoyed the comforts of a first-class suite. The ship, completed after the fall of the Confed, was state-of-the-art interstellar travel, a luxury boat for those with stads to burn; it was like being in a resort town that could fly.

"How much are you worth, anyway?" Sleel asked.

They were in one of the restaurants, where the price of a single meal could easily equal a month's rent for a middle-class family. They were both enjoying the special of the day, Green Moon beef. Reason sipped at an expensive blue wine, Mtuan Azure; Sleel, working, didn't usually do strong chem; instead, he drank splash, as mild as beer. The smell of the meat was rich, the taste exquisite, and Sleel savored the texture and flavor.

"I could scrape up perhaps a hundred million standards," Reason said. "Depending on property values around the galaxy at any given time."

Sleel nodded, chewing on a mouthful of the steak. Big money didn't impress him.

"So, where to?" Reason asked. "I assume you have something more specific in mind than the entire Bibi Arusi System?"

"Yep."

"And I must say I was somewhat surprised that you booked passage for us under our own names."

Sleel swallowed the steak and grinned. "No, you weren't."

Reason tilted his head slightly to one side. "Oh?"

Sleel leaned back in his chair, automatically scanning the

dining room again. He had done so a dozen times during the meal and now as then, there was no apparent threat. None of the waiters had offered to cut Sleel's steak for him with a black sword. "You didn't get to be the best thief in the galaxy by being stupid. And you didn't stay out of Confed jails for more than half a century by accident. I think maybe you're being a bit disingenuous here, old man."

Reason chuckled. "Why, Sleel. Where'd you learn a word like that?"

Sleel said, "Where's the best place to hide something?"

Reason didn't ponder that one. "Where nobody will think of looking. I didn't know you were a fan of Poe."

"Mostly the poetry," Sleel said. "But I liked 'The Purloined Letter.' Emile made us read it. Where's the next best place?"

"Where they know where it is but can't get to it."

"What I figure," Sleel said. "Now, we can hide where nobody will ever find us, but that limits things. You'll always be looking over your shoulder."

"I am anyway."

"Maybe, but you've managed to stay ahead of the game until now. First we take care of the guys with swords, then we worry about other stuff."

"All right. Meaning . . . ?"

"We go somewhere where they can find us but can't get to us—unless they do it on our terms. Then we got time to figure out who is behind this and take them out."

"Cut off the head and the body dies?"

"It worked against the Confed," Sleel said.

Reason nodded. "That makes sense. So, where are we going?"

"To The Brambles," Sleel said.

Reason shook his head. "That will be a neat trick. I'm given to understand that there are only a handful of people in the whole galaxy who can go there without spending a year getting the needed permissions and documentations to visit. They don't encourage visitors."

Sleel's smile was tight and bitter. "I know somebody," he said. "Let me tell you a story."

There were three worlds in the Bibi Arusi System: Mwan-amamke, Mtu, and Rangi ya majani Mwezi, the Green Moon.

The center planet, the backrocket-lanes Mtu, had but few things of galactic note upon it, Sleel said, some decent wines, colorful silks—but it did have The Brambles.

The area known as The Brambles covered almost four thousand square kilometers on the semitropical side of the fourth continent, Ua Ngumi, which translated roughly meant, "Flower Fist."

Much had been written about The Brambles: that it was the largest briar patch in the galaxy; that it contained—depending upon whom asked—either mankind's salvation or damnation. That it was the most brilliant botany experiment ever conducted. So important an idea was it that the Confederation had left it virtually alone for more than fifty years, no small accomplishment in itself, rather than risk interfering with its mission.

Even *stupid* Confed officials wanted to live forever.

For the unique plant that formed the dense sticker bush that was The Brambles might hold within its nodular roots the secret to an unlimited life span.

To be sure, there were already drugs that increased productive human lives considerably. The *Bindodo* vine, the genetic grandmother from which the bramble bush—*Uzima edmondia*—had been developed, was native to the Green Moon, and its adaptogenic properties had already given mankind and its mues up to a hundred and fifty useful years. That seemed to be the limit, however. Even eliminating most diseases, discounting accidents or murder, anything over a hundred and sixty or eighty T.S. years was still far beyond man's grasp. Past this, normal cells hayflicked and died, and while no "death-hormone" had been discovered, *some*thing wore out. Certain cancerous growths could be kept going virtually forever, but though scientists had been trying for hundreds of years, no way to impart the benefits of this growth to people without the side-effects had been uncovered.

Until *U. edmondia.*

Maybe.

Sampson Lewis Edmonds, acknowledged as the most brilliant applied botanist to have ever lived, along with his wife, Elith Liotulia, considered the *second*-most brilliant botanist in galactic history, had apparently worked a biological miracle upon the offshoot *Bindodo* cuttings they had transplanted to

Mtu. The growth had a number of names, though those who worked with it usually just called it bramble. The resulting plant, though not a true *Rubus*, certainly looked the part. At maturity, it was estimated that a thigh-thick trunk would reach perhaps two meters before spreading up into a weeping-willowlike spray that would rise another twenty meters. This would then spill over in a graceful arch that dangled the ends of the straight and barbed branches all the way back to the ground. The bramble at maturity would look like nothing so much as a giant, sparsely leaved blackberry bush, bigger than a house, without fruit, but with wicked thorns. It would be incredibly tough, the fibers of the branches being dense and very flexible; deep rooted, and genetically engineered to resist disease, insects and even fire. The wood would make great pipes for smoking, or violin bows.

The real achievement, however, would lie in a fist-shaped knot of burl that lay just under the ground between the trunk and roots. The size of a man's head, this burl would contain, if everything went as hoped for, a chemical compound that would safely allow human cells to bypass the Hayflick Limit without side effects—by a factor of five to seven.

Such a chemical elixir would give the possibility of an eight-hundred- to thousand-year life span. And various permutations of such a substance might, even if the primary purpose failed, cure virtually every known disease.

Certainly this was enough to keep the Confed from meddling in things. The payoff would be priceless, if it worked. Nobody wanted to risk killing this particular goose.

There was, however, a catch:

From first planting to maturity, it would take at least seventy-five years. The oldest patch of *U. edmondia* was but fifty years old. Although the plant achieved its full height within ten or fifteen years, the burl would not be ready for harvest for at least another three score after that. Computer projections and growth curves all predicted that the biological chemical factory that was the burl *should* work as designed, but there was no way to hurry it. Something about the processing defied artificial attempts to speed it up; certainly it had been tried. Tests on the fifty-year-old bramble showed that there was a good probability it would work, but there was no way to be *sure* until push came to shove at the end. Until then, the small army of biologists and support personnel would simply have to wait and see.

If it worked, then Sampson Lewis Edmonds and Elith Liotulia would etch so deeply a place in history it would never be erased as long as men lived—and men would live a long, *long* time indeed. A betting man wouldn't make much profit going against it, so the oddsmakers said. Current numbers were nine to one in favor, growing more likely all the time. Everybody wanted this one to work.

Reason blinked. "You certainly know an awful lot about all this," he said.

They were back in their rooms. The *Pachelbel* continued spanning vast distances using its Bender drive, moving faster effectively in an eyeblink than light did in a hour. Or not moving at all, depending on how you interpreted the physics.

Sleel nodded. "Yeah, I know about it."

"I wouldn't have thought that a matador would be so up on esoteric biology."

Sleel shrugged.

Reason looked at Sleel. "You didn't learn about this in the matadors, though, did you?"

"No. Before."

"You want to tell me?"

"Not really, but what the hell. I grew up there, in The Brambles."

"Your parents were scientists? They work with the plants?"

Sleel took a deep breath and let it out. "Yeah, you might say that. They *invented* the damned stuff."

Reason blinked, astonished, but whatever else he was, he wasn't slow. "Sampson Lewis Edmonds? Elith Liotulia?"

"Yeah."

"The initials. S-l-e-e—"

"Yeah," Sleel cut in.

"Well, I'll be damned."

"Not while I work for you. Afterward, maybe."

FIVE _____

THE BOY WAS caught in the tree.

He was only ten or twelve meters up, where the ascending and straight branches were still thick enough to support the weight of a nine-year-old, and where the thorns were long but well spaced and usually easy to avoid.

Usually easy to avoid.

As sometimes happened, the wrist-thick risers would cross in long and narrow X-shapes. Normally this was good, 'cause it gave more support to a climber. This time, though, it just happened that three or four thorns bunched up on the inside of the top angle of the X, and when he'd put one foot there, the pressure had lodged his thin boot smack in the middle of the thorns. When he'd tried to move, he found he was caught. He'd tried to shake his foot loose, but that hadn't worked. He'd tried to pull his boot off, but the angles of the thorns only dug them in deeper. Some of the little spikes, each as long as his forefinger and needle-sharp, pointed upward and some of them pointed down, and at least two of them went completely through the boot's plastic and into his ankle. They hurt, and he'd cried for a while, but that hadn't done any good. He was caught, and unless somebody came to help him, he was going to stay caught.

It was almost noon; he could tell by the way the light slanted through the upper part of the arches. It was hot and damp, like usual, and he was dressed for climbing, with his no-snag suit on, so he was hotter still. The smell of the flowers above him filled the hot air with a rich dusty-spice odor, sharp and heavy in his sinuses.

Let go! He jerked his leg, but that only made another thorn stab his foot. Ow! Ow! *Ow!*

He was about a klick from home, on Prime Row, maybe five hundred boles away from First Tree. These were the largest of the crop, a long time from being harvested but still almost as big as they were going to get. The rows ran on for kilometers and kilometers; he'd once gone with his father in the fanner as far away as eight thousand boles and they hadn't even been close to the end. From Prime, you could see the way the boles came up, arrow-straight rows, each row with its arch of branches that came back to the ground, so that it looked like dozens and dozens of tunnels going off to the end of the world. There were planets where you could see the sky in other than long strips between rows of trees, he had seen them in edcom holoprojics, but they didn't seem real to him. It was hard to imagine such places. Sometimes he dreamed about being on a world where there were only scattered trees. Frightening dreams they were, being exposed out in the open under the big sky.

Stuck in a tree. The other children would never let him live it down. It was bad enough that he was the youngest at Prime Tree Station. And the smallest. It was going to be a lot worse if one of the teeners spotted him up here and laughed. And they would laugh, sure as shit stinks. They laughed at him a lot because he was so clumsy and so small. He couldn't keep up with them, and when their parents made them take him along for games or outings, they resented him. It wasn't his fault; he didn't want to go!

Well, that wasn't true. He *did* want to go, but not like that. He wanted them to like him, only they didn't.

He tried again to twist his foot out of the clamp that held it fast. One of the thorns sank deeper into his flesh. He could feel a trickle of blood run down to his toes inside the boot. Ow! Oh, ow! Somebody *please*!

His parents didn't understand. They looked at him like he was some kind of bug that had wandered into their house. His father would blink at him and look puzzled, as if he'd never

seen him before. When his father was in the lab, he snapped
out orders and had people running every which way. And his
father was brilliant, a genius, everybody said so and it was
even in the ed programs. His mother, too. They were two of the
smartest people in the whole *galaxy*, everybody knew that.
Everybody.

Why hadn't any of that come to him? Why was he so stupid
and clumsy and afraid of everything? Even too little to climb,
the other children said, taunting him. Can't think, can't move,
can't do *squat*!

What did they expect? That he would be as smart as his
parents? *No*body was as smart as they were! Why did *he* have
to be? He couldn't. No way. And he was too little to be worth
leaf puke, too. Couldn't even *climb*!

Oh, yeah? Well, he'd show them. He would climb a tree and
pick a flower, they grew only up near where the arch began,
and when the other children saw him walking around with one
of the white flowers under his arm, then they'd see!

Right. Only thing was, now he was stuck and that was bad.
Now he couldn't show anybody anything because he was going
to stay here until he died. Nobody would even miss him. Not
his parents. Not the other children. One day maybe they would
look up and wonder why he wasn't around, but nobody would
worry about it and nobody would even care.

Feeling pretty sorry for himself, he glanced up toward the
canopy. He'd almost made it. There was one of the handsized
flowers only another three meters or so away. You weren't
supposed to pick them, but all the children did. A few flowers
wouldn't make any difference, everybody knew that. The bugs
didn't bother them, 'cept the pol-bees, and that was okay. They
didn't fall off, the flowers, but just shriveled up at the end of
each growing season and eventually turned into a little black
lump. The new flowers came out of the lumps next season. It
was against the law to pick them, but nobody ever said
anything about it unless it was an outsider who did it,
somebody who didn't live here. Rules were different for
outsiders; the rules were designed to protect the trees from
them because the trees were worth a whole lot. Scientists who
lived here were allowed to experiment on the trees but

outsiders who did anything damaging to The Brambles went to rehab or jail, even. The Confed didn't let just anybody come here, and those who did had better be real careful.

A long time passed. At one point he had to untab his pants and pee, and that looked pretty interesting. He'd never peed that far before. Odd how it broke up and turned into a spray of droplets before it hit the ground.

More time went by. He was getting pretty hungry and thirsty. He had a chocolate bar in the pocket of his no-snags and he carefully ate half of it, saving the rest for later. It made him thirstier to eat it, but it tasted real good.

He didn't have a chrono with him, he'd worried that it would get snagged, so he didn't know exactly what time it was, but it was getting pretty late. The sun dropped so that it wasn't far from dark. He figured he'd been in the tree for almost eight hours.

He was lucky that his foot was caught in such a way that he could lean almost all of his weight against one of the branches; even so, he was sore from where his hip and side pressed against the springy wood. Good thing there weren't any thorns there.

Just before dark, he heard somebody calling his name.

After a few moments, two of the older boys, Morl and Lutain, came into sight below, about eight meters away. They were yelling. First they would shout out his name. Then they would add something nasty, like, "Where are you, you dickless little turd?" Or "Come out, whizz-brain fuckoff!"

At first he was thrilled to see them. He almost yelled back. Then the shame of his position and his embarrassment overwhelmed him. He didn't *want* them to see him. He would never, ever live it down, they would tease him until he died, that he got stuck in a tree. Sure, it had probably happened to other children, but that didn't matter. They would laugh at him, they would call him names, and it would be better to die up here than to have to suffer that.

The two older boys passed under his perch, and he kept silent. They didn't think to look up. Good.

When night came, the so-ho crickets started singing, that over and over *so-ho, so-ho*, the sound that gave them their names. There weren't any wild animals or anything that would bother him, even if they could climb up and get to him, but now he was afraid. He wished he had yelled to the boys now. Maybe he really *was* going to die up here in this tree, and that terrified him.

A couple of times he saw lights flashing under distant rows, and he yelled, but nobody heard him. Through a break in the canopy to his left, he could see the Green Moon rising, and the Spearcaster constellation and Big Red star glimmering in the soggy skies. Probably it was going to rain; it usually did at least once a day and it hadn't yet. He was going to die in a tree, all alone, in the rain, and nobody would save him. If he was going to get away, it would be up to him.

But there wasn't any way. He had tried a thousand times to move his foot and it was not going anywhere, no matter how hard he twisted or jerked. His foot had gone numb; the thorns didn't even hurt anymore. He tried hanging all his weight on his hands on one branch, then the other, to spread them away, but that hadn't worked. He tried pulling them together and separating them apart. No good. He'd checked his pockets for anything that could help and there wasn't anything. Sure, he had his penknife, but the blade was only three centimeters long and the wood was almost impossible to cut. And the thorns were harder than the branches; it took a saw or a laser to shear through one of them. He was doomed. Trapped.

Going to die . . .

The idea happened when he gave up and realized he wasn't going to get away. It was so simple he felt real stupid for not having thought of it before. Damn! Stupid!

He pulled his penknife and squatted as best he could. Careful, he had to be real careful, he couldn't drop the knife because it was his only chance.

In the dark and alone, the boy began to cut at his boot. It took a while, but finally he managed to slice away most of it. The thorns were still stuck into him, but it was the boot sole jammed into the crotch of the branches that mostly held his foot trapped.

The Green Moon gave him enough light so he could see that only three thorns were stuck into him. His blood looked black, but there wasn't all that much of it, and it had mostly dried. With his hands, he shoved the boot sole into the springy trap, pressing as hard as he could. It was awkward, but by bouncing on the hard plastic, he managed to back the thorns off a little.

Good as it was going to get.

He straightened and gripped tightly with both hands the branch upon which most of his weight rested. He couldn't cut the thorns and probably they wouldn't break, either, but they weren't stuck into his bones or anything.

His skin and muscle weren't as hard as the spikes that held him.

He took a deep breath and jerked his trapped leg upward, as hard as he could.

The needle-sharp thorns dug bloody furrows in his foot and ankle. It hurt, it *hurt*! Ow, ow, *ow*! But he was free!

His ankle was bleeding and it hurt, but he cried from relief and not the pain. He was free. All he had to do now was climb down and go home.

But the boy who would someday call himself Sleel didn't do that. Instead, he climbed up. To get the flower he'd come for.

When he arrived home with the flower, one boot missing and his bare foot and ankle bloody, it was his mother who saw him first.

"Where have you been?" she asked. "We were worried about you. Are you all right?" She seemed distracted, and she stood back three meters, watching him as if he were a new specimen of bramble she wanted to examine, but one still in quarantine so she couldn't get too close.

"I went to get this," he said, holding the flower out.

"Oh, You've damaged your ankle, haven't you?"

"It's only a scratch."

"Where is your boot?"

"I lost it."

"Well. Well, okay. Go and have the diagnoster look at your leg. And get cleaned up and fix yourself something to eat. Your father and I have a holoconference at twenty-one hundred, and it's almost time."

"Yes, Mother."

With that, his mother bustled off to turn on the holoproj for their conference. She had not swept him off his feet or hugged him, but at least she had noticed he was missing. That was pretty amazing.

His father, passing by, nodded at the boy. "Evening," he said. "You have a good day?"

"Yes, Father."

"That's nice."

If he noticed the boy's bloody ankle or missing boot, he made no mention of it. He didn't act as if he had been aware that his son had been gone at all. When his mother had said "we," she must have meant herself.

His father walked away, no longer interested in his son. The boy looked at the flower in his hand. He dropped it onto the floor and stepped on it with his injured foot. He ground the white petals into the plastic. The cleaning din would suck up the ruined flower and the floor would be none the worse for it; likely his parents wouldn't even notice the mess. His parents had never laid a hand on him in anger. He sometimes wished they would. Even being beaten was probably better than being ignored.

At nine, the boy who would become Sleel had begun to realize that if he wanted to get along in the galaxy, he would have to take care of himself, that nobody else was going to do it. If he couldn't do it on his own, it wasn't going to get done. Well, okay. If that's how it had to be, fuck it. He would take care of himself. Somehow—

Sleel came out of sleep suddenly, wide awake. There didn't seem to be anything wrong; the door squeal was armed and quiet, Reason snoring in the next room. He shook his head. It was just a bad dream, he told himself. An old tape. It doesn't matter anymore, what happened to you as a kid. It really doesn't matter.

SIX

THE HOUSE OF Black Steel was steeped in tradition but not so much that it refused to acknowledge the march of time. Technology had its uses, and Cierto was not a man to handicap himself when it came to certain devices. A viral matrix computer ran the household, insofar as security and communications went, and his stealthware was as good as any but the cutting-edge top-secret Republic military and political gear. Money was a grease that made many things run smoothly, and even when the Confed squatted most heavily upon its citizens, the House of Black Steel had never come close to missing a meal. Cierto was born rich and if he spent a million standards a year and lived to be a hundred and fifty, he would still die rich.

Yes. Money bought security plans and how to get around them; money gave his students devices that would do things Cierto's grandfather would have considered miracles; money talked and when it did, almost everybody listened with respect.

Even so, there came a time when money alone was not enough. His students had thus far failed to remove the final stain upon the family honor, and that stain now sought to continue its vile existence, hiring protection. It was time to become more serious about this task, Cierto knew.

He sat in the hub of his control center, surrounded by holoprojic pictures dancing colorfully upon the air, by machineries worth a king's ransom. The casa was quiet, the students out doing field exercises in the forest that made up the southern quarter of the estate. Only the household dins puttered about, cleaning and polishing, and the house was empty of human life, save for Cierto himself. He had preparations to make before he took to the dueling arena, business to conduct before he was prepared to cleanse the final speck of dirt from his grandfather's boots, and much of that preparatory work could be done here. Calls would be made, favors asked and granted in return, more of the valuable lubricant of the family fortune sprayed upon abrasive places. In the end it would be as Cierto wished it to be, as it had always been for his family. What the Ciertos wanted was, if at all possible, done. And with heads held high.

He was not a *betyldese* operator, able to converse in several esoteric com languages at once, but it was not necessary. His machineries did what he needed. His skills lay elsewhere.

Cierto glanced up at the Latin signature that shone upon the bases of each of the holoproj images, the family motto that was part of nearly everything in the casa in one form or another: *Potius mori quam foedari.*

Death before dishonor.

Ah, sí, that was always the way of it. The *Código de Honor* was all for his family, the alpha and omega, and it was infused with mother's milk into the souls of the children of the Ciertos. One did not go against it. Ever. If one did, the consequences were swift and painful. Cierto could never forget what had happened on the morning of his eleventh birthday.

Hoja parried Enrique's cut with his own foil and riposted, a deep lunge at the other boy's heart. Enrique danced away, and the foil's buttoned tip fell short. Enrique slid to *en garde* and waved his weapon in tight circles, grinning.

Hoja's heads-up display timer flashed off the seconds. Only twenty seconds left in the match and Hoja was down a point. A clean touch was needed were he to win, and Enrique knew it. All Enrique had to do was stay out of range and the match was his. At twelve, Enrique was slightly taller than Hoja, and somewhat more muscular, aside from being a year older. Plus his father was the fencing master, and so he surely must be coached in techniques that the younger Hoja did not know. It was not fair.

Fifteen seconds left. Enrique grinned and made a weak attack, designed to kill nothing but time. Hoja dodged it easily.

Hoja saw his chance as the other boy shuffled back, and he took it. With five seconds remaining, Hoja leaped forward in a wild lunge, foil extended fully.

He was short by no more than a centimeter, but Enrique was hunched forward and his arm hid the miss from where their fathers stood watching.

"*Touché!*" Hoja yelled.

The timer chimed and the match was over. The boys saluted each other, then the fencing master.

Enrique removed his face mask and shook his head. "I did not feel it. Are you sure?"

"Sí, can you not see the mark on your suit where the button hit?" Hoja pulled his own face guard off and shook his hair. Sweat flew.

Enrique looked down. "No, but if you say so, then it must be. Congratulations."

Hoja felt a stab of guilt, but only a small one. The hardwired fencing suits were capable of recording each touch so that there could be no doubt, but the Patrón had disabled this aspect of the electronics as a matter of routine—and of honor. Lesser men might need such things to assure truth, but the *Casa del Acero Negro* did not. To imply otherwise would be an insult to the duelists.

Hoja's triumph soured when he looked at his father, who wore a frown. The Patrón was watching a holoprojic replay of the match, and the ceiling camera's eye had not been blocked by Enrique's position. The image shifted to a closeup of the foil approaching Enrique's chest, slowing as the Patrón commanded. It was clear that Hoja's weapon had stopped short of the touch.

The Patrón waved one hand in anger and the image vanished. He looked down at his son. "Hoja. Come here."

The boy swallowed, fear thick in his throat. "Sí, Patrón?"

The senior Cierto wore the sword of his grandfather, the magnificent weapon that would someday pass to Hoja, the finest blade in all the galaxy. He pulled the sword from its sheath and turned it so that the edge was up. "You claimed a touch," his father said.

"Sí, Patrón, I thought it so."

"No, you did not. You cheated."

"But—Patrón—"

"Hold out your right arm."

"Patrón—?"

"Now!"

Trembling, Hoja did as he was told, the foil pointing straight ahead.

His father lowered the thick spine of the sword slowly so that its full weight rested upon Hoja's forearm just above his wrist. The blade was heavy, and it took more than a little effort to hold his arm steady. How long would he have to hold it up? Already his arms were tired from the match; surely the Patrón could not expect him to support this heavy blade on his outstretched arm for very long. He could feel his shoulder starting to burn from the combined weights of the sword and foil. How long?

He needn't have worried about that. Moving so quickly that the black steel was only a blur, Hoja's father whipped the sword up and down, smashing the thick spine of the blade into his son's arm.

Hoja could not stop his surprised yelp as the ulna and radius snapped. His arm actually *bent* upward around the dull edge, as if the hard bones were made of flexcord. The sight and sensation filled him with nausea. He barely stopped himself from vomiting.

For some reason, he did not drop the foil, but managed to keep his grip on it. He reached over and clutched at the broken bones with his other hand, squeezing them. He felt them grate together under his fingers and almost passed out from the fiery pain. Ah—!

"Thus do you pay for staining our honor," his father said. His voice was cold, without anger, and that made it worse. "Do you understand?"

Hoja wanted to cry, but he held the tears back. Tears were for the weak. "S-Sí, P-Patrón." Bile burned in his throat.

"Go and have your arm orthobonded. And consider yourself fortunate that you did not drop your weapon, for if you had, I would have broken the other arm, too."

With that, his father turned and strode away.

The pain had been sharp, piercing to his depths, but the medics repaired the damaged bone and took away the hurt. The mild swelling subsided after a few days and the arm was as good as before, but the shame and the lesson would never be forgotten. Never.

Cierto even now felt shame at the old memory. Ah, yes, the lessons had been hard, but they had taken root and grown, making him into a man. It was time to begin thinking about having a son of his own. He had select sperm and ova frozen in his private bank that could be grown to provide an acceptable child. Of course, he would prefer to meet a woman with fire as bright as his own to be the mother of his son. The old ways had some merit. Certainly it was more pleasurable to implant his seed in a hot and living receptacle, be she willing or not, than to have his semen mixed with an egg in a Healy chamber to be grown to term. A baby grown in the natural way might not be chemically distinguishable from one raised in a machine womb but Cierto was convinced that children with biomothers inherited some of their spirit. And spirit was an important part of honor.

Yes. After the family honor was cleansed, it would be time to select the proper mother for his son. To assure that the House of Black Steel would have the correct heir. To teach him the ways of honor and the sword, so that he might become, as Hoja Cierto had become, a man among men. But first there was this thief to slay. And his matador along with him.

Kildee Wu walked behind the line of kendo students with her split-bamboo sword, the straight *shinai*, watching as they exchanged *shomen*, cuts to the center of the forehead. The line shuffled forward and with feet still in motion, snapped their bamboo blades down on the padded *men* helmets of their opponents, giving loud and simultaneous *kiai*! with their strikes. Passing through, they would pivot, and wait as the other line repeated the action. There were only eight valid strikes in this mostly classical style of academic *ryu-hai*, seven cuts and one thrust. It was all very precise and very limited and that was what attracted so many of the students. Kendo per se was not a battlefield free-for-all, but as rigid as the rules for classical *haiku*. Most of these students would not go beyond the bamboo *shinai* or the *bokuto*, the wooden sword. A few might progress to the live blade, but not many. The advanced classes were more interesting, but it was only when those students went beyond even that that Wu was truly engaged. Classical *kata* had its proper place, certain basics were the same—the laws of motion only allowed so many efficient ways for a human to behave—but until *zanshin* was reached, it was all play. To be a true warrior with the sword required total unity of body and spirit and blade. Anything less was not enough.

"Hee-yo!" the second line yelled, bare and callused feet scooting across the flame-patterned wood.

Wu nodded, opening her perception to the students, seeking as always that spirit, the *ki* which would identify one of them as worthy for higher teaching. These were her beginners, but they ranged in experience from a few weeks to two years. A spiritual breakthrough could happen at any time for a number of reasons and she kept herself alert for such. A master of the sword could be born in an eyeblink, and she did not want to miss the birth if it happened near her. It had been her sister who had aided in her own transformation, and had she not been there, Kildee Wu could have wasted years floundering.

"Hee-yah!"

"*Hidari-men*," Kildee ordered, advancing to the next attack, the oblique cut at the left temple.

The students obeyed.

Teaching was not about money, though she charged steep rates. That was more to keep the idly curious away. No, teaching was about finding the perfect student, and with the perfect student, the teacher would become both *sensei* and student herself, for a perfect student taught as much as he learned. This basic kendo class was little more than a filter, a net, in which she hoped to catch the perfect student. There were several who had come close, but the fish she wanted had not yet swum into her *dojo*.

Ah, well. She could be patient. Many teachers waited fifty years for the right one. Her school had been open for a mere eight years. No time at all.

"Hee-yah!" Came the clack of the bamboo on the *men*.

"Again," she said. There was something amiss, some out-of-synch move, or perhaps it was just in a student's intent. She focused her attention yet sharper, probing as she watched the two lines. Twelve of them, seven men and five women, moving relatively well, even the newcomers. What was it she sensed? Some flaw in the energies, something beyond normal perceptions.

The black *bogu* armor squeaked on the students as they cut and *kiai*ed. A good attack; all the *shinai* clacked as one. "Good," she said. But the nagging problem was still there despite the precision. On the left, definitely. Toward the other end. Had to be one of the last two students.

Wu moved toward them, unable to pin the feeling down.

"Again."

Shuffle, *cut*! *Kiai*. *Clack*.

The tall red-haired woman Shanti, face hidden under the helmet, moved with grace; she had been training for almost two years. The shorter figure on the end, Ells, had only been training for a few weeks, but he moved almost equally well. He had, he said, some background in other arts; those skills seemed to transfer to kendo.

Her instructor's eye was not good enough.

Wu took a deep breath and when she allowed it to escape, she sent her intellectual controller with it. *Zanshin*, that sense of total *awareness*, claimed her. It was not a state entered into lightly, nor was it easy to achieve. Its intent was to become one with the sword, one with the cosmos, one with all, and normally reaching it was reserved for perfect formal *kata* or actual battle. It was like a precious and rare liquor at this stage of Wu's development, to be sipped sparingly and savored with great care. A true master could slip in and out of *zanshin* at will, but Wu was years away from that; she still had to work at it.

Ells. It was Ells.

Precisely what it was she couldn't say. *Zanshin* was not telepathy or even empathy, but there was *some*thing. It was in the way he held his weapon. Was there something wrong with his *shinai*? Or perhaps he was injured and splinting against pain? Something definitely on his mind.

"Hold," Wu said.

Obediently the students froze.

"Ells?"

"Are you all right?"

"I'm fine."

Something false in his reply. A faint finger of danger tapped Wu's solar plexus lightly.

"The rest of you continue. Move to *migi-men*."

The students squared themselves for the attack. Ells's partner would fence with the air, conjuring his own vision of an opponent.

To Ells, Wu said, "Over here."

She walked past him and toward the far end of the *dojo*. It did not matter that her back was to him; the *zanshin* wrapped her in its awareness so that every step he took, every breath, every rustle gave her ears his position; the pressure of the air transmitted the feeling of his relationship to her. She felt the heat of his body, the essence of his *ki*.

So when he attacked she felt him coming.

Wu sidestepped easily as Ells lunged and cut down with his *shinai*; she twirled and whipped her own split bamboo blade around in a horizontal cut that caught Ells at the base of his skull. The bamboo was light and meant to give when it hit, but the back of his helmet was open, since kendo did not allow such strikes. The force of her cut was enough to send Ells sprawling facedown upon the floor.

One of the other students said, "Holy fuck!"

He's gone mad, she thought. If he had hit her, it would have done little damage, even though she wasn't wearing her *men*. What was the point?

Ells rolled, but his *bogu* made it awkward, and as he staggered to his feet, trying to raise his *shinai*, Wu moved in, put the tip of her weapon to the padding over his throat and pushed him backward until he hit the wall.

He dropped his *shinai* and raised his hands. He was suddenly full of fear; Wu could feel that as the *zanshin* continued to flow through her.

She lowered her sword. What in the hell—?

Her heightened awareness blasted at her: *Danger*!

Ells sprang at her, a springblade knife in his hand, produced from under his *bogu*. He thrust for her eye, a killing attack.

Full kendo armor covers most of the upper body, the head and neck from the front, the shoulders and the hands and wrists. But there are gaps where the chest and stomach protector, the *tare*, is pared away to allow the arms free movement. When an attacker raises his arms for a cut, the axillae are exposed.

Wu shifted and pivoted and drove her *shinai* into Ells's right armpit as hard as she could.

The point of a *shinai* is dull and rounded, covered with a thick leather cap that holds the four springy "blades" of the split bamboo together at the end. The padding and flexibility of the *shinai* normally make it unlikely to inflict damage; it is designed to deliver full-power strikes without causing damage. It is not a deadly weapon as is the sword it represents.

Such was the power of Wu's strike that the *shinai* bent, shattered, and the jagged ends of two of the pieces slid between Ells's third and fourth ribs and deep into his flesh.

Ells tumbled, literally knocked sideways off his feet. He slammed into the floor, tried to come up, but was unable to rise.

Wu's students stood staring at her and Ells in amazement.

Surely, Wu thought, their wonder was no less than her own.

SEVEN

THE BOXCAR DROPPED toward the surface of Mtu from high orbit, heading toward the port in northeastern Ua Ngumi. Not where Sleel wanted to go, but the main port at Bandari was currently experiencing the effects of a Force Three tropical cyclone, with winds gusting as high as two hundred and thirty-five kilometers per hour. They didn't give them cute names on Mtu, only numbers; this was the ninth hurricane of the season and the biggest. Even the lumpy boxcar would be hard pressed in such winds, so all traffic from offworld was going to Mende, almost eight hundred klicks away from the border of The Brambles. The big whirlies would beat themselves to exhaustion on the plateaus and mountains of Ua Ngumi long before reaching the border, and only the dregs of rain would wash down upon the precisely planted trees, doing them little harm. Even if the storms could somehow manage to hang together long enough to get that far, the deep-rooted and flexible trees would hardly suffer. They had been designed to be hardy, and probably would not lose more than a few leaves in the worst winds.

Sleel leaned back in the cushioned seat and flicked on the holoproj image picked up by the boxcar's external cameras. It had been twenty years since he'd been here, but it didn't look any different from this high up. He couldn't see the briar patch from this glide path, but there were other land- and seamarks he recognized. The Cape of Misery, looking like a smashed thumb off the coast of Churaland; the warm, reddish waters of

51

the Damu Sea current where it met the cooler blue of the Samawati Ocean. The Hook-and-Eye of the Jino Mountains, free of cloud. Twenty years, half his life, and it came back as if no time at all had elapsed since he'd last made planetfall here.

Welcome home, Sleel.

Damn.

Next to him, Reason said, "Last time I visited here was probably thirty-five years back."

"A theft?"

"Yes. One of the dozen or so perfect jobs I ever did. There was a rare document, a paper letter written by Abraham Lincoln, at the museum in Jangwa City."

"The old capital, on the edge of the Great Desert," Sleel said. "Who's Abraham Lincoln?"

"Pre-space politician or king of some kind, as I recall. Gave women the vote or somelike. I had a collector who fancied such things, so I got it for him."

"Just like that."

He chuckled. "Well, no, it wasn't quite that easy, but I was hot in those days. I'd just built the second generation of my electronic suppressors—"

"Reason's can opener," Sleel put it.

"Not my name for it, but yes. The museum's security was pretty good, but they didn't really expect anybody to put out major energies to steal the letter. You could only ransom it, or sell it to a collector willing to hide it—it was hardly something you could take to the neighborhood pawnshop. So I got in and out without working up a big sweat."

Sleel nodded. "And what makes it a 'perfect job'?"

"They had the thing sealed inside a polarized thincris container full of inert gas so the paper wouldn't decompose any more than it already had. I had one of my ops pix it and then had a duplicate made of the case and letter. A very good duplicate. When I took the real one, I left the fake."

Sleel got it. "You mean they never even knew the real letter was gone?"

"Far as I know, they're still showing the copy around."

Sleel laughed. A perfect theft, sure enough, if nobody knew it happened.

The boxcar attendant approached them. Sleel watched the man carefully, but he only wanted to deliver a message to Reason. He passed the thin wafer of the White Radio text to the old man, smiled, and went on his way.

"That from Earth?"

"Yes."

Sleel had okayed the transaction, since they were traveling under their own names and not trying to hide. More bait for their unseen enemy.

Reason slipped the wafer into the seatback reader in front of him. The holoproj lit up, white words on a blue background. "Ah. Apparently Officer Bligh survived the attack. She is recovering inside a Healy at the local medical center."

Sleel shook his head. "So I see. We can zip all over the galaxy, we got tech gear that would have made us demi-gods a few hundred years ago on Earth, and here we are getting attacked by guys with fucking *swords*. Iron Age stuff. It's unreal."

It was Reason's turn to nod. "Yes."

Sleel leaned back as the boxcar started a slow turn to the right. There was nothing else helpful in the message from Earth. Well. He had some contacts. People who waved swords in this age were likely to show up in certain places.

The Musashi Flex was one. Maybe it was time to give Dirisha a call. Just for information, of course, not for help.

During the early days of Mtu's settlement, an old-style maglev train system had been extensively used. The feeder lines were mostly gone, but the main tracks were still in place and still used, mostly for moving cargo though there were also a few passenger trains working. The trains had been designed to run at high speeds and the wind didn't bother them, even a hurricane wasn't much of an impediment. A falling tree large enough to overcome the low-powered repel fields installed to keep odds and ends off the tracks would be a major problem, but crews were employed to make certain such things did not end up crossing the path of the trains.

As Reason and Sleel entered their private compartment, the older man said, "So what if the crew misses a tree blown over by the winds?"

"We hit it at four hundred klicks an hour and it does some damage."

"Pleasant thought. It doesn't worry you?"

"Nope. I worked as a safety tech two summers when I was a teener. We never missed one. Anything big enough to get through the field is real visible. If the sensors don't spot it—and they never missed one when I was working—a din or a human will eyeball it. If the track doesn't read clear before the train starts its run, it doesn't leave. It falls during the run, the train slows down so somebody can remove the problem."

"All well and good," Reason said, "but what happens if something blows over onto the track right in front of the train?"

"What happens if you get hit by a meteorite crossing the street? Life is full of risk."

"Odd, coming from a professional bodyguard."

He grinned. "I don't do earthquakes or *tsunamis* either."

After they were seated it was only a few minutes before the train lifted and began its run. The trip would take less than two hours to reach the border of The Brambles. That was as far as the train went. People who had business past that would have to find other ways to travel—assuming they could pass the entrance strictures.

Sleel felt a flutter in his belly, as if something alive there were suddenly made unhappy. Getting into The Brambles wouldn't be a problem; his status as a matador alone would probably pass him, plus he was a native, *plus* his parents were who they were. That didn't worry him.

Seeing his parents again after twenty years, though, that was something else, even though he was pretty certain he had chosen to come back here for that as much as anything. There were lots of places to hole up and see trouble coming, but none of them would let him show his parents what he had become. Sure, he wore the orthoskins of a hired guard, but there was more to him than met the eye. Much more.

Not enough to satisfy himself, of course, but maybe enough

to satisfy his parents. It was the "maybe" that made him nervous.

A little voice laughed inside his head. *Hell, Sleel, they probably haven't even noticed you're gone yet.*

How about you just shut the fuck up, okay? That's not funny.

Oh, but it is!

Kildee Wu had to think and to look at the situation before the local medics arrived to take her attacker away. So she hadn't yet called the medics—or the cools, even though the attack had been intended to do her deadly harm. The *shinai* Ells had used was more than it seemed at first glance. The bamboo slats, normally sanded so that they would be smooth and not catch on an opponent's *bogu*, had instead been cut in such a way as to leave sharp edges. And something darker than the pale bamboo glistened on the edges, something that had a dank smell when held close to an inquiring nose. Chem, she guessed, and whether it was deadly or not was hard to say, but, given Ells's try with the knife after he lost his *shinai*, she would bet it was poison dabbed on the sharpened edges. One of her advanced students was a medic with access to scanning gear; she could have him analyze it for her.

Ells had meant to kill her.

Why?

More important than the attack, since it had failed, was the motive behind it. People didn't just up and kill other people without reason, not unless they were mentally disturbed. Ells had planned this in advance; Wu was certain that he had joined her *dojo* with the intent already formed, and that kind of premeditation might spring from madness, but it didn't make sense. It took intent to prepare a practice sword as a killing weapon, especially as carefully as Ells had done it.

Before the medics arrived, best if she could determine why Ells wanted her dead.

She'd had her students carry the wounded man into her office, where he was sprawled now upon the couch. The class had been dismissed and she and Ells were alone. He was not particularly comfortable, one lung collapsed as it was, and having trouble breathing, but she didn't think he was in imminent danger of dying. The shards of shattered bamboo were still buried in him, sticking out of his side.

Wu squatted next to the couch.

"Why?"

Ells managed to shake his head. Was not going to tell her.

She reached out and lightly touched one of the bamboo spears embedded in him, wiggling it with her fingertip.

Ells groaned. "Don't, that hurts!"

"If I hit this with the heel of my hand, I expect I can drive it all the way into your heart, if it isn't touching it already."

His already pale face seemed to go whiter.

"I haven't called the medics yet. I could have com problems and you could bleed to death and get cold enough so they couldn't bring you back."

"You . . . wouldn't."

"Tell me why."

Ells stared at her, looking for truth. He must have found it. He started to talk. What he said was most interesting. When he was done, Wu called the medics. She watched him carefully until the medical team arrived and took him.

Well. It looked as if she would be leaving Koji for a time. An ancient score had come to light. An old story from long before she had been born, materializing out of the past like a ghost to haunt her. She would have preferred that it had not, but there was no help for it. She would have to attend to it.

It was a matter of honor.

EIGHT

IN THE HOUSE of Black Steel, Cierto the Patrón considered his recently collected data. Most of it was straightforward enough: his quarry had fled Earth for the world of Mtu, in the company of the matador identified as Sleel. Once there, they had boarded a train—a train, how quaint!—and traveled across the continent to the border of the scientific station colloquially known as The Brambles. Local records showed that the pair had been admitted into the station—an achievement of no small difficulty, Cierto was able to determine. From there, there were no more specifics as to where the two men had gone, at least nothing available to Cierto's stealthware.

The master of the casa stood alone in his private gym, facing a stolid-looking oversize lac generated for wrist-strengthening exercises. The lac shuffled in and brought its blade—a two-handed Mtian broadsword—down in a headsplitter cut.

Cierto stepped back and brought his right hand up with his own sword in an upward block, absorbing the force of the blow. It jarred his wrist, arm and shoulder. As the lac lifted its heavy weapon for another cut, Cierto shifted his sword to his left hand, tossing it easily without looking. He caught the handle and turned his body slightly, sliding his right foot back, leaving his left foot forward.

So. The thief had run, not unexpected. But surely a man who had lived most of his life looking over his shoulder for pursuit by various authorities should be more adept at hiding his trail?

The lac whipped the broadsword down.

Cierto blocked.

The *clang* was realistic enough, as was the vibration that tested Cierto's grip and arm. The lac shuffled forward for its next attack, a lunge for the heart. Cierto tossed the sword back to his right hand.

The lac thrust the point of its sword at the man.

Cierto used an inward block, holding his sword point up and snapping it across his chest. The lac's stab was deflected; it passed harmlessly next to Cierto's left shoulder. Cierto shifted grips once again for the next attack, the balancing sinister to the previous dexter.

Thrust—

Inward block—

The next attacks were high, a looping slice to Cierto's neck, first on his right, then the opposite side. Outward blocks stopped both.

The final attacks of the programmed series were low, stabs at the man's groin, identical moves on the lac's part, but once again requiring that Cierto switch hands to meet them. Upward, outward, inward, downward. In theory, a man could cover his entire body with just these four blocks; they were basic to nearly all martial arts, armed or empty-handed. Since a sword was merely an extension of the hand, the moves looked similar to those of a karate player or *Sengatist*. The difference was that a missed karate block would be cause for a damaging blow from a fist, whereas a miss here was worth death from a razored edge.

The lac bowed slightly and assumed a defensive pose, so that Cierto could become the attacker.

"Off," Cierto said.

The lac shimmered and was gone.

No, he did not need to practice these skills on an artificiality. He had wasted enough precious ammunition on this old thief who continued to live and plague his house. It was time indeed for the Patrón to take the field and demonstrate what must be done.

As the ground cart rolled through the lanes toward Prime, Sleel felt the pressure of the sameness around him. Occasionally there was a break in the trees, where one had died and been replaced with a younger one, but by and large the continuity was there. They didn't seem to have grown very much in twenty years, he'd expected that.

Sleel and Reason were alone in the cart, a programmed unit supposedly sealed until it arrived at its destination. As a teener, Sleel had learned how to reprogram the carts; most people who lived in The Brambles knew how to do that. The carts had originally been a Confederation safeguard, designed to ferry outside people to and from the various guarded locations, not allowing them to stop and poke around on their own. When the Republic arose from the ruin of the Confederation, the carts were left in place, since they worked well enough, but the penalties for misusing them had gone down. The little vehicles continued to roll on their cushioned wheels, the plastic exteriors age-worn, the seats inside sagging and hardly comfortable. Still, they were a lot faster than walking. The tops were hard and clear plastic, so a good view—such as there was to see—could be had, save when the yellow-brown pollen from the trees accumulated on the carts and blurred things. Locals who had money could buy flitters or hoppers if they wanted, and many had, but the carts were still used because they were free.

"Amazing," Reason said. "I had no idea how extensive these things were. A whole country of giant sticker bushes."

"Yeah, well, if the stuff works, they're gonna want a lot of it. It's a big galaxy."

"You have an insider's knowledge; you think the longevity chem won't work?"

Sleel shook his head. "No, it'll work. My parents don't make that kind of error." Yeah, they're great with plants, it's people they can't handle.

"Do they know we're coming?"

"I thought I'd surprise them."

Sleel shifted to stare through the pollen-dusty plastic. No, he hadn't called them. Probably even if he had, they would have forgotten about it within a few minutes. They were both still fairly young, early seventies, but they were also narrowly focused. An only son coming home after more than two decades would hardly rank in the same category as a patent graft or a new theory about enhanced photosynthesis.

"How much farther?"

"Another hour," Sleel said. "I think I'll just grab a little sleep. Wake me if a webbit tries to attack the cart."

Sleel closed his eyes and deepened his breathing, but he was not about to drift into sleep's welcome oblivion. Just as well, given his dreams of late.

Going home. Well, it hadn't been home for a long time, but it was one of the few constants in his life. Maybe they'd be glad to see him. Maybe he could impress them with what he'd done. Yeah. Right. And maybe he could learn to fly by waving his arms.

The boxcar to the ship leaving Koji was scheduled for a midday lift and Wu had her seat confirmed. The port was in Rakkaus, the City of Love, and it was a town unto itself. Wu carried her sword inside an officially sealed security travel tube, hanging from a strap over her left shoulder, and what little else she'd packed in a small bag slung over the other shoulder. She had almost an hour before boarding, and she wandered through the port, looking at the displays. Since this was Koji, most of the holoprojic or real displays had religious themes. Here were the Tillbedjare Artifacts, or a stylized rendering of them, the Hand and Eye and Mind; a few meters away the Libhober display showed the Prophet Stekarie achieving his cosmic flash of Oneness. Here sat the Buddha, contemplating the Eightfold Way; there the Trimenagists Shifting Triangle pulsed and glowed, beckoning. The Siblings of the Shroud had a computer to answer questions. The Jesuits manned a recruiting station. And past that—

Past that was a war memorial.

Wu stopped in front of the memorial and stared at it. It was an endlessly changing projection of faces, taken from ID graphs, people and mues, children, men, women, dozens of them, but each dissolving into another face within a few seconds, timed so that the effect was almost hypnotic. Bearded men transformed into smooth-faced boys, old women into younger ones, mues into basic stocks. As each face faded and

was replaced, the colors of skin and hair and eyes shifted
through the ranges of all races and configurations. The family
of man was indeed vast, including in it genetically altered
brothers and sisters who stretched the boundaries far and wide.
These were the faces of those who had died during the galactic
revolution that had toppled the Confed, millions of them, and
it would take a lot longer than any one person could stand here
to see the cycle through. There was no sound, no identification
attached to the images, just the continuing pulse of humanity.

Whenever she traveled, Wu would pause here for a few
moments. Somewhere in those constantly altering faces was
her sister. She had never seen her appear; she was in the viral
matrix of the computer's program, just as she continued in
Wu's own memory. A heroine of the revolution she had been.

Ah, sister. If I could only have a few minutes with you, to
say all I never got to say.

Wu turned away. So many faces. It sometimes overwhelmed
her to think about it. The numbers of those who had died had
no meaning, but looking upon this memorial made them real.
The sons and daughters and fathers and mothers and uncles and
cousins who had been caught in the sweep of history and taken
away from those who had loved them continued to pulse
behind her, but she could not look. She wanted to see her
sister, and yet, she did not think she could bear it if ever she
finally did.

On the floor under the display were various items left by
those who had come to see the memorial. Holographs, flowers,
medals, a candy bar, coins, tiny world flags and other things
that had some meaning to those who had left them, and perhaps
once to those who silently appeared and faded in the flux above
them. Offerings to memory they were, and even though a
service din came and cleaned them all up once a day, the floor
was never bare here.

It must be getting close to boarding time.

Wu walked away from the memorial.

Sleel and Reason arrived at Prime and the cart rolled to a
quiet stop, then opened itself. What luggage they had was

easily carried, small personal items bought in port, a change of clothes, little else. They had left in a hurry.

Sleel's breath came and went in a sigh as he stepped out onto the land of his birth and childhood. The smell was all too familiar, the feel of the air, the heat of the tropical sun. Sweat gathered under his orthoskins, seeking evaporation and failing to find it.

"Little warm," Reason observed.

"Yeah. This way."

The main complex was shaped roughly like a letter G. The top curve was of biolabs and climate-controlled greenhouses, of which there were five separate-but-joined-by-tubeway buildings. The back of the letter was given over to four supply and stores buildings, as well as a formal gathering hall, almost never used. The base of the curve was a pair of large shops for maintenance of dins and other machineries, and a power plant. The inverted and reversed L-angle consisted of housing; single, double and family units sufficient to hold fifty families in moderate comfort. Sleel's parents' unit was the last one on the inside tip, past the center of the G. Prime was the size of a small village, and stocked fully, easily self-sufficient for more than three years.

When Sleel and Reason arrived, there was nobody else in sight, save a pair of old exterior dins set to maintain the grounds. One of the robots lurched to the left on a damaged tread and had to keep correcting itself, moving in a jerky fan-shaped pattern.

Sleel laughed.

"Something funny about a lame din?"

"Not by itself. Only, that din was doing the same thing when I saw it last."

"You sure it's the same one?"

"Yeah. I carved my initials into it with a grafting laser, see?" He pointed at the lurching robot.

"Poor maintenance?" Reason said.

"Nah. They probably fixed it a dozen times. Things just don't program well, have to replace the whole brain and it's easier to patch it than replace it."

"Odd philosophy."

"They're all scientists here, they spend a lot of time in the future and not the present. Old cliche, but true, they tend to be dreamy about the little things." Yeah. Dreamy about things like food, shelter and . . . children.

The cube looked the same from the outside. The wear-ever plastic was a little more faded from the effects of weather, a paler blue than he remembered. The exterior gardens had different growths in them, but that had changed fairly frequently even when he'd lived here.

They walked to the entrance and Sleel palmed the ancient lock. The thin plastic door squeaked as it rolled open on its warped track. Sleel shook his head. It shouldn't surprise him that they hadn't changed the lock.

"Just going to walk in?" Reason asked.

"Sure."

The two men entered the cube, a spacious one by local standards. Living area, dining-kitchen, three bedrooms—his parents had never slept in the same room that Sleel had known about—two offices, three freshers. They dropped their gear.

"Doesn't seem as if anybody is home," Reason ventured.

"They're here," Sleel said.

Sure enough, after a few seconds, his mother peered around the doorway into her office. "Yes? Something?"

"Hello, Mother," Sleel said.

The woman blinked. Twenty years hadn't done much to her that he could tell. The lines were deeper, the hair all gray instead of just mostly that color. She looked smaller, but that figured. And she could have been wearing that same set of jumper coveralls when he'd left.

Elith Liotulia blinked again, as if unable to process what her eyes beheld. Then: "Oh. Oh. How are you?"

"Fine," Sleel said. "This is Jersey Reason, the famous thief."

"Ex-thief," Reason said, smiling.

"Oh. How nice. Well. Come in. Make yourself comfortable. I have a report to finish. I'll be with you later."

With that, she ducked back into her office.

Sleel's face felt tight, the thin smile chiseled into his features set as if it were made of stone.

Reason said, "How long has it been since she's seen you?"

"A little over twenty years."

"Good God."

"Wait until you meet my father."

With that, Sleel led Reason to his father's office.

Sampson Lewis Edmonds sat in the center of a computer work station, surrounded on three sides by machineries that hummed and purred with bioelectronic effort, his back to the door.

"Hello, Father," Sleel said.

The man spared them a glance away from his computations, took in the two, and nodded. "Busy," he said. He turned back to his work.

Sleel's frozen smile stayed in place. He nodded and turned away. That had always been enough, that single word. It was dismissal needing no amplification: *Busy.*

How in the name of any sexual god had these two ever managed to produce a child? Had they done it while working together, never missing a single datum between insertion and ejaculation? Sleel sighed.

"This way," he said.

Except for whatever the cleaning dins had done to it, his room was the same as he had left it. There were two beds, for when he had infrequent company who wanted to sleep alone. Toward the end of his life here, there had been a few who'd shared his bed with him; if his parents had noticed or cared, they had never said.

"We'll stay here. You can have either bed you want."

Reason nodded. He tossed his bags on the guest bed.

Sleel put his own gear on his bed. *Welcome home, son. It's so nice to see you again. How has your life been?*

Sleel shook his head. What exactly did you expect, pal? A parade? Well, no. But maybe something other than *Oh, have you been gone?*

Some things never changed.

NINE

IN THE DINING room, Sleel worked the com, linking into the White Radio net that spanned the inhabited galaxy. The name was a double misnomer, being that Desmond White had not invented it, though he had paid for it, and neither was it radio. The invention was more properly known in scientific circles as the A-17 Chronometric/E-RE-PN Impiotic Particle Acceleration/Reception Augmenter, and for that reason it quickly came to be called White Radio. What it did was allow communication across light years with very small time lags, and for some reason no one had ever been able to determine exactly, the longer the distance, the shorter the lag. In the early days, the computer augmentation had problems with the color, but that was long since corrected, so when Sleel called Dirisha, she looked as though she could be in the next room.

"Well, well," Dirisha said. "I thought sure you'd be in jail again by now." The chocolate-colored woman sat in front of her com in a bedroom, nude except for her spetsdöds. A thin sheen of sweat shined on her, highlighting her tight muscles.

Geneva lay on the bed behind Dirisha, and save for her weapons, she was also naked. "Hey, Sleel!" the blonde yelled from the bed. She waved.

Sleel grinned. The last time the three of them had been together he had fulfilled a major fantasy, and felt for a few hours during it that there was indeed some justice in the galaxy. These two were the brightest, deadliest and most beautiful women anywhere, at least in Sleel's experience. They were salt

and pepper, dark and pale, lovers since the years of training at
the Villa. He'd tried for longer than that to get Dirisha to sleep
with him, since the days they'd been bouncers at the Jade
Flower on Greaves, and finally, she and Geneva *both* had
agreed at the same time. Some justice, sure enough.

"Hello, Dirisha. Geneva. Did I interrupt something?"

"Nah. We wouldn't have answered the com if we'd been
really busy. How's it going, deuce?"

"You know me, no problems I can't handle."

She laughed. "Same old Sleel. What's up?"

"I need some information. You used to walk the Flex."

"Long time ago."

"You ever run into anybody who used a black sword? Some
odd kind of steel, not anodized or painted or anything, black all
the way through."

Dirisha thought about it for a few seconds. "I never fought
them. I heard about a couple, just streetscat, but never saw
them work myself."

"A couple of them?"

"It was about the time I left to go look up Emile when he was
doing his Pen impersonation on Renault. I didn't do a lot of
weapon work myself, those who did tended to find each other
to play with, but there were a few who waved blades."

"You have any contacts who might know?"

"This important?"

"No, I just wanted to spend a week's worth of stads calling
halfway across the universe to pass the time of day."

Geneva laughed and sat up on the bed. "You need to work
on that, Sleel. Not cutting enough. Needs more irony."

"Fuck you, brat," he said. That was Dirisha's pet name for
Geneva, but they'd given him use of it. He grinned when he
said it.

"Oh, yeah? Last time I offered, you said you were too
tired."

"I never said that."

"Okay, you didn't *say* it, but the physical evidence was
overwhelming. Or should I say underwhelming?"

"Any time you want a return match . . ." Sleel said.

"Ooh, Dirisha, listen, idle threats!"

"I'll check around, you want," Dirisha said.

"I'd appreciate it."

"This biz?"

"Yeah. You remember Jersey Reason? He's my client."

Dirisha smiled, white teeth shining against her dark skin. "Say hello to the old man for me." There was a short pause. "You doing okay with it? Need any help?"

"Nah, piece of easy, I just need to check some things out." He kept his voice even.

"All right. My com get the right number?"

"Yeah, I'm not hiding."

Dirisha glanced up at the corner of her screen. "Mtu?"

He felt himself grow tight, but he forced a smile. "Yeah, home for a visit to my parents."

Geneva slid off the bed and came to sit next to Dirisha. She put one pale hand on the darker woman's shoulder. The contrast in skin color was attractive. "Christo, *you* have parents?" Geneva said. "My. Will wonders never cease? I thought maybe you sprang full-size from the forehead of some god."

"A natural mistake," he said. "Gimme a call if you get something."

"Later, Sleel."

When the holoproj faded, Sleel found himself shaking his head. Those two were part of his real family. He found that he missed them, though he wouldn't have admitted that to them. Or to anybody else.

Behind him, Reason said, "I just caught the fade-out. How are your fellow matadors doing?"

"Fine. They're visiting the casinos on Vishnu."

"Expensive com from here."

"My parents can afford it. And they'll never notice it, anyhow. All their bills go through a manager and he's learned to expect weird things from them."

Sleel glanced at his timepiece. "Almost eighteen. I'd better call the catering service and tell them there are two more of us for supper."

Reason looked puzzled.

"Neither my father nor my mother will remember that we

are here. They have all their meals delivered, same time every day. A din brings the food and rings a loud bell until one of my parents stirs enough to shut it off manually. Otherwise they'd probably starve."

"I hope you won't take offense, but your parents are passing strange."

Sleel laughed, a short, sharp sound. "You might just qualify as a master of understatement with that one."

The vessel carrying Kildee Wu to Rift was one of the old Melanie-class hoppers, an ancient ship from the height of the Confed's reign. In those days, travel schedules were based on policy and not practicality, and so the ship had been appointed with enough luxuries and space for voyages that could last months for some passengers. There were parks, convoluted walking paths through genetically stunted small forests, streams and ponds, and individual cubicles built to resemble tiny houses. Named *The Skate*, the ship was a study in deception, for although it created the illusion of size and space, it was scarely larger than a standard troop ship. The arts of *bonsai* and architectural eyeweave had peaked in such vessels, and even when you knew you were being fooled, it still looked like a small village.

Wu wandered along one of the paths, listening to the sounds of artificial birds and the tread-actuated buzz and rasp of various insects. The pull was a standard one-gee. A permanent repeating holoproj overhead showed a sunshiny blue sky with fleecy clouds, and a gentle breeze wafted through the trees carrying the scent of pine. The sounds and lights and smells were all artfully designed to convince a walker that he or she was in a real, albeit a tiny, wood, but like the old flat wall paintings of *trompe l'œil*, there was a not-real feeling about it all. Something deep within her sensed the illusory nature of her surroundings; still, it was pleasant enough. And a walk in the forest without company allowed her space enough to reach for the inner calm she needed. Although Wu meditated regularly using various martial disciplines, she wanted her spirit to be like a still pool for the task to come. It mattered not how sharp a woman's blade was, could she not wield it with dispassion.

Attachment to victory or even technique was bad. In sword-play, there was no past and no future, only *now*, and nothing must be allowed to pull or push the moment.

Wu laughed at herself. Right. As if such high-mindedness could make it so. Her *sensei*, Master Ven, would be whacking her with the bamboo in this moment, were she sitting *zazen*, no doubt about it. Don't think, *be*! he would roar. She kept the smile after the laugh, remembering the old man. Now there was one who'd had control of his art. His last battle was the stuff of legends. He had challenged five of the best swordplay-ers in the Musashi Flex to a duel, five against his one, and met them in combat using a wooden blade against their steel. After defeating them, he had sat *seiza*, bowed once, and achieved *satori*, after which he left the shell of his body behind by sheer force of will. He had been eighty years old.

Wu wished she could have seen it. Of the four players who survived the encounter with her master, she had spoken to three, and all of them had come away radically changed. One had put down the sword and gone into a religious order. One had secluded himself, seeing no one for six months, to ponder his life. One had begun a full-time study under Master Ven's then most highly ranked student, Kildee's uncle. The fourth player committed suicide before Kildee could reach her.

Master Ven was a man who had lived his life exactly as he wished, and left it when he thought the moment penultimate. Every player of note in the Musashi Flex had heard the story, and though it sometimes was amplified in the telling, it was amazing enough in fact. The great Musashi himself had used a wooden sword near the end of his career, but never against five opponents at once.

Wu hoped that when her time came, she could leave life with as much grace as her master.

Given the mission she was on, that time might be near.

So she walked through the pretend forest, striving for inner quietness, seeking to become one with her self. She had a long way to go, she knew, both in space and in time. Ah, well, a woman had to do what a woman had to do, and demons take the rest. That made her smile, too.

• • •

Cierto's fortune was such that he need not be limited to commercial star hoppers as were ordinary men. His ship, *The Lanza*, was sufficient to transport fifty passengers in extreme comfort, with a range of nearly that number of light years before resupply was needed. On this voyage, there were only ten passengers, including himself. His top four fencing students, two men and two women, were on board, as was a three-person team of expert computerists who could electronically forge nearly any document. There was also a pair of biologists who had expertise relating to the guarded plants upon the world to which they traveled. Already the forgers were at work on positioning materials needed to secure legitimate entry into the area called The Brambles, and the scientists were preparing briefings for Cierto and his students regarding the same place.

The grease of many standards made for smooth workings, Cierto thought for perhaps the thousandth time.

He stood in the ship's gymnasium, a small space, but adequate for his needs. Once on Mtu he would be contacted by a certain disaffected scientist who had quit or been fired from the project, depending upon which story you chose to believe, and learn more about the place where his quarry had fled. After that, it would be only a matter of time before the thief was made to pay for his crime. Honor would be served, finally.

Sleel's parents emerged from their offices, called by the food delivery din's loud bell. The pair of them brought to mind nothing so much as soggy butterflies emerging from their cocoons, not quite finished with their metamorphosis, blinking against unaccustomed brightness and a new life.

Already seated at the table with Reason, Sleel watched them come. Here were two people unsuited to reality, he thought. Certainly not qualified to be parents. You had to have a license to carry a weapon or pilot a flitter or to run a business, and none of those came close to the responsibilities of caring for children, but civilization had not seen the light regarding that yet.

The two scientists arrived at the table and regarded Sleel and

Reason, blinking and with some puzzlement, as though the matador and his charge had appeared there by magic.

"Mother. Father. This is Jersey Reason."

His parents nodded, almost as one, and sat.

The din circled the table on quiet rollers, setting small microwave steam trays in front of each diner.

Elith Liotulia opened the cover of her tray. The smell of soypro and blue beans mushroomed up in a small cloud of hot vapor. And some kind of fruit pie, probably lolaberry, Sleel thought. His mother looked at the food for a moment, then up at Sleel. "How are you?" And as an afterthought, she added, "Son?"

"Fine."

"Um." She stirred the steaming collection of beans around with her spork. "It has been a while since we've seen you. How have you spent your time?"

Sleel could not suppress a chuckle. "For the last twenty years? Oh, this and that."

Sampson Lewis Edmonds shoveled soypro into his mouth, then hastily reached for the glass of water to cool the too-hot bite of cutlet. When he had drenched the heat, he said, "What is the uniform?"

"I am a matador, Father. A bodyguard."

Edmonds nodded absently, and grunted as he took another bite of soypro. The term meant nothing to him; he had not heard of the matadors. "A bodyguard." The tone was disapproving.

Sleel, unable to stop himself, rushed in to defend against the metaphorically raised eyebrow. "I've done other things," he said, too quickly.

"Really?" his mother said.

"I went to Bocca when I left here."

"And—?" his father said.

"I graduated with signal honors. Third in a class of seventeen hundred, a doctorate in poetic literature, with a minor in anthrokinetics."

"A doctorate," his mother said. "That's nice."

"Not in botany, though," his father said. "And only third."

The spot that Sleel had managed to squeeze into a tiny

sphere over the years suddenly expanded under his sternum, filling him with emptiness again. Just like that, it stole his heart and soul and made him hollow once again.

Aching, Sleel rushed ahead. "I also wrote several novels that were well received. Under the name of Gerard Repe."

Reason stared at Sleel. "*You* are Gerard Repe? The man of mystery? The author nobody sees? My God, why aren't you living in a palace? Repe's books have sold in the tens of millions. I've read all six of them. First time I finished *Heartsick* I cried myself to sleep."

"I gave all the money to charity. Established a foundation that attends to orphaned children."

"That was nice of you," his mother said.

Sleel felt the pressure of Reason's gaze and amazement. The older man muttered, "Disingenuous. *There* was an understatement. My God. You're a genius and I never suspected."

"Yeah, and don't forget I was a hero of the Revolution," Sleel said.

"Revolution?" his father said, around a mouthful of blue beans.

Sleel's laugh was bitter; it came up from his depths, full of all the years. How could you impress a man who was so out of touch with life that he missed—he *missed*!—the upheaval that rearranged the entire galaxy?

"That's nice," his mother said. On some level Sleel knew she could feel his pain, had always been able to feel it, but had never known what to do about it. It affected her just enough to make her vaguely uncomfortable. If his father felt anything similar, it had never shown.

If he wrote this scene in a novel, nobody would believe it, Sleel thought. But Sleel felt the old wounds reopen afresh, as if no time had passed, as if he were still sixteen and vowing to do something to impress them or die. Nothing impressed them, nothing outside their own deep but very narrow expertise.

Sleel did what he always did when he wanted to see his parents smile. That way, he could pretend they were smiling at him. "So, how's the new variation coming?"

There was always a new variation, always.

Both his parents lit up as if they'd been jolted with a sudden charge of high energy. They both smiled. They both started talking at once:

"—genome reconfiguration optimizes photosynthetic processes—"

"—model augmentation indicates an increased reproductive rate equal to the current maximums—"

"—which alters the chemical composition by almost nine percent, low, but obviously only a transitional sequence that can be improved—"

"—however the Liebig Constant will not be reached for another six generations unless the Gesner Effect can be recapitulated without the Hooker Variant—"

Sleel allowed the botanical patois to wash over him as he had allowed it during his entire life with them, smiling and nodding as if he understood it all. It was like a simultaneous lecture from two brilliant professors to a doctoral class, and even an expert would be hard pressed to keep up with either, much less both at the same time. But it was a game Sleel knew all too well. Even at five years old he could play it and fool them. How anyone could look at a small child smiling and nodding as they spewed such esoterica and think he understood had always escaped him. He smiled and chewed it up and swallowed it into that void where his heart and soul should be.

Some things change frequently, some things seldom, some things never.

Thought of the day from Sleel, the hollow man.

TEN

When Kildee Wu arrived on Rift, she had no trouble finding *La Casa del Acero Negro*. Or in reaching the Romantic Enclave and the gates of the estate itself.

Ah, sí, fem, this is indeed the famous House of Black Steel, the guard told her. No, you cannot see it from this location, it is far beyond the fence, but it is a magnificent structure. Here, here is a holocard with a picture for you, compliments of El Patrón. Sí, is permitted to use your camera for pictures. No, the Patrón is offworld at the moment. No, the guard did not know to where he journeyed, but then, your pardon, even if well paid and charged with great responsibility, he was after all only a guard.

The master of the *casa* was apparently unworried if anyone knew where he had gone, Wu found when she checked at the port where one of his personal boxcars was normally berthed. His starship, *The Lanza*, had departed only a week ago for orbit around Mtu, in the Bibi Arusi System. Though the information officer at the port did not know why such a man would wish to spend his time on such a backward planet, the motives of the very rich were sometimes hard to fathom, no? They are not like ordinary people such as we, the officer allowed.

Indeed not, Wu said.

She walked through the port, thinking. While the school brought in fair money and she had spent little of it over the years, she was not rich. Should she wait here for Cierto's return? Or should she buy another ticket and follow him? Both had their advantages and disadvantages. On the one hand, she could be fairly certain the man would arrive here eventually. When that might happen was another thing but she knew how to be patient. On the other hand, this was Cierto's base, and he would be strongest on his home grounds. Meeting him in a neutral setting could be to her advantage.

He was only a week ahead of her, and Mtu was only that far away by Bender drive. A man with his own starship should be relatively easy to find on an agroworld like Mtu.

Yes. Go there and find him, then.

The scientist, who called himself Cembor Jaan, was a nervous, sweaty man, dark hair and skin, and full of bitterness against those who had cast him aside. He was only too eager to spill whatever he knew about The Brambles to Cierto.

They sat in a suite at the largest and most expensive hotel in Bandari, itself the largest city on the planet, though large was a relative term. Less than a million people lived here, mostly basic stock, with perhaps ten percent of them assorted mues.

Two of Cierto's students, Miguel and Juanita, stood guard just outside the door to this, the biggest of the eight rooms in the suite; the other students, Luis and Doña, were stationed at the entrances in the hallway. The rooms had been swept for listening devices, of which there had been none.

Jaan said, "The defenses were the best the Confed could devise when they were first installed. Nothing without clearance is allowed to overfly the area, save at orbital heights, and these satellites are all tracked. Any craft below that is warned by automatic transmissions; if they do not change course, they are shot down.

"There is the fence, of course. Anyone attempting to climb or cut through it is pinpointed on the security sensors. Guards can reach any area of the perimeter within a few minutes from one of the two hundred stations just inside the wire. And there are sensors underground to prevent digging.

"While the entire complex is too vast to cover every square meter with movement sensors, there are enough of them strategically located to make movement for more than a klick or two very risky. Armed guards patrol key lanes among the trees, as do heat reader dins."

Cierto waved one hand in dismissal. Circumventing even the best security was not impossible; for every device invented to stop someone, a counterdevice was almost always created. His own estate's security was similar, though probably of a lesser degree of thoroughness. No, merely being able to get into an area the size of a country was not the problem. Locating the quarry exactly and arranging all the steps necessary to take him were apt to be more difficult. Still, with the proper equipment and a certain level of adeptness, it could be done.

"Tell me," he said. "This plant, will it burn?"

In the days after their arrival, Sleel and Reason could have easily fallen into a very dull routine. Sleel's parents lived in their world, unaffected by and nearly oblivious of their guests. The weather was hot and muggy, activities outside of the scientific work almost nonexistent, and by and large, the two men were ignored. Sleel worked out, practiced shooting, and waited for Dirisha to get back to him with whatever information she could find. Of course, he also tied into the local nets, checking for what he expected, somebody come looking for them.

As a matador, Sleel knew there were no truly secure places. But like the old castles which had specially built floors that creaked and sang when trod upon, getting to the center of The Brambles would require a certain amount of noise. The trick was in knowing what to listen for.

So he trained and listened and waited. Like watching an intricate game of *Go* or chess, it was slow, at times boring, even when lives were at risk. Still, it had to be done.

Three weeks after they had arrived, there came a distant electronic creak at the entrance to the castle.

Sleel heard it during his morning scan of the security database he had built.

There was a private ship hanging in high orbit over the world.

On Earth or Mason or Vishnu or any one of a dozen other planets thick with humanity, a private ship would draw little attention. Even though the monies needed for interstellar travel were vast compared to what an ordinary middle-class citizen had, there were in the galaxy hundreds of thousands of those rich enough to afford such things. Here on Mtu, the main visitors were scientists, and they usually came by commercial transport or foundation charters, science per se being not nearly so well-paying a career field as entertainment or sports. According to Sleel's sources at Orbital Control, this vessel was registered to a corporation on Rift, in the Delta System. The ship was called *The Lanza*.

Not a major warning bell, but enough to tickle Sleel's attention. A small creak, maybe only the settling of the house caused by a temperature change. Or maybe not. Sleel plugged it into his consciousness, and made a few calls to check it out further.

Dirisha called back that same afternoon.

"Yo, Sleel."

"Dirisha. Where's the blonde shadow?"

"Geneva's at the swimming pool inciting lust in half the casino's transient population."

They both smiled.

"I got something for you on one of the swordplayers. The guy I heard about was considered the best at the edged stuff for a time. About fourteen, fifteen years back. He did nineteen duels in the last six months we can track him."

Sleel heard a trace of something in her voice. He said, "That a lot?"

"Yeah. In a busy year I did maybe six. A dozen in that time would be considered pushing it, least in the top ranks. Guy liked to fight. He had eighteen wins; twelve were outright kills, six were wounded badly enough so they barely made it even with full-medical rides. He used a black sword."

"Sounds like what I'm looking for. Eighteen wins, you said, but nineteen fights?"

"Yep. There aren't any official records on the nineteenth fight. The word is, in the last one, our boy lost a foot. He went away after that, no further mention of him in the Flex. Probably regrew the foot and retired. Not many old players in the dance. It's a game for the young and stupid, mostly. The smart ones get out, they survive long enough."

"What about the player who beat him?"

"No record on them. They didn't claim the victory and Cierto never said."

"Cierto."

"Yeah, that's the guy with the black sword. Hoja Cierto, from Rift."

Oh, ho, Sleel thought. Rift, as in private ship hanging in the sky up there is from Rift.

Sleel found Reason lying under the shade of a big umbrella, sipping at a drink he'd programmed the dispense-din to make. Something with a lot of color in it, red and blue and even a touch of green. The older man was reading something, the words of which were barely visible, the holoproj washed dim by the reflected tropical sunlight even here in the shadows.

"We got company," Sleel said.

"Oh?"

"A ship owned by one Hoja Cierto of the planet Rift is hanging offworld in a parking orbit. Mean anything to you?"

Reason touched a control on his reader and the dim text vanished. He appeared thoughtful. "Doesn't resonate offhand," he said. "Rift."

"In Delta," Sleel offered.

"I know where it is. I'm trying to remember if I've ever been there." He shook his head. "I can't recall anything. Certainly not recently."

"How recent is recently?"

"Thirty years."

Sleel nodded. "All right. It would be nice to know *why*, but it's more important to know *who* at this point. I've got a couple of worms digging for information on this guy."

"Cierto," Reason said. "No, the name doesn't mean anything to me. Are we certain that is who it is?"

"No. He could be lending his ship out, I suppose. But according to Dirisha, this guy likes to play with swords. Black swords."

"Ah."

"Yeah. And he's got a lot of money if he owns his own starship; he'll probably figure out a way to get into The Brambles."

"Despite the security?"

"I can think of three or four ways without taxing my brain."

"What do we do?"

"We don't stay here. There's a camp about a hundred and fifty klicks away, used by one of the local religious groups for retreats. It'll be empty this time of year. We'll go there." Whatever his parents were or were not, Sleel wouldn't bring deadly danger to their cube. It had been a while since he'd lived here, but he knew the territory. Once thing nice about an orchard with a lifetime harvest cycle was that it stayed pretty much the same. The advantages were his when it came to terrain, and also when it came to training, he figured. Like he had told Dirisha, it was a piece of easy.

Still, just in case, he ought to pick up a few things. If the bad guys knew he was guarding Reason, and surely they must, given what had happened to the last would-be assassin on Earth, then they would plug that into their equation. It would be good to alter that picture before they came to call.

Getting to Mtu was easy enough. Finding the ship she wanted was not much more difficult. It was up there, all right, circling at the outer limits of the atmosphere, as regular as a pulse timer. Getting to it was another matter.

Wu sat in a booth at a theme restaurant, working her way through a meal of Lagomustardorian waterfowl. Supposedly it was fresh and supposedly it was steeped in a genuine *mchele* and *namna ya tunda* sauce, but Wu had trouble believing that either was true. The bird was tough and the sauce awfully bland for the normally fiery rice-and-strawberry liquor.

The restaurant, on the edge of the tourist quarter, was somewhat better appointed. It had as its focus the early history of the Wild South on the neighboring world of Mwanamamke, complete with holographic representations of a vast *struthio* ranch. The large and ungainly flightless birds, half again the size of a tall man, most of the height being legs and neck, padded back and forth across the grasslands of the high plateau

with appropriate sound effects, squawks, trills, mating whistles
and the thud of splay-feet. To Wu's left, where a gilded rope
prevented the unwary from smacking nose first into the wall
hidden by the holoproj, a pair of *struthio* went through an
arcane mating dance, bobbing and stretching, doing small
leaps back and forth, singing in raspy tones to each other. The
female was the aggressor in this ritual, nature's balance on the
plain having produced fewer of them than of the male birds;
too, the female was the bearer of the brighter plumage.

The female, having excited the male so that a small and
glistening purple penis now peeped from his downy feathers,
turned and presented to him in a half squat. The male mounted
her, having to rise up onto his toes to accomplish the insertion.
As he began to thrust, the female beat her vestigial wings in
time to his movements. The act of copulation itself lasted no
more than a few seconds. The male withdrew, shook himself
into a fluffy state, smoothed his feathers, then turned and
padded off. The female straightened from her crouch and went
in the opposite direction. Neither bird looked back at the other.

Seemed like a lot of dancing for such a short climax, Wu
thought. Must be particularly intense for the birds. Whatever,
it was more interesting than the meal.

Wu did not think that Cierto had come all the way to this
world merely to fly round and round it; likely he would come
down sooner or later, had he not done so already. She had
begun discreet inquiries, hiring a local private investigative
firm to that end. As long as his ship was still up there, she
guessed that Cierto would be here. True, this was not an
appropriate assumption, any more than the one that Cierto
hadn't come here simply to circle in orbit. One was not
supposed to assume *anything*; Master Ven had always been
quite explicit about that. Still, sometimes it was hard to be in
the moment and not jump to that juicy conclusion just ahead in
the path.

Wu sighed and pushed away the remains of her supper.
There was nothing wrong with personal ambition—Master Ven
had taught her that, too—unless it got in the way of spiritual
progress. The paths of power and magic were seductive; a
seeker must stay on guard to avoid being lured into a dead-end
road. It was all too easy to become rich or famous or

influential, were such things all that one wished to accomplish. The growth of spirit required much more than these and they could easily stunt that growth, did not one tread with great care. Master Ven himself had been the most powerful man Wu had ever known, yet only a handful of people had ever seen it, for he was careful to keep it hidden unless there was a great need for demonstration. She had never seen him walk on water, but there was a part of her past her rational mind that would have believed him had he ever said he could.

This thing with Cierto was a personal goal, an ambition, and Wu must take care that she not allow it to block her way. Easier thought than done, however.

Behind her, another pair of giant birds began to dance. She shifted to watch them.

An old man came into the restaurant. He wore a standard gray business one-piece and sandals and looked ordinary enough, save for the old-style tripolar droud sockets on the sides of his shaved skull. He walked to where Wu sat and nodded at her. "Fem Wu?"

"Yes?"

"I'm Scanner, from the agency. We spoke earlier on the com."

The transmission had been without visuals, but Wu recognized the scratchy voice. "Please sit down."

The old man did. "I've located our subject. He has a suite at the Vivu Hotel. There are seven others with him from offworld, including the boxcar pilot, and at least one local staying there. His people have been making inquiries about The Brambles."

Wu nodded. "You are very efficient."

The old man tapped one of his drouds. "Electron dances can tell you a lot, if you know where to look."

"Anything else?"

"Our subject has just bought a small chemical manufacturing plant in Pau; that's a little industrial town about forty klicks away from here."

"A chemical plant?"

"It mostly produces several forms of chlorine, bottled gas, blocks, and a granulated dry powder. The various aspects are used primarily where UV or US water treatment is impractical. Swimming pools and small drinking-water tanks, like that."

"Odd," Wu said.

Scanner shrugged.

"And where is Cierto now?"

"As of thirty minutes ago, in transit to the plant at Pua."

Wu shook her head, puzzled. Certainly Cierto's business was his own, but it did seem passing strange that he would travel all the way across the galaxy to personally buy something like this.

"Thank you," Wu said to Scanner. "I appreciate your skill and speed."

The old man smiled. "Years of practice."

"Any of my retainer left?"

"About half."

"Keep it."

"You're too generous, Fem Wu. You want an opinion?"

"Sure."

"The chlorine plant has a contract to deliver in The Brambles; been doing it for years."

"So?"

"So, unless you have a stack of clearances, you can't get into the place. Tight security. You know what they're doing there?"

"I've heard."

"Well, hopping the fence is dangerous, apt to get you killed, and incomings and outgoings are checked. But if you wanted to get past the guards, owning a hovervan that has been making the trip for years would be one way to go about it."

Wu nodded again. "All right. But why would he want to sneak into The Brambles?"

"Got me. I'm just saying he probably can, if he wants."

Wu considered that. Buying the chem plant would make more sense if there was some ulterior motive involved.

"Thanks again," she said.

"All part of the service, fem." As he stood, he measured her with a look. "As one kind of dancer to another."

She nodded once, acknowledging his call. He might be old, but his eyes and the mind behind them were still sharp.

Now, the question was: why did Cierto want to go into The Brambles?

ELEVEN

"ALL IS IN readiness, Patrón," Miguel said.

The morning's heat had already started to rise, the tropical foliage steaming under the bright sun, the air vaporous and heavy over the chemical plant. The sharp stink of the chlorinating compound stabbed at Cierto's nostrils as he stood next to the hovervan watching the final plastic barrel of the stuff being loaded.

"Very well. Tell it to me again."

Miguel, a squat and muscular man of twenty-two, nodded once. "Luis and Juanita are en route in their vans. Juanita is already within the compound; Luis will be arriving at the border within a few moments. The scientist has rigged Luis's van for the diversion. Doña is on-station and ready to bring up the escape vehicle. Your suit is inside, as are the two gliders." He indicated the van with a glance. "All of the identification materials have been logged and vetted. The quarry has been positively located and the maps and overlays are in the van's computer. The quarry is alone with the single guard. Everything is just as planned."

Cierto rubbed at his lower lip with one finger. "Very well. Let us depart."

He and Miguel entered the van. The young man moved to the control seat while Cierto went to put on his special clothing. This was a third-generation shiftsuit, which gave the wearer the ability to match a stationary background almost to the point of invisibility. Seated upon a barrel in the back of the van, a man wearing such a disguise would appear to be part of the truck's wall even in bright light. In addition, the shiftsuit had been lined with spidersilk panel armor, so that it was roughly equivalent to class-two military gear. Wearing such, with the hood and matching face shield, would not only make a man virtually undetectable by human eyes, but also impervious to many personal hand weapons. It was not as good as a full class-one hardsuit, or even the new issue softsuits—a powerful thrust from a sharp knife would surely pierce it, for instance—but it *would* stop a spetsdöd dart. A special pouch on the left side hid his sword; on his right hip, a shielded holster contained a 12mm Rynar projectile pistol. This weapon held a magazine containing nine squashed-ceramic frangible bullets that could be driven to very high velocity by electromagnetic pulses. His armor wouldn't stop these, either. The thief should die by Cierto's blade, true enough, but the matador need merely be gotten out of the way with whatever means necessary.

Each of his students also had such gear ready for use at the proper time. True, it was bulky and it tended to slow one's moments, but the advantages outweighed the disadvantages for this encounter. It was hot, even with the built-in regulators, but in the cooled compartment of the van this was no problem. With luck, he would only have to wear the suit outside for a brief time.

As he dressed, Cierto reviewed the plan once again. It was simple enough. Miguel had a delivery flight that would take them within a few kilometers of where the old thief was hiding. At an appropriate place, he and Miguel would leave the vehicle and fly between the rows of trees using small delta-wing gliders powered with tiny, silent repulsors. The hovervan would continue toward its distant destination on robotic controls. It would overfly the stop and either be shot down or eventually crash on its own, but by then, Cierto would be long gone.

Juanita would perform a similar action with her van. Luis would also join them, via glider, but not before he allowed his van to supposedly develop repellor trouble. After Luis called for help, his van would crash into the trees.

The scientist had explained it to Cierto with a kind of delight. "Certain chemicals when mixed produce a delayed but very intense form of combustion. These chlorinated granules, for instance, are relatively harmless when dry, see?" He dipped one hand into the white grains and allowed them to sift through his fingers back into the container, a metal bowl that held about a liter of the material.

"This is common hydraulic fluid," the tame scientist said, holding up a clear cup filled with a reddish liquid. "It is used in wing controls, landing gear and such. By itself it is harmless. Mix it with the chlorinating compound, however—" With that, he dumped the liquid into the bowl with the granules. "And the combination proves to be something else altogether." The scientist glanced at his timepiece.

Cierto looked at the sludge formed by the liquid and the granules. It bubbled a little, but nothing else seemed to be happening. "Very impressive," he said, his voice dry.

"It takes about four minutes," the scientist said. He continued to monitor the time. "Please stand back, Patrón."

Cierto moved back to a spot indicated by the scientist, five meters away from the mixture. A strong odor, bitter and sharp, reached him, and a smallish amount of smoke arose from the bowl. The time dragged. "I don't see—"

A pillar of flame erupted from the bowl, reaching three meters into the air with a sudden roar, as if spewed forth by a mythological dragon. The heat of it singed Cierto's eyebrows and the hair on the back of his hands even at this distance. This *was* impressive.

"Ah," Cierto said.

"Sí, Patrón. If a van carrying a load of such granulated chlorine compound crashes and spills much of it, and if the hydraulic lines of the van which contain more than a dozen liters of the liquid should also rupture . . ."

"Hot enough to light the trees?"

"Sí, Patrón. More than hot enough."

"Trees that are potentially worth millions, perhaps even billions each, will ignite. I expect that will draw considerable attention."

"As you say, Patrón."

Now dressed in the shiftsuit, Cierto smiled at the memory. A simple plan, but one which would have an excellent chance of success. Local authorities would be busy worrying about their crop. While they concentrated on extinguishing the fire, Cierto and three of his students would kill the old thief and his guard, and rendezvous with Doña where she waited with the escape vehicle. If they had trouble with guards while leaving, those guards would be dealt with, and before anyone could figure out what had happened, they would be on his private ship and into Bender space.

Honor would be satisfied, at last.

The camp was reached by road only from the east. The three buildings that comprised the main part were upon a hill deemed too rocky to level and use for planting, so the single road wound around and over mostly bare rock and dirt, with some small scrub growth and grasses being the only vegetation. From the hill, a man had good views of the canopy of bramble extending off in all directions below.

While intentionally rustic, the camp was not without some modern facilities. Sleel had the computer up and had installed in it a security program. The matadors had contacts all over the galaxy, and it was not difficult to spend a goodly chunk of Reason's money upon defensive materials.

Sleel explained it to Reason.

"I've got half a dozen AA lances around the perimeter of the hill," he said. "Although there isn't supposed to be any air traffic without official clearance, that's just in case anybody comes calling from the air. They do, they get spiked.

"There are button sensors scattered around the base of the hill, with a cluster along the road, so anybody comes that way, we see 'em."

Sleel held up a small rectangle of black plastic. "This is a black-market spetsdöd load. Explosive rounds. Punches a neat little cone-shaped crater in anything softer than carbonex or steel when it hits it. In case our bad guys have developed an immunity to my other dart chem."

"I didn't think spetsdöds were supposed to be lethal."

"Learn something new even at your age, hey?"

Sleel produced a small pocket pistol. "This is a 6mm needler, fires capacitor rounds, about thirty thousand volts each. Builds up the charge when it spins through the muoplastic barrel. Kind of like a real mild version of the military Spasm load, it'll lock a guy into tetany long enough to knock him down and keep him twitching for ten minutes. Like a taser, but without wires." He handed the gun to Reason.

"I don't much like guns," the older man said.

"I'm not asking you to make love to it, just keep it around. Try not to shoot me or yourself with it. You got fourteen shots in a magazine; here is a spare. There are more than twenty-eight of them, we're in trouble."

Sleel grinned.

"You think they are coming here."

"Oh, yeah. I haven't figured out how or when, but they're coming. So far they have shown us they are determined, but not too adept, so I figure we either end it here or catch us one who can tell us where to go to finish it. If we can grab one before he passes out."

"So that's it?"

"The good ones are simple. Unless you have a better idea."

"No."

Sleel looked through the plastic window in the main room of the largest building in the camp. The hot sky was cloudy on one edge, promising a thunderstorm before the day wore out. He was ready. More than ready, he was anxious for an attack. It was time to do what he knew how to do, to prove to himself that he was good at something.

Come on, elbowsuckers. Come and try me.

Whatever Cierto was up to, Wu didn't think it was in any way good. The man was arrogant, rich, amoral, and deadly, not a pleasant combination. She had watched him enter the hovervan and leave, heading toward The Brambles, and it occurred to her that something nasty was about to transpire.

What, she wondered, could she do about it?

She used her personal com to put in a call to Scanner.

"No," the old man said, "I don't think I can get you into The Brambles, least not so fast as to be able to tail somebody."

In the shade of a broad-leaved tree with orange bark, Wu nodded to herself. "Thanks anyway."

"What I can do, I can tap into the mapsats and footprint him for you."

"Come again?"

"Mapping satellites that overfly The Brambles. These things have optical resolution that can read the time on a guy's wristwatch from twenty thousand klicks. There are sixty or seventy of them orbiting up there officially, not even counting the sub rosa spysats I can access. Give me your location and the direction the van took."

Wu did so.

"Hold on a second; I have to translate that into binary grid numbers. Okay . . . got it. It's a little tricky, switching from unit to unit here . . . there he is. Fortunately there isn't a lot of air traffic over The Brambles. Yep, there's the flight plan, that's our boy. He's on course and heading for a scheduled delivery at Madini, that's about six hundred klicks from where you are. Oops, now he's moving out of range. I need to see what's coming up crossways . . . it'll be a couple of minutes before I can patch into something to see him again."

Wu shook her head, amazed.

"All right, here's what I'll do. I'll find out where he goes and then follow him when he comes back. I'll give you a call when he's where you can reach him, that okay?"

"Great."

"Okay. Discom."

Wu tucked her com unit back into a little square and crowed it to her belt. Well. Whatever Cierto was up to in The Brambles, she could catch him when he returned. Wonderful stuff, technology.

Meanwhile, maybe she could get in a little practice with her sword. One could never be too good. Especially now.

Sleel felt a chill, despite the day's warmth, as he moved about the camp. He was like a tracking beast searching for some sign of intrusion. He scanned the skies and road, seeing nothing amiss, but feeling that prickly coolness on his skin that went with danger. His inquiries had come up mostly dry. He knew that the passengers of the private ship were groundside, checked into a hotel in Bandari, but they weren't in their rooms. A list of applications to enter The Brambles did not include Cierto's name, but Sleel also did not assume the man was entirely stupid. Even though local records showed that no visitors had been approved for entry past the guarded borders for today, the tickle in Sleel's belly would not stay still. Danger was coming; Sleel knew it in that part of his mind that lived past reason and logic. The old reptile brain Dirisha used to prattle on about, that part was alert, nose in the air, sniffing for death and smelling its dank stench. How and when it didn't know, but soon. It knew that.

Sleel checked the explosive loads in his left spotsdöd again, a thing he had done five times already today. The right hand weapon still contained the stepped-up version of shocktox, the animal trank. Even though Sleel was less concerned with sparing life than Emile or some of the other matadors, there was no point in using more force than was needed to stop the threat. Sleel figured that if somebody tried to kill you, all bets were off, insofar as their right to keep using the community air went; still, explaining a pile of bodies could sometimes get difficult. Best to save the killing stroke until there was a real need for it.

He was outside the main building, perched upon a small grassy hillock that rose a few meters higher than the rest of the hill. The sunlight splashed everywhere, the bugs buzzed back and forth, the air was thick with humidity. It was quiet enough.

Sleel looked at his tracker. Reason's transmitter sent to the tiny four-centimeter screen a small green dot that pulsed in time to his heartbeat. The man seemed calm enough. That was good. Sleel didn't doubt his own ability, especially given what these geeps had thrown at him so far. It was almost a shame to have to bring it to a close. Almost, but not quite.

Inside the hovervan, Miguel said, "Thirty seconds, Patrón." His voice was muffled by the protective helmet and face shield of the shiftsuit he now wore.

Cierto nodded absently. "I am ready." The trip thus far had been almost uneventful. The guards at the border had performed a cursory inspection, and neither Cierto nor the glider parts had been in any jeopardy. Such fools would not last long in his employ. Immediately after clearing the border, Miguel had put the vehicle on automatic and begun to assemble the gliders. There was a bad moment when one of the spunfiber struts jammed, due to some grains of the chlorinating compound which had adhered to it from where it had been hidden. Fortunately it was a problem easily resolved. Now, both gliders were rigged, the small and quiet motors purring in readiness.

Miguel touched a control and the rear door of the van retracted. They were cruising at perhaps two hundred kilometers per hour and the warmer air from outside swirled around them. Miguel glanced at his timer. "Five seconds, Patrón."

Cierto moved to the edge of the doorway. The filmy delta-shaped wing of his glider was fan-folded closed to allow movement inside the van; once he leaped out, a tug would pop the wing open. Although they were perhaps a thousand meters above the tops of the trees, Cierto had only a touch of fear about the jump. He had tested this particular glider on a dozen such drops and it had performed flawlessly—

"Go, Patrón!"

Cierto leaped into the empty air, to his left as they had practiced. Miguel was immediately behind him, angling right.

There was a moment of gut-twisting free-fall before the wing snapped out and locked into place; then Cierto was flying in the hot daylight, still dropping rapidly, but now in a controlled glide. In a moment, he and Miguel would be between two rows of the ubiquitous trees and safe from detection. Any radar tracking the van would show only a quick strobe of them before they were gone, and unless the simadam operating it happened to be looking right at the scope at that precise instant, they would never be noticed at all.

Wu was in a flat patch of grass on the edge of a public park, dancing with her sword. She had gathered a small and curious crowd, but she did not allow this to bother her as she moved. The single chime of her com on her belt did interrupt her *kata*, though.

"Yes?"

"Scanner here. The two men inside the chem van just bailed out."

"Huh?"

"Yep, my crossover sat just happened to be coming online when they did it. They hopped out the back and opened some kind of ultralight aircraft, then went into the trees."

Wu considered this. "What about the van?"

"It's all by itself and continuing on course. Be interesting to see how far it gets past there before the AAA guns pot it."

"Can you follow the two men?"

"Sorry, no. They are under the canopy."

"Damn."

"I have an idea where they are going, though."

"Where?"

"There's a religious retreat, a camp, a dozen klicks away from where our boys left the van. Nothing else for more than a hundred kilometers 'cept trees. I doubt those gliders have much of a range. Plus, I've been sorta keeping an eye on some of the other chem plant delivery vans. A couple of them are heading in that same general direction."

"Any ideas as to what it might mean?"

"Well, no. The camp is empty, except for two men who filed an internal flight plan for it a few days ago. They are one Jersey Reason and somebody who calls himself Sleel."

"Sleel!"

"You know him? He records as a local boy."

"Not personally, but if he's who I think he is, I know of him. He's a matador, one of Khadaji's original crew."

"Well, that would explain things, wouldn't it? A bodyguard and his client, holed up in what ought to be a pretty safe place. Looks like your man Cierto has biz with them."

Wu felt her belly grow tight. This was bad. Somebody was going to die. The real question was: who?

TWELVE

SLEEL LOOKED AT the infocrawl on the computer's holoproj and whistled. "Man," he said.

Behind him, Reason came to look at the picture formed in the air above the comp. "A fire?"

"Yeah. Couple hundred klicks from here."

The miniature version of the distant fire blazed high into the scaled-down sky.

"I thought the trees were flame-resistant."

"They are, but almost anything will burn if you crank the heat up enough."

"What does it mean?"

"Mean's company is on the way here," Sleel said, automatically checking his spetsdöds.

"Because there's a fire two hundred kilometers away from us?"

"These trees are worth their weight in platinum right now," Sleel said, "and likely will be worth a lot more than that when they come to term. Everybody who can lift a shovel or man a hose will be heading there to put the fire out. Security will stay on-station, but they'll be watching on the 'proj. Something that might get attention on a dull day could slide when people get busy. I would say we got ourselves a nice, fat diversion here." He nodded at the tiny flames of the projection.

"We'd better get ready."

Cierto glided to a soft landing next to where Juanita and Luis awaited. Miguel brought his craft down directly behind Cierto. The pair of them quickly shed the harnesses connecting them to the lightweight gliders, folded the wings, and put the devices next to the trunks of the line of trees to their left.

"Is the diversion established?"

"Sí, Patrón," Luis said, grinning. "Half a kilometer of the trees are *en fuego*."

"How far to the target?"

Juanita said, "Less than a kilometer. That way."

Cierto nodded. "All right. Light your suits. No radio contact, line-of-sight-laser coms only. This matador will have security. We can defeat much of it, but if anybody sneezes and reveals us, that person dies by my hand, *comprende*?"

There was a soft chorus of acknowledgments from the students.

"*Bueno*. Let us go and bag our quarry."

"Scanner?"

"Here, Fem Wu. I've got the camp in view, it's easier 'cause it isn't moving, but it looks quiet. It sits in a fairly cleared area, lot of rocks, and the perimeter is clean—

"Damn. My eye is gone. The next one is three minutes away. I'll keep you apprised."

Wu nodded at the empty air. Cierto was about to do something, and she guessed it was to try and assassinate this Jersey Reason. The matadors were the best bodyguards in the galaxy, Wu knew this, but the odds were bad. Cierto was a dangerous foe, he was likely well armed and he had the support of others and a mountain of money upon which to stand. She would not wish to be in the matador Sleel's position.

Well. If it came to violence, the chances were that either Cierto or Sleel or both would be killed. If Cierto died, then her own mission was finished. But if he survived, what would he do then?

Wu sat on the short grass in the warm sunshine and considered the problem. If Cierto killed the two men and lived through the adventure, then it was not likely that he would spend any time picnicking in the trees afterward. No, he had broken more than a few laws, not even counting the murder, so he would probably wish to depart this fair world with all due speed. Which would *probably* mean that Cierto would proceed directly to where his boxcar was berthed for a quick lift to his ship's orbit.

Wu could hardly spend a great deal of time skulking around the port without being noticed, but if Cierto's departure was apt to be no more than a few hours away, she could certainly manage to watch the boxcar for that long.

She stood. Yes. It made sense, even though it went against Master Ven's law of no-expectations, that Cierto would be leaving shortly. If she hoped to catch him, there would be the best place.

She went looking for a flitter to taxi her to the port.

"Anything?" Reason asked. He had the needle gun tucked into his belt and he nervously touched the gun's butt as he spoke.

Sleel watched the security screens that lit the air over the com. The radar said the skies were empty; the sensors at the base of the hill were silent; the cameras trained on the road showed no traffic. Even so, Sleel felt an impending sense of threat. "No, we're clear. But tell you what, you sit and watch the screens. You hear or see anything, gimme a yell. I'm going to go out and take a look around with my own eyes."

Reason nodded and slid into the control seat as Sleel stood. "This is the perimeter alert—" he began.

"Teach your grandfather how to suck eggs," Reason said.

"Huh?"

"Old proverb. Means I know as much about how to operate this gear as you do."

"Right. Sorry."

"I just remembered something," Reason said. "I was on Rift for a job about fifty, fifty-five years ago."

Sleel looked interested. "Yeah?"

"I was still pretty young. I was working for another thief, part of his crew. There were four or five of us, as I recall."

"What did you steal?"

Reason shook his head. "I don't know. Never did. I was the escape driver. I drove the groundcar, an old crate with polyglas wheels, thing ran on broadcast power but we had it rigged with a battery in case we got shut down. Whatever it was was pretty small; the guy I worked for managed to keep it in a shirt pocket. Least that's what he patted when I asked did it go all right."

"Not much help there. You remember the place where it happened?"

"Not really. Rich man's estate out in the middle of no-where."

Sleel thought about it. "Can't be this guy, he's only forty-something T.S. He wouldn't have been a hormone storm in his father's loins yet."

"Just thought I'd mention it."

Sleel nodded, then went outside.

It was past noon, into the hottest part of the day. Heat spiraled up from the ground, heavier from the exposed rocks, in shimmering waves. Sleel walked and looked for any sign of trouble. A chokebird *chawk-chawk*ed as it flew past, and the insects sang their songs, but there was nothing amiss that Sleel could see.

Something was wrong, he could *feel* it, but the ground below the hill was empty and quiet.

Damn.

Luis whispered from two meters away. "There, Patrón, the guard. I can shoot him from here—"

"No," Cierto commanded. The man in orthoskins atop the hill peering into the distance was easily a hundred and fifty meters away. Too far for a handgun like those they carried, even with an expert marksman like Luis behind the weapon. "Wait until we get closer."

"As you wish, Patrón."

Cierto heard the impatience in Luis's voice and he smiled at it. It did not matter what the young man *thought*, only what he *did*, and as long as he obeyed, that was the only important fact. Luis could not see his smile, Cierto knew; it was as invisible as Luis was to his own eyes, a shimmer that was nearly a perfect match to the background from virtually all angles. The matador

atop the hill could be looking right at the four of them and not
see them.

As for the sensors they had already passed, well, they were
excellent devices but hardly a match for the confounders Cierto
and his trio of students carried. At a cost of a hundred thousand
standards each, the confounders had better work.

Abruptly the matador turned away and moved from sight.

"Climb with great care," Cierto said. "Do not disturb the
rocks."

"Sleel?"

Sleel was wearing short-range dentiphones and need do
nothing more than grit his teeth once to be able to reply.
"Yeah."

"I got a funny signal on the sensors."

"On my way."

Sleel hurried toward the main building.

Inside, the older man pointed at the ground sensor projection. "Look at this."

"Looks clear to me."

"Yes, but it's *too* clear. This group of twelve here is reading
perfectly blank."

"So are all the others."

"Not quite. There's a ground effect from the hot rocks, here
and here, see."

"So?"

"So, there are a lot of hot rocks around this group, too. Why
aren't they picking up clutter the same way?"

"Who knows? Were they before?"

"According to the recording, yeah."

Sleel felt a cold finger touch his heart, then slide its way
down into his bowels and begin stirring hard. Uh-oh. "Con-
founder," he said. It was not a question.

"A real good one," Reason said.

He'd underestimated them, based on the previous attacks.
Bad mistake. He knew better.

"Go get in the flitter," Sleel said. "You get a signal from me
saying 'Go,' you punch it right through the door and fan like
hell away from here with your distress beacon screaming. I

think we got company and they didn't bother to touch the doorchime before they came in."

"Sleel—"

"It is not a suggestion. Do it."

Reason sighed and gave him a short nod.

Sleel went to the building's rear entrance, away from the too-clean sensors, and went through the door at a run, diving and rolling on the hard ground, coming up into a combat crouch, both spetsdöds questing for targets.

Nothing.

He started to rise, then sensed something to his right. The air was . . . blurry about fifteen meters away.

Shiftsuit blurry.

Sleel didn't think; he snapped his arm out and fired. If he were wrong, he'd have wasted a demistad's worth of ammo, he could live with that—

Spetsdöd darts moved relatively slow compared to some projectiles. A man with sharp eyes could see one, were the air clear and the sun bright. Sleel saw the dart fly. Then he saw it stop in midair.

Armor—!

He dived just as a dark object seemed to materialize next to the spetsdöd's frozen dart. That would be an unshielded gun of some kind. Sleel didn't stop to note the make and caliber. He looped into a second roll, straightened and opened out prone on the ground, jamming a sharp rock into his left thigh hard enough to tear the orthoskins and bruise him pretty good. He swung his left hand around and fired twice, a double-tap, one on each side of the gun coming to bear on him.

The explosive round to the right of the invisible target's weapon found its mark. The *whump!* was loud. Part of the shiftsuit's grid shorted out and, like a broken-up holoproj signal, the outlines of a short, heavyset man flickered in and out. The suit's backup computer tried to compensate but could only manage the bottom half of the outfit. What appeared to be the top half of a man toppled and fell onto its side. Sleel fired another explosive round and it hit the downed attacker about where his nose ought to be under the mask. The mask shattered and the half-body flopped onto its back.

Sleel leaped up, but the sudden pain in his leg where he'd hit the rock caused him to lurch to one side. It was lucky, because the gunner behind him, who was yelling, "Miguel!" missed with her first shot.

Sleel spun, but the second shot took his already injured leg out, knocking him sprawling. He twisted as he fell and fanned off four shots. Two of them hit the woman—it sounded like a woman—and she screamed and went down. Her suit was better, it maintained its integrity, but the blood pumping from within her quickly stained the outside of the figure as it ran down to pool in the dirt.

He spared his knee a glance.

Half of the joint was gone, the remaining part wasn't ever going to be useful again, and he wasn't going anywhere unless he hopped or crawled. Too soon to hurt, too.

Sleel bit down on his dentcom control. "Go, Jersey. Now!"

He heard the flitter's fans rev and he rolled onto his back and pulled a bungee strap from his belt and slapped it around his shattered knee. The strap tightened and slowed the flow of blood from the gaping wound.

The door to the garage rolled up and the flitter drifted out. It was no more than thirty meters away. Sleel propped himself on his right elbow and waved at Reason. "Go on! Get the fuck out of here!"

But Reason fanned the flitter toward Sleel.

"No, you stupid dickhead! Lift! Lift!" He waved Reason off.

Reason put the flitter down two meters away and cycled the door open.

"Goddammit, no, go, get the hell away from here!"

The older man hopped out of the flitter and moved to grab Sleel.

"Far enough, thief!" a deep male voice called.

Sleel turned to try and locate the source of the sound. There, only five meters or so away, a shimmer—

Sleel raised the left spetsdöd, but before he could acquire the target, another blur to his left shimmered and became fully visible. It pointed a handgun at him.

Sleel jammed his forefinger toward the second target and the spetsdöd went off at the same instant the other's weapon fired. His shot took the attacker at throat level, but the other's projectile hit Sleel's outstretched wrist, and his hand and spetsdöd shattered into bloody fragments of bone and sinew and plastic and metal. The blast splashed into Sleel's face, blinding him. He fell onto his back and wiped at his face. Slivers of sharp bone stabbed into his palm as he wiped them from where they stuck into his face. His left eye was dark, and when he touched the socket, it was full of nothing but hot ooze and more fragments of bone. Not a good day for his left side, he thought, and almost laughed at the insanity of the inappropriate thought.

Now it hurt. All over.

He felt Reason grab his clothing by his shoulder and tug. Sleel raised his left arm and saw that there was, oddly enough, almost no blood flowing from the destroyed wrist. That was nice.

"Leave him," the male voice came.

Sleel twisted and saw another figure shimmering into view. A tall man who pulled from a sheath on his side a long, nearly straight-bladed sword.

Sleel was going into shock, but he tried. He pulled his right arm across his body—it seemed to weigh tons—and triggered his remaining spetsdöd. The darts spattered against the suited figure harmlessly until the weapon ran dry. The man laughed.

He could reload the weapon with explosive rounds—

—if he had another hand to do it with.

The man in the shiftsuit reached up and pulled his face shield off. Sleel didn't recognize the face.

Neither, apparently, did Reason.

"Do you not know me, thief? You stole from my family. From my grandfather." He had some kind of lilting accent.

Reason shook his head, but he did not lose control. He still had the needler tucked into his belt. He pulled it.

The man put his face shield back down and raised the sword. He started toward Reason.

The old man triggered the weapon. Sleel saw that his aim was good, all of the needles hit right over the heart, but the armor under the suit stopped them. Reason dropped the useless gun.

Sleel shoved at the ground with his hand, trying to rise enough to block the attacker and allow Reason time to escape. The world went gray from the effort. He put everything he had into it, managed to get to his good knee and elbow.

The oncoming attacker didn't bother to dirty his sword, he just reached out and shoved Sleel over with one boot. Sleel struggled to come up again; but it was beyond him. He was forced to lie there as the swordsman came within range of Reason.

The old man might have made it back into the flitter if he'd tried, but he just stood facing the swordsman.

"For honor," the man said, and swung the black sword.

Reason's head fell and bounced once, then rolled over to rest against's Sleel's smashed leg. The half-blind matador screamed, a wordless cry of utter rage and anger, but it was choked off as the gray claimed him for itself.

THIRTEEN _____

CIERTO WALKED EASILY toward where the gliders were. Doña would be on her way toward the pick-up point, having made her legitimate deliveries in the chemical company's van. Cierto would fly the few klicks to meet her for the rendezvous and they would leave this world as soon as possible.

Cierto had the hood and face cover of the suit pushed back, and the day's heat did not bother him now. He felt strong and able and pleased with himself. The electrical storm that had been gathering itself was approaching, but he would be away before it arrived. Distant thunder rumbled long after the lightning flashes.

Cierto skidded on a patch of loose soil. He grinned. Careful. It would not do that he fall and break an ankle on the way back from such a victory. The thief was dead, the matador guarding him was doubtless drawing his final breaths as his life seeped from his grievous wounds. He had been skilled, that one, able to detect and slay Juanita, Miguel and Luis despite the suits, but in the end, he had lost the fight. They were overrated, these matadors, Cierto decided. But this was not important.

What *was* important was that the blot from more than five decades past had been at last erased. True, there had been some cost. So many of his students gone to join their own ancestors. He would particularly miss Juanita; she had been a good fuck, and was learning how to be a great one.

The thought of her made him grow hard, a sensation at best mixed under the tight suit. He often became aroused after a duel. Ah, well. Doña would suffice. She had not yet learned to enjoy that which Cierto liked most, but she would submit. Teaching her to take pleasure from her pain would happen in time. Besides, the galaxy was full of women. He would start a new class, bring in new students, and among them he would fine one or more who could be taught all that he required.

Ah, sí. Life was sweet. Never more so than in the moments after one's life was risked and retained.

Smiling, Cierto walked through the trees.

Wu waited at the port. Although there were sections that were kept fairly secure, with guards of both human and electronic stripe, the area near the private boxcars was relatively easy to enter. A clip-badge stolen from a maintenance worker Wu bumped into was sufficient to get her past the unmanned gate; once she was inside the compound, no one seemed to take any particular notice of her. Her baggage, including her sword inside its security tube, was stacked neatly on a small cart and Wu pushed this along briskly, striving to appear as if she knew exactly where she was going.

Cierto's boxcar was parked in a row of similar orbital shuttles outside of a large repair hangar. Heat rose in waves from the plastcrete. Wu found a cooler spot in the shade of the hangar and moved into it. She began to go through her bag, unpacking and repacking it. She had learned that people tended to leave you alone if you looked busy. It did not matter so much as to what you were busy doing, as long as you seemed occupied and intent. Cierto's boxcar was perhaps thirty meters away and being fueled and made ready to lift. Just as she suspected.

Her com chimed. Scanner.

"Yes?"

"Fem, there's been a new development. Happened between passes."

Wu listened as he described the scene at the religious retreat deep within The Brambles. "At least four bodies, maybe others. None of 'em in a position where I can tell who they are, so I don't know if Cierto is one of them; there's a thunderstorm blocking my visuals. I can see with UV and US and doppler but

I can't get the detail, even with the computer-augs. Nothing moving down there now."

Wu said, "No point in staying with it, Scanner. Whatever is done is done."

"You're at the port," he said. Not a question.

"Yes."

"Officially, I have no idea why, but unoffically, good luck."

"Thanks. Discom."

She took a deep breath. If Cierto lived, he would be coming here very soon. She reached for the plastic tube that held her sword. In theory, such tubes could not be opened without special tools and codes, and also in theory, to open one without these tools and codes would cause a transmission to the nearest spaceport security office. In fact, there were ways around such things and Wu knew these ways. Still, she would hold off until the last possible instant, to save herself the problems that came with flashing a bare sword in a restricted area.

The rain on his face brought Sleel back from the gray.

He blinked against the downpour and for a moment, didn't know where he was or what had happened to him. It came back with a jolt like a spear into his belly.

Jersey Reason's head lay on the ground next to him, the rain washing down on its half-closed eyes.

Sleel could barely move. The effort to roll onto his side was monumental, hardly worth it, but he knew if he did not do something, he was going to die. The left side of his body was a wreck. No hand, no eye, not much of a knee.

A meter and a half away was the flitter. He had to get to it. His client was dead, there were others dead here, and if he couldn't get to the flitter, he would follow them wherever they were.

Lightning flashed and sizzled and the boom of thunder treaded immediately upon its heels. The light and sound jarred him. On his right side, Sleel began to millimeter himself along, digging into the wet ground with his elbow, pushing with his good foot. It hurt to move, to breathe, to exist, and it got worse. The gray returned for him, but Sleel fought it off. He had never felt such agony. Bloody ooze from his torn wrist ran with the rivulets of rain water. His shattered knee throbbed as if it were being pounded by a madman with a hammer. The water ran into his eye and he had to blink it away to see.

He managed half a meter. It took him an eon.

Another half a meter. Another eon.

The door to the flitter was open but the threshold was twenty centimeters above the mud. Sleel grabbed it and pulled. Managed to get one elbow hooked over the edge. The effort exhausted him. He stopped.

There was a vouch in the main building, but even if he could call it, it would never be able to get to him. The thing was designed for smooth surfaces; it would surely bog down in the mire. Didn't matter. He couldn't call it anyway. But there was a medical kit in the flitter. Very basic, pressure patches and a few medications, but if he could get to it, it might be able to keep him alive long enough to get the flitter operative.

And then what?

Worry about that if you get that far, Sleel.

It took everything he had to stay conscious and drag himself into the flitter far enough to reach the aid kit. He opened the kit and turned it over, dumping its contents onto the flitter's floor. He pawed through the stuff, found a skinpopper of dorph, and pressed it against the artery in his neck. A flush of warmth came over him, dulling the pain so that it was nearly gone. A second popper full of stimulant against the blood vessel sharpened his thoughts and brought him back from the edge a little more. He used his teeth and good hand to peel and trigger patches for his eye, wrist and knee. The microprocessors in the patches were rudimentary, but enough for the stupecomp to know to seal the wounds properly and begin coagulating the blood that wasn't already doing it on its own.

He probably was going to die anyway, and this was as good as it was going to get. The flitter had a voxcontrol, and Sleel used it. "Door close, lift to eighty meters and hold," he said. The rain pounded on the flitter's roof as the vehicle obeyed, raising above the soaked hillside. He managed to achieve the seat.

If he began yelling for help on the the emergency band,

somebody might get to him in time to keep him alive. He'd lost a lot of blood and he was in shock, but a full ride in a Healy could repair a lot of damage. He'd lost limbs before and survived.

But if he called for help, the man with the black sword who had killed his client was probably going to get away. His client was dead, Sleel had failed, and staying alive didn't mean a whole lot, knowing that.

"Radar scan," Sleel said. "Aircraft within fifty klicks."

The flitter's computer gave him two.

"Identify aircraft."

Blip One, the computer told him, was a fertilizer truck from Sindano en route to Mkufu; Blip Two was a chem delivery van returning from Dhahabu to Pua. According to filed flight plans.

Sleel's chemmed brain considered this information, jumping back and forth rapidly under the influence of the stimulant. Mkufu was a work station in the middle of nowhere. Where was Pua? Ah, yes, he remembered, thirty or forty klicks outside of Bandari. Okay, he knew that. What did it mean?

Think, Sleel, think! If you had just killed somebody and also left several of your own dead, where would *you* go? Farther into the woods? Or would you want to get the hell away from here?

The port was at Bandari.

"Overtake Blip Two," Sleel said. "Full throttle."

The flitter accelerated enough to press Sleel back into the control seat.

The rendezvous was uneventful. The glider was able to match speeds with the slow-moving van, and Cierto glided right into the rear of the vehicle to a stand-up landing. The van was nearly empty, only a couple of barrels of the chem remaining, plus a few dry tanks being taken back to be refilled with liquids or gasses. He shed the glider, tossed it out of the van, and called to Doña.

"Put the van on autopilot," he said. "And come back here." He began to remove his suit. The border was more than an hour away, plenty of time to exhaust himself in Doña's various receptacles.

"Patrón?" she said as she entered the rear of the van. "What of the others?"

"They will not be coming," he said. He grinned. "But I surely will." He reached for her.

Despite the addition of a second popper of stimulant and of pain abatement chem, Sleel felt himself drifting. Remembering things he would just as soon forget. His graduation from primary ed, neither parent in attendance. His hospital stay when he broke his back after a fall, neither parent coming to see him while the boneglue set.

Damn—

The radar screen beeped, pulling Sleel back into the present. "Distance to Blip?"

Thirty-five kilometers, the computer said. Holding.

"Increase speed," Sleel ordered.

The computer was unable to comply, it told him. They were currently traveling at allowable maximum.

"Emergency override."

Nature of emergency?

"Personal medical, you stupid fucking piece of shit!"

Acknowledged, the computer said. The fans whirred a bit faster, but not much. The flitter had not been built for speed. It began to gain on the van, but slowly.

Wu took deep breaths, working to center herself, to bring both balance and readiness to her body and mind. Scanner had called again to report the position of the chem van. It was heading toward her, and allowing for a brief inspection stop at the border, would be here in less than an hour. Plenty of time to prepare herself.

Cierto thrust with his hips as hard as he could. His weight rested entirely on his hands and groin. Beneath him facedown on the van floor, Doña moaned. Buried to his base, he climaxed for the second time. Yes! Yes!

Sleel realized that even with the stop at the border, the van was going to reach the port half an hour ahead of him. If there was transportation waiting—and surely there would be—then likely he would miss his quarry. The thought of them lifting and getting offworld burned him, bubbling like molten metal in his soul.

No. Couldn't allow that.

There were invisible lanes in the air approaching the border, strict height and width limits to be obeyed. Straying outside of these was just cause to be fired upon by the perimeter guns. No emergency override would convince this flitter's comp to venture from those lanes. It had been a long time since Sleel had disconnected the control unit from one of these flitters, but he still remembered how.

The computer squawked and blared the built-in warning as Sleel uncoupled it from the controls. In a moment, he was flying on manual. He had, he knew, a slim chance of making it. The perimeter guards were robotically operated, but had to be controlled by humans. The decision to fire was not automatic; somebody had to make it. And as he dropped the flitter to a height sufficient to clear the fence by less than a meter, Sleel hoped that whoever was watching the scopes would allow puzzlement to slow their responses. He had a couple of things going for him: first, the guards were more concerned with keeping people out than in; second, shooting at something that low would necessarily cause some splashback if it were hit, and anything close would suffer from it.

"Flitter one-oh-seven, you are out of approach," came the voice over the com.

Stall, Sleel. "Control, I have a computer malfunction here! I'm trying to override!"

"Say the nature of the malfunction, one-oh-seven."

"I don't know, the computer is not responding to diagnostic commands."

The fence drew nearer. The operator talking to Sleel must be sweating blood; Sleel would be in his place. "One-oh-seven, kill main power and put the vehicle into an emergency glide."

"Right," Sleel said.

The fence loomed a klick ahead; Sleel could see it.

"One-oh-seven, kill your main!"

"I'm trying! The control is dead!"

"Goddammit!" the man on the ground said.

What would he do in the man's place? A local flitter, with a native of record in control, a declared emergency? Sleel was a matador, albeit an inept one it seemed, but he would blow the elbowsucker right out of the air. The guard on the ground had probably never had occasion to fire his weaponry except in a drill, and this didn't slot neatly, now did it? What would he do?

Sleel added to his discomfort. "Oh, Christo, I'm going to hit the fence!"

"Ah, fuck!" the man on the ground said.

And the flitter flew over the perimeter unmolested, just missing the top of the fence.

Sleel immediately dropped the craft so that it was nearly touching the ground and doglegged left. By the time the guard realized he had been fooled, Sleel had the flitter behind the plastcrete groundcar stop, where the guns couldn't hit it. He shut the com off; no point in listening to all those threats.

He'd bought himself a few minutes. The van ought to be no more than a couple of kilometers ahead. There was a fair amount of traffic toward the port; that ought to slow the van even more. Maybe he could still catch it. He could hook the radar back up, but that would take time. He could see the van with his remaining eye if he got that close.

If he caught it, he would ram it. He was going to die anyhow, what the fuck.

Cierto, sated, sat next to Doña in the van's cab. They were approaching the port and the shuttle to his ship. All had gone well. Not as well as he had hoped, but it was the end that was important, and it had been nearly achieved. Once aboard his ship, it would be finished.

Wu saw the van approaching, spiraling down for a landing. She clutched the tube that held her sword, ready to extract it with the popper she'd attached to it. The van would settle just there, a hundred meters away. She stayed in the shadows of the hangar as the vehicle came to rest, fanning up dust and grit, then started toward it. If she circled around behind, she could use the line of boxcars for cover; they would not see her until she was almost on them.

Sleel approached the port. There was the chem van, and there, just alighting from it, two people. Looked to be a man and a woman from this height. Sleel's jaw muscles tightened. Easier to take out two pedestrians than the van.

The flitter shook as if kicked by a giant's boot.

What—?

The rearview cameras showed the problem. A flashing light atop the hopper behind him identified them as cools. Military police, looked like. He couldn't hear them, his com was off, but they were firing on him. Well. It didn't matter, he only had a couple hundred meters to go—

Another projectile hit the flitter, and with the boot that kicked it sideways came an explosion, followed by a grinding of stacked plastic that abruptly stopped.

Got the rear fan, Sleel thought.

The flitter slewed and began to fall. The computer would have compensated with the remaining fans, but Sleel had it on manual and he only had one hand. He reached for the control tab.

Not going to make it, he saw, as he slapped at the sensitive tab.

Shit—!

"Patrón!" Doña screamed, pointing at the sky.

Cierto turned and saw a flitter coming toward him.

Behind the flitter was a police hopper. It fired on the flitter. The rocket's explosion sprayed hot debris when it hit. The police vehicle fired again. The flitter rocked from the second explosion and began to fall out of control.

"*Dios!*" Cierto said. It was going to land right on top of him! Then he realized that the flitter would hit well short of where he and Doña stood.

The police vessel sheared away. Madness for them to be shooting here, Cierto thought. The flitter's remaining fans whined, its repellors strained, it seemed about to pull up, but it crashed into the ground fifty meters away. Cierto saw the pilot clearly as the windshield shattered.

The matador!

Impossible.

He was struggling to get out of the ruined craft's automatic seat restraints. He was lucky; the flitter had not hit nearly as hard as it could have. Then the man slumped in the restraints. Dead or unconscious.

"Quickly, to the boxcar," Cierto ordered. Police would be here soon and he had no desire to be here when they arrived.

Doña followed her Patrón to the shuttle.

The flitter crashed almost in front of Wu, blocking her view of Cierto. She started to circle around it, then saw the man inside. He was bloody, his eyepatched face covered with his own gore. He wore the uniform of a matador.

A low hum began to rise from the downed flitter, until the sound began to be painful to her ears. Something was overloading in the flitter. The engine was going to go, and likely it would spatter the craft every which way, along with anybody close to it. Or in it.

Wu had no time to ponder a decision. Cierto was fast approaching escape. The matador inside the flitter was probably dying if not already dead and surely would be if the flitter blew apart.

Life or death?

Kildee Wu chose.

Part Two
Tread Down
The Sword

FOURTEEN _____

SLEEL AWOKE AND wondered where he was. Several things combined to give him an answer at about the same time: the smell of recirculated and too-sterile air, the clear but slightly fogged thincris plate twenty centimeters in front of his eye when he opened it, and even though he was naked, the realization that he was not cold, nor was he hot.

So he was in a Healy, coming out of an induced recovery slumber. It only took a moment to determine that his left eye, wrist and knee were covered or wrapped in the rubbery but shell-like tentacles of a Zigg-Roth generator's extrusions, with injuries being fed a complex formula of enzymes and proteins and nanogear. He felt no pain. In fact, he felt great, pumped, he knew, full of endorphins and enkephalins and gods knew what other wonderful chems. There were people who got addicted to rides in the medicator coffins; they never wanted to get out. Sleel had spent enough time in the things himself, having various body parts regenerated and otherwise deadly wounds staunched. Contrary to what a lot of folks thought, the term "Healy" had nothing to do with healing per se; it was simply an odd coincidence that the inventor of the original machineries had been named that. All of which was interesting, but now the question was: what had he done to deserve this? His recent memories were in a warm fog, just out of reach and sight and he couldn't recall how he had come to be chewed up this way. Like he was standing on a sandy beach somewhere, his near past at sea with the gulls and fishes. Nothing but sand and gentle surf around him.

The alpha brainwave detector chirped, telling Sleel and anybody with a monitor tuned in that he was awake. Well, shit. You can't run and you can't hide.

A woman's face appeared outside the medical box and peered down at Sleel. He looked back at it. Oriental stock, this face, with short, dark hair framing it. Violet eyes, smile lines, young, thirty or thereabout he figured. Some depth to it, the face, and very attractive. She wore pale blue skintights and a gray *gi*-style jacket; that was as much as he could see from this angle. And she was familiar, too, though he couldn't put a name to the image.

"Welcome back," the woman said.

Sleel managed half a smile with the part of his own face not covered by the Zigg-Roth's semiflexible shell. "Thanks. Where have I been? And how did I get here?"

The woman smiled. Sleel liked the expression. Nice teeth, some real amusement.

"You are in the Bandari Mediplex. How much do you need filled in?"

Sleel hated this. It was bad enough his spetsdöds were gone, worse that he didn't know anything about his situation here. If knowledge was power, then he was about as strong as a newborn and damp hummingbird. Start simple, then. "You a medic?"

A repeat of the smile. "No. A friend of the family. I brought you here for a tuneup. I'm Kildee Wu."

Sleel blinked. "Not related to Mayli Wu, by any chance?"

"My sister," she said.

Sleel blinked again, trying to cover his astonishment. Now he knew why she looked familiar. Mayli had a sister. He would be double damned. "Small galaxy," he said.

That shock cleared away some of his mental fog. Too much clarity. He remembered all of a moment seeing Jersey Reason's head lying on the ground. *That* ugly note brought forth a stormy symphony of memories, rolling over Sleel and his beach like a wave, a hurricane-driven breaker that pounded and foamed and knocked him tumbling.

Oh, fuck.

"You okay?" Wu asked.

"Yeah. Fine. He got away. Cierto."

"Yes."

It was too much. Sleel felt the emotions welling, filling him to overflowing. He wanted to scream, and if he had tried to speak in that instant, he would have choked on the words and tears. Bleakness raged in him. He had failed. Failed big. He bit his tongue to keep from using it.

"I know part of it," she said. "About the attack at the retreat. You were hurt but you followed him to the port. Crashed your flitter before you could stop him. That broke a few bones and ruptured your spleen, along with a few other odds and ends to add to what you already had. The medics said your chances were only one in three when they boxed you in there. You'd lost a lot of blood by the time they started the surgical lasers. You are lucky."

"Yeah, lucky. How long have I been in r-sleep?"

"Three weeks."

Sleel shook his head, not easy with the eye covering. "How do you figure into all of this?"

"I have some business with Cierto," she said. The smile was gone and her face set into a harder cast. "I came across you while I was looking for him." She lightened her tone and broke the harsh mask with another smile, a smaller one this time. "Good to meet you after all this time. Mayli spoke highly of you."

Sleel managed a chuckle. "I bet she did."

"My sister thought you had great potential," Wu said.

"Huh?" Here was another astonishment for him. Sleel had always taken great care to keep his relationship with Mayli antagonistic, or competitive, at least. He had worked long and hard on his facade to keep anybody from getting past it. She couldn't have pierced it.

"Yes," Wu said. "She said you were the biggest liar she had ever met."

Sleel smiled, relieved. He was safe. "Well, I suppose I might have told a few stories—"

She cut him off, but gently. "No. Mayli's gift was that she

always could see past the manufactured to the truth; before she was a medic, before she was a whore, before she was a matador, even as a child she could do that. You never fooled her, Sleel. She knew who you were. Right from the first. She told me."

If the woman had punched through the thick lid of the Healy and smashed him in the solar plexus she could not have stunned Sleel more.

She said, "You've had some visitors and callers. When you feel up to it, you can replay the recordings on the Healy's reader. I've got some business to take care of, but I'll be back later."

And with that, she was gone.

Sleel lay there, trapped, revealed, all his built-up persona stripped away, and he had never felt more defenseless. He had failed as a matador, lost his client, and his protective wall was no more than rubble in front of this woman, as it had apparently been for her sister. He couldn't do anything right.

For that, why wasn't he in detention? Not that he would be going anywhere on his own for a while, but he had broken a few laws, local, planetary and galactic.

Shit.

Cierto sat in the tub of swirling hot water on the balcony outside his bedroom and watched the sun paint the sky in deep reds and flashy oranges as it set. He sipped at the stem of bubbly clear wine; he allowed himself one such intoxicant each day, and savored it that much more for its scarcity. The hot water throbbed about him, soothing after the two-hour session in the gym, alleviating the aches of sinew and muscle.

For the hundredth time, Cierto replayed in his mind the memory of his victory on Rift, the slaying of the thief. In mental slomo the man's head fell and hit the ground yet again, bringing as it always did the smile to Cierto's thin lips. He had a recording of it, of course, but for now, memory was better.

And also now, there was more: the woman. He had seen her at the port, moving for him, and the wonder of that still amazed him. There she was, full of the fire that a blind man could see, holding the plastic tube which surely contained a sword. She would have challenged him, he was certain of it, had not the flitter containing the dying matador crashed just then. She had turned away, had gone to attend to the man in the flitter.

The Patrón of the House of Black Steel sipped at his champagne, angry at the memory. In that moment at the port, he wished that she had come for him. Even now he felt an irrational stab of jealousy that she had chosen to attend to the matador rather than try his blade. He would have killed her then, of course, and rightly so, but now with the luxury of time to consider it, he had decided that he was glad he had not had to slay her. Such a woman should not be wasted. Such a woman should be utilized.

He smiled once again into the last of his wine. Ah, yes, there was a particular use to which he could put this spirited woman, now that he had cleared the stain from his family's name. She would be perfect for it. And it would be so very ironic, would it not?

Cierto carefully placed the wine stem into its holder and slid deeper into the swirling waters of the carved marble tub. The heat massaged his neck and shoulders, the peppermint-scented foam frothing up past his chin, tickling his nose. Already a plan had been put into motion. In a short while things would come to fruition. Life was ever so sweet and about to become sweeter still.

Wu went to the park for her daily workout. Part of her usual audience had gathered, waiting for her to begin. There were old men with no better place to go seated on the benches watching her, a couple of martial arts students, women with babies in strollers, a local cool who nervously fingered his chemical baton. Wu guessed that the cool was wondering if he could take her in a one-on-one, and she thought he had decided he could. She acknowledged the people with a short nod. She removed her jacket. Took her sword from its carrying case. Began her stretches.

As she loosened her hamstrings, she considered her actions of late. She had not planned to stay on this world after turning Sleel over to the medics. At first she told herself that she only wanted to be certain that a man her sister had loved and respected would live, but it was more than that. There was something about him that called to her, some aura that was ill-defined but definitely there. Much of her training with the sword touched upon the spirit, that easy-to-say-but-hard-to-see aspect of the arts that were at once the core and boundaries of them. During those times in which she had achieved *zanshin*, it was easy enough to feel. Other times, it was not so simple. There was something in Sleel's spirit, some resonance that touched her, and while she could not pin it down squarely, it was enough that it was there. She had learned to trust those feelings, fleeting as they sometimes were, and when she could see or hear or feel them, they had never failed to prove worthwhile.

She rolled her shoulders and twisted back and forth, loosening the muscles along her spine and in her lower back.

So, Cierto could wait. In the tai chi balance of things, he was a very much *yang* objective, and too much of that could overbalance a woman, make her lose her center. *Yin* must be nourished, and while Sleel did not seem on the surface to be anything but flint, accepting the easily seen could sometimes be a mistake.

Ah, yes, she told herself, as much a mistake as allowing desire to get in the way of truth. Take care that this is not the case here, Kee Wu.

She reached for her sword. Perhaps she could cut away the illusions today. One could always hope, right?

Sleel watched the holoproj above the clear plate of the Healy, his one eye making the picture flat. The recorded images were otherwise crisp and lifelike, of Dirisha and Geneva looking directly into the visitor cam mounted to give the patient's point of view.

"Well, well, there surely must be a whole slew of gods who look out for fools, that you got one all to yourself, Sleel." The black woman smiled. "You should buy stock in this company." She patted the medicator. "You sure get enough use out of the damned things."

Geneva, always less flip, looked more serious. She was on

the edge of tears. "You should have called us for help, goddammit!"

Dirisha put one hand on Geneva's arm. "The brat's right, deuce. That's what friends are for. We don't have so many we can afford to lose any, even a piss-poor one like you. Get well, Sleel. Listen to Kee Wu. Give us a com when you wake up."

Sleel touched the control. He'd been out for three weeks; Dirisha and Geneva had come to see him less than a week after he'd been boxed. Must have left for Rift the same day he'd crashed the flitter. Damn. Apparently they trusted Mayli's sister.

He started the holoproj again, scanning through the messages. Bork had called. So had Emile and Juete. There was a com from Rajeem Carlos, former President of the Republic. He had spoken to some people about the matter, and Sleel needn't worry about criminal charges. Ah. Calls from Grandle Diggs, Tork Ramson, plus half a dozen members of his matador class—Christo, it was like old home week here. Sleel shut the messages off. He'd have to watch and listen to them later. Something was wrong with his good eye at the moment; he couldn't see too well. Must be something in the recirculated air making him tear up so bad. Somebody looking at him would think he was crying.

FIFTEEN

IT WAS NOT Hoja Cierto's habit to admit strangers into his sanctum. If men or mues were unknown personally to the master of the house, research was done. By the time he sat across from any new visitor to his domain, Cierto would know as much about them as possible. In some cases, more than a sister would know about her brother, or a father about his own son.

The man who sat stiffly upon the genetically grown dinosaur-leather couch went by the name of Ricard Ells. He was a kind of bounty hunter who survived by tracking down small-time felons who had jumped bond, finding runaway spouses and children, and locating odds and ends. Ells had spent a week recently in a medical kiosk having repaired injuries sustained in a fight on Koji, the Holy World. Not all that unusual, for despite its name, some religions tended toward the way of the old god Mars. Ells had been tight-lipped about the source of his injuries and there was no existing record of who had nearly killed him by driving what the medics had described as several large splinters of bamboo nearly into the man's heart. Ells had come to claim the reward posted for information on black steel. He had brought with him a small recording sphere which purported to contain images of a sword made of the material.

"Show it to me," Cierto commanded. Several had claimed to have discovered this before; thus far, none of the claims had proved valid. One man had come across a sword made here that had somehow become lost. Others were either outright fakes or similar, but not the true material. The reward for information was somewhat less than that for an actual example. Cierto wondered if perhaps this man had attempted to steal a weapon and had met resistance.

Ells moved somewhat stiffly to the computer console and slotted the infoball.

Cierto leaned back in his own form-chair, a custom orthopedia designed for him alone. The soft machineries hummed with soothing sonics as they molded the special fabric to his contours.

The holoproj lit. The resolution was clean, the colors sharp, even though the camera had obviously been hidden upon Ells's person and must have been quite small. The picture was only a little jerky, and Cierto, who knew something of such things, determined that the compensation system for the virtualcam work was less than the best available. Still, the image was adequate. There on a polished wooden stand was a Japanese-style sword, *katana* pattern. There was nothing obvious to give the uninitiated a scale, but from the size of the *tsuba*, Cierto guessed that the weapon was larger than a medium-sword, a *wakizashi*, or a short-sword, a *tanto*. A *daito*, then, over two *shaku* in length. An ancient measurement, a *shaku* was about thirty centimeters, if Cierto recalled it right. The ensheathed weapon wore a lacquered white scabbard, the guard was stainless or nickeled steel, and the handle appeared to be white ray hide in black silk diamond-turning pattern, with a butt cap to match the *tsuba*.

The workmanship on the parts he could see appeared excellent, but one could tell little from a recording. The trust test of a sword was in how it felt in one's hands.

"Very nice," Cierto said, "but the blade could be purple under the scabbard."

"Just a moment."

The picture fuzzed and refocused. Now there was a woman kneeling, the angle showing her back. She was dressed in split skirt and *gi*. The camera panned down to the woman's left and zoomed, framing the sword lying on the mat next to the woman's left hip. The woman picked up the sword and blurred into a *kata*, the sword flashing darkly into the *dojo*'s air. The camera operator widened the angle, trying to keep up, but missed the next move. By the time the recording caught her, the woman was whipping the sword furiously through a complex series of attacks and defenses, thrusts and feints and cuts. The blade ghosted through the moves like the prop of a copter, so fast it seemed like a dark sheet at times. Definitely black. And wielded with considerable skill, even though it was merely a *kata*.

"Stop picture," Cierto said.

The computer obediently froze the image.

"Reverse play, quarter speed."

The recording tracked backward. When the blurry sword slowed for a high block, Cierto said, "Freeze frame. Quarter screen, left upper, full enhance, true colors."

The comp augmented the image, moving in tight on the sword.

Well, well.

Handmade swords were never exactly alike; had this one been a duplicate of any from the House of Black Steel he would have known for certain that it was a fake. Cierto knew the whorls of the folded metal and the temper lines along the edges of the three dozen weapons produced here as well as he did the lines in the palms of his own hands. Even those that had belonged to the students who had failed would eventually be returned here, when enough stads found their way into the right pockets.

This sword was not one of his.

It was a *katana*, and save for one, the *casa* had never made the style. They were more cutters than piercers, and that lacked a certain finesse in Cierto's mind. The single one such blade produced here was safe in the underground vault thirty meters below where Cierto sat—or it had been this morning.

"Push in," Cierto said to the computer.

The sword grew larger. The tempering along the cutting edge was done by using special clays, and after heating and polishing, left a distinctive pattern of lighter metal where it was harder. The patterns had names, and this one was either a flame or perhaps a three-cedar; the computer could not make it clear enough to be certain. In any event, the temper line was not one of the more common ones. Would the maker of a fake blade bother with something so esoteric?

Hmm. This might just be what Cierto had always feared. Someone else with the family secret; worse, someone who knew how to use it. He had to have this sword, to determine its age—and everything else possible about it.

"And where is this place?" Cierto said to Ells.

The man smiled, a thin, cagey expression. "There was a matter of a reward."

Cierto wanted to laugh, but held it. What a fool. He had no understanding of his position. "Of course." Cierto waved his hands at the compute. "Give me your credit cube number and it will be transferred to your account." The amount was nothing; he would have paid ten times as much if this sword was what he felt certain it was.

The image hung in the air. And what did the woman look like who moved so well with his family's secret? "Computer, wide angle, normal speed."

The image altered and began to move again. When the woman spun and faced the camera, Cierto said, "Stop, enhance still image."

When he saw the woman's face, he did laugh. Ells did not understand and Cierto did not bother to enlighten him.

Truly, Cierto thought, truly there must be gods and they must have warped senses of humor. How else to explain such a thing?

When the lid of the Healy fanned open, Sleel sat up slowly. Even though the machine had stimmed his muscles to hold their tone, he wanted to give his heart a chance to keep the blood flowing to his brain. His knee was virtually healed, the new eye was mostly formed and only a few weeks away from being fully grown, and the left hand was well past bud stage, with small but perfect fingers. He would be fitted with the first of a series of robotic glove prostheses to give him useful function until the hand reached normal size. That would take about two months. He was as well physically as this machine could make him.

"You look better," Wu said from the doorway.

"I don't feel any better."

"I brought you something," she said. She held in her hand a single spetsdöd with its plastic flesh backing.

Sleel shook his head. "Keep it. I don't deserve to wear it."

The woman nodded, as if to herself. "What will you do now?"

"Why should you care?"

"Because my sister did."

Sleel slid out of the Healy through the egress slot and stood, testing his weight on the new knee. Weak, but no problem.

"Yeah, well, that was a long time ago. She's not here and you don't have to take her place."

"You know how she died?"

Sleel nodded. "Yeah. I was there."

"Will you tell me about it?"

"It's old stuff, better to let it lie." He took a couple of tentative steps. Never know the knee had been blasted into organic goo from the way it now worked. The flesh was hairless, brighter and unscarred but that would eventually fade and change until it looked like the rest of the leg. If he lived that long. He was still naked, but the woman had seen him that way often enough in the last few weeks. It was a little chilly, though.

She opened a cabinet and pulled a robe from it, tossing the garment to Sleel. He caught it with his good hand.

"She was my sister. I want to know."

Sleel put the robe on, tabbing it shut. After the weeks of nudity, even the soft material felt rough against his skin. "All right. I'll tell you. Let's take a walk."

Wu listened as Sleel told her the story, trying to picture it.

"It was on Earth, during the last push of the revolution. There was a power station on the small continent, Australia, just south of a place called Lake Disappointment. We were supposed to knock the grid offline, to cut the juice. There were six of us: Mayli, Dirisha, Geneva, Bork, Red—he was Geneva's father—and me.

"We got into the station okay, even though it was heavily guarded. We got it done, set the explosives, and were leaving when it went sour. Everybody started shooting. Mayli, Red and I, we got hit. Bork—you know about him and Mayli?"

"Yes. They were lovers. Mayli thought he was the most gentle man she had ever known."

Sleel managed a half smile at that. "Bork could tear off your leg and beat an army to death with it, if he wanted. Anyway, Mayli got hit first. Autocarbine, firing explosive antipersonnel rounds. She took one right in the heart, she must have died instantly. We didn't leave our own behind. Red gave covering fire and Bork picked Mayli up. Then Red caught it. Bork grabbed him, too."

Sleel stared down the medical center's corridor. His stare was unfocused. Wu watched his face, feeling the power play in him.

"I lost it," he said quietly, as if from a great distance. "I went deadbrain stupid." He shook himself, as if shaking water from his face after a shower. "I took a couple of hits, lost a foot and the prosthetic arm I was wearing at the time. I went down, should have died there, but Dirisha covered us, took out the rest of the troopers, and then Bork came back for us. Picked me up like a baby and threw me into the back of the escape vehicle. We had a vouch, but it was too late for Mayli or Red. They died. I didn't."

A long moment passed. "You think about it a lot," she said.

"Yeah. Yeah, I do. If I'd been a little bit faster, if I hadn't been wearing that stupid fucking slow arm, maybe I could have saved them."

She touched his shoulder. "That's a big weight, Sleel. You couldn't have won the revolution by yourself. The others had to have known the risks. Mayli certainly did."

"Yeah, maybe." He didn't sound convinced of that.

The two of them continued to walk. An old woman wearing a pair of plastic exolegs hobbled past, going in the opposite direction, the hydraulics in the supports humming softly with her steps. She smiled at them. Wu smiled back.

"What will you do now?"

Sleel shook his head. "I don't know. I lost my client. I can't be a matador anymore."

"They wouldn't kick you out because of that."

"It's not them. It's me. I can't do it. I fucked it up, just like I fucked up the rest of my life."

Wu stopped. Sleel managed another step before he came to a halt. He looked at her.

"Come with me," she said.

"Where? Why?"

"Does it matter?"

He laughed, a short, sharp sound, almost, she thought, a sob. "No. I guess it doesn't matter."

"Fine," she said. "Then we'll go home to Koji."

SIXTEEN

SLEEL SAT IN a tiny, mostly artificial park, listening to the calls of fake birds. The sounds could have been recorded from real birds, though they were probably computer-generated copies. Birds and calls and park were inside a starship, *The Skate*, the same one that had brought Kildee Wu to Rift, so she had said. And so here he was, traveling through Bender space on a vessel named after a fish, in the company of a woman named after a bird. Kee, she had asked him to call her.

His new eye itched. It worked now, though he still had to wear a droptac lens to correct for astigmatism and myopia, both of which would supposedly clear up when the eye was fully matured. He'd never had an eye done before, but it seemed to work as well as the old one. It was interesting to have binocular vision again after the one-eyed flatness of the last few weeks.

The left knee worked fine, and was actually in better shape than the old right one, there being no wear on the ligaments and new bone.

The prosthetic glove he wore was a bit clunky. It looked like a real hand, the plastic flesh tinted to nearly a perfect match for Sleel's own skin. Apparently there was a medical specialization that concerned itself almost solely with the cosmetic aspects of such things. A tech with a computer chose from thousands of tones and shadings so that the fake would be indistinguishable from the real. A long way from the crude matching that Red had done for the spetsdöd bases when he'd issued Sleel weapons back at the Villa years ago. Underneath, the new hand was larger and itself workable, though still too small to function alone with the full-sized forearm muscles. The nerve impulses to the hand were mostly right, the induction pickups routing them to the glove better than the ones in the robotic arm he'd once worn, but there was still a tiny gap between the thought and the movement. The sensitivity left something to be desired, too. Not a problem as long as you allowed for it, he wouldn't be crushing things, but even the best robotics could not match a human hand perfectly.

He still had not gotten used to going without spetsdöds. Both the artificial and his real hand appeared incomplete without the weapons, and Sleel felt naked, even though he forced himself to forgo the dart guns. He had made a bad mistake, he had lost his client, and there was no way around it. He didn't want to call himself a matador anymore; he did not deserve the name.

The fake birds chirped, reacting to someone approaching along the path. Sleel looked up to see Kee Wu. She wore sandals and shorts and a fluffy short-sleeved blouse, and seemed to be enjoying the warmth of the pretend-sunshine. Very nicely built, Kee Wu, and in another lifetime, Sleel would have been making an effort to play man/woman games with her. Not today.

"Sleel."

"Kee."

He stood.

"You don't have to leave," she said.

"Yeah, I do. I've been putting it off, but I have to call Reason's son and tell him about Jersey. He has a right to hear it from me. Just like you did about Mayli." Sleel shook his head. "Seems like I'm around a lot when good people die."

Kee Wu did not speak to this.

"So, I guess I'll go back to my room and put in a com to Solov."

She blinked. "Solov? This man named his son 'Solov'?"

"Yeah. I thought he had a weird sense of humor when I heard that, too."

She smiled and shook her head. "I hope I don't hang funny names on my children if I ever have any."

"I don't guess I'd have a Sleel Junior, either. See you later."
Sleel left her there and went back to his room.

Solov Reason looked nothing like his father. The image on
the holoproj was of a fifty-something man, thick and long dark
hair shot full of gray, with a serious expression and a certain
gravity to him. A good, upstanding citizen, to judge from his
conservative PrimeSat gray suit and neck tattoos. Sleel knew
that the look wasn't altogether accurate, because Solov had
gotten into some trouble once that required Dirisha's help to get
him out of. According to what he recalled, Reason's son now
managed some kind of resort on the Great Barrier Reef on
Earth.

Sleel had struggled through the explanation. When he
managed to finish, Reason nodded, after a short time-lag.
"Sounds as if he made his own choice, just as he always did.
You've nothing to be sorry for."

"Excuse me? I let them kill him."

"Not if he could have escaped. You told him to, right?"

"Yes, but—"

"Sleel, my father was living on borrowed time. He knew it;
he'd told me that more than once. He should have died before
I was born, he cheated the Skull-and-Bones dozens of times.
Every day was a gift, he used to say. If luck had looked the
other way, he would have died at the age of twenty."

"A lot of people could say that," Sleel said.

"Perhaps. But a lot of people don't. My father made his
peace with the cosmos a long time ago. He told me he would
know when his number came up for recycling. Sure, he hired
you to protect him, he wouldn't just roll over and die unless he
knew it was time, but up on that hill with you, he accepted it."

"I can't."

"I can," Reason said. "My father lived a long and exciting
time; he did nearly everything he wanted to do when he wanted
to do it. He had family, money, a certain kind of fame, or
maybe infamy. He was the best at what he chose to do. Not
many can say that."

After Sleel broke the communication, he sat and stared at the
wall. If Jersey's son had screamed and foamed and castigated
him for failing to protect his father, Sleel would have felt

better. That he had been calm and accepting did not go with
Sleel's sense of shame. If Sleel had done his job, Jersey would
still be breathing. Sure, the old geep should have taken off like
he'd been told to do, probably he could have gotten away
clean. But it never should have come to that. That was Sleel's
fault. He'd been living that cock-of-the-galaxy facade for so
long he'd halfway come to believe it. He had badly underestimated a deadly enemy and the mistake had been fatal for a
man who had hired him to keep him alive. Hubris. That was
the bottom line, now, wasn't it? No way around that one. No
way.

Kee Wu felt a coolness touch her as she sat in the ship's little
park, as if a ghostly hand had brushed her spine. She turned,
but there was no one else in sight. The sensation was one she
had felt before, usually when she noticed she was being
watched by someone. Riding a public trans or sometimes when
she was working out in crowded places. Every now and then,
she would get the cool tingle when she spotted a hidden
surveillance camera. Odd that she should feel it now. Maybe
there was a spycam set up to watch the park?

She stood and wandered, trying to look aimless, but could
not see either an observer or a hidden camera. After a few
minutes the feeling abated, though it did not go away entirely.
She shrugged it off. She was, she decided, being paranoid.
There was no reason anybody should be watching her in
particular, and if a surveillance eye happened to be focused on
her, well, that was part of living in civilization.

She left the convoluted trail and went to find a restaurant.

The recording was excellent, Cierto noted, and he mentally
added a bonus to the operative's pay. The woman sat in a small
"outdoor" cafe on the starship, sipping at tea—the brand was
included with the report—and having a light lunch. Some kind
of fish, a vegetable salad, bread.

She knew she was being watched.

As Cierto replayed the recording for the third time, he
looked for the moment again. There, in the park, as she sat
upon the bench listening to the birds and insects, there had

come a moment of . . . awareness. Very subtle; she didn't leap up and begin digging through the shrubbery for a watcher, but she knew, even though she had given but the slightest sign. He had missed it on the first playing, caught it on the second, and now confirmed it to himself on the third viewing.

Cierto leaned back in the form-chair and smiled. Wonderful. Truly a dangerous opponent, this woman. Of course, he had known that already; this merely confirmed it. The years had not made her duller, but had sharpened her edges. Ah, but such a woman would be perfect once she had been conquered. The winning of her would not be easy, but that made the victory plunge all that much sweeter, did it not? And the House of Black Steel did not ask for ease, but for challenge.

The operative's report indicated that the wounded matador, still healing, traveled with Fem Kildee Wu as she returned to Koji. That caused a frown to flit across Cierto's features. Why? Surely a woman like Wu could not be attracted to a man who had proven himself as inept as this matador. Perhaps it was pity. Or was it something else? Cierto had other operatives poking into Wu's and this man Sleel's pasts, and if there was some other connection between them, it would be uncovered in due course. Meanwhile, he would not concern himself overly with this development. This Sleel had even stopped carrying his weapons, and certainly his spirit had been broken on that rocky hill where Cierto had beaten him. He had seen it before; brave men made cowards when they had been thoroughly overcome. He had done it to others himself often enough when he had walked the Flex—

He frowned. There were some bad memories that way, too. But that was long ago, and much had changed since.

Now Cierto chuckled to himself. A man was allowed to be young and stupid, and were he lucky, he would survive to become older and wiser. He had done both. More, he had learned patience. There was no hurry in any of this. Some dishes were better eaten cold, and one had to wait for the temperature to drop before dining. When he took his pleasure with Kildee Wu, it would be at the proper moment; nothing less would serve.

After all, she was to be the mother of his son, and such a thing must be perfect.

It had been a long time since Sleel had been to Koji. He didn't remember much about it; his visit had been short, part of his research for one of Gerard Repe's books. He knew that Shtotsanto, the Holy City, was where Emile's teacher Pen had been recruited by the prerevolutionaries setting themselves up against the Confed. But that was history. Sleel wasn't sure why he had agreed to come here with Kee Wu. It was probably because he didn't have anywhere else to go. He had learned that old literary lesson well enough: You couldn't go home again. If there had been any doubts after seeing where he had grown up, they had been erased.

His parents had not come to see him while he was in the medical center. He hadn't really expected them to do so, but down deep had been a glimmer of hope that they would. That hope had been snuffed. Maybe for good this time.

"This way," Kee said.

There were churches, kloysters, temples, synagogues, zendos, kyrkas and other houses of religion that Sleel did not recognize, all scattered through the port city as thick as slot machines in a gambling town. The rental flitter took him and Kee Wu through the port and into the outskirts of the place, then across a patch of empty woods and rolling farmland. Night came, and the lights of civilization were thin. Sleel stared through the window at the darkness, staying quiet, watching but not really seeing. He found himself nodding off, but it seemed too much effort to keep awake.

Wu watched Sleel sleep as they drew nearer her *dojo*. They had left Rakkaus three hours ago, the programmed flitter would have them in Kyrktorn in a few minutes. The village was small enough so there was not much of a pool of potential students there. Wu wanted those who sought to study with her to have to overcome a few obstacles before they ever stepped into her *dojo*. There was no listing for it on the comlink and she did not advertise. To find and get to her were hardly major chores, but few people wandered in accidentally. Those who came through her doors generally did so because they were seeking what she offered and had done some research to locate it. Not much of an entrance exam, but it screened out the merely curious.

Sleel slept, his forehead pressed against the flitter's window, oblivious to the sometimes bumpy ride.

Now, why had she brought him with her? He was sunk in the depths of self-pity and such a thing did not move her. True, he had been with Mayli when she had died, but Kee Wu did not live in the past to the extent that she had made her sister into a saint to be worshipped. He and she had a mutual enemy, but that in itself was hardly enough. So, why?

She watched the plastic window fog with his expelled breath, clearing between exhalations. Why did she burden herself with this man? The reason danced outside her reasoning mind, a shadow against the darkness, enough that she was aware of it but not enough that she could tell what it was. That would have to do for now. Just as she had learned to sense a sword cut coming at her when sometimes she could not actually see it, there was about this man some sense of *some*thing that had made her realize he was important to her.

The flitter slowed. The *dojo* was just ahead, the village mostly asleep at this hour, early though it was.

"Sleel," she said softly.

He came awake instantly, no sleep fog in his eyes when he looked at her. He knew where he was, she saw; there was no disorientation. Also in that moment she saw a depth she had not seen in him before. The moment passed.

"We're here."

His lips set tight, and he gave her a short nod. "Okay."

Was this a mistake? Should she have taken on this crippled man? Well, she guessed she would find out.

SEVENTEEN

THE EARLY SPRING night was only a little chilly, not enough for a jacket or heat threads. Sleel's breath hardly fogged the air as he walked along the quiet street. It was late, nearly midnight, and save for a few people exercising themselves or their pets, he was mostly alone. Kyrktorn was a small town, maybe ten thousand people altogether, and the majority of residents apparently went to bed early, which suited Sleel.

There were sufficient street lights so that it was the darkness that seemed to pool here and there. This part of the town was mostly flat and residential, multiplexes and single- or double-family dwellings. The small yards had neatly trimmed ground cover, grasses or vines, with a fair number of assorted species of trees ranging from shrub-size to thirty meters or more high. Night birds peeped in a few of the taller trees. One of the birds had a cry that sounded like nothing so much as "*Heyfool!*" and Sleel wondered if some warped god had put the damned bird there for his personal benefit.

Sleel's boots sounded quite loud on the plastcrete walk. An occasional flitter fanned by, raising a little dust, its fans humming for a long way in the quiet.

In the weeks that he had been in Kee's village, he had spent a lot of time walking. At first it was to rehabilitate the knee, developing strength in the new muscles. The new hand was bare now, grown enough to be usable on its own without the glove, though not altogether full-sized. The eye was as good as it had ever been, probably better, since it was relatively unworn.

He was able to do the sumito pattern, and he did that a few times a week, but the walking had become his chief focus. He didn't keep track of it exactly, but he probably averaged twenty or twenty-five klicks a day. Rain or shine, cold or warm, Sleel walked, trying not to think, and failing at that most of the time. Now and then, however, he did manage to lose himself in the crisscrossing of Kee's town. That was reason enough to continue it.

"Evening," a man across the street called to him, waving. The man, dressed in a long cloth poncho, was walking his small dog, a floppy-eared, short-haired, stubby-legged beast of several colors. The dog bayed once at Sleel, then went back to sniffing out the urine trails of his distant canine cousins. Sleel had seen the man and dog a dozen times on his night walks. He waved back without any real enthusiasm.

Ahead, a streetsweeper grumbled past the corner on the cross-street, warning lights flashing as it slowly made cleaner the already clean road. Sleel watched the flashing yellow and blue lights. It looked like some kind of organic thing, a dinosaurlike beast bellowing softly to itself as it grazed on civilization's dirt.

Sleel knew what his problem was. Psychologically speaking, he was still recovering from the shock of his failure. But knowing why lightened his depression not in the slightest. He ate, he slept, he stared into the distance, he answered when spoken to, and he walked, for hours at a time.

The smell of the dampened dust behind the streetsweeper reached him as Sleel neared the corner. Kee had been very understanding. He had offered to pay her for lodging and she had shaken her head and smiled. She didn't question him, didn't demand anything, mostly just left him alone. She taught her classes, went about her business, and he saw her briefly now and then. That suited him, too.

And so Sleel had become familiar with the streets and alleys and walkways of Kyrktorn in the ways only a walker can know. His body was nearly healed, but his mind was still crippled, and while he knew that, he couldn't bring himself to care. His life was maybe a third over if something like a meteor didn't drop out of the sky and kill him, and he had nothing to show for it.

Poor Sleel, he thought. Poor, sad, miserable fucking Sleel.

Cierto tended to his students. Among the new ones, there were six for whom he had hopes. Eight months, a year from now, and these six would, with sufficient training, be better than average swordplayers. As Cierto watched them practice lunges in the gym, he smiled. They were part of his plan, these six. They would be a gift to his unborn, to his yet-unconceived son. It was not given to many men to be able to give such a thing to their children, but Cierto was not just any man. *His* son would have a hero for a father, a man of honor and courage, and his mother too would be brave and adept. He would be able to demonstrate that to his son, Cierto knew, even if the boy's mother were not around when he came of an age to appreciate it. These six would be instrumental in that demonstration.

So, eight months, a year, and his carefully laid plan would come to fruition. Just as he had slain the thief who had dishonored him, so would Cierto achieve his next goal, of fathering a son to inherit his sword. He would raise the boy by the Code, and he would make his child in his own image. Such was his duty.

And in this case, such would also be his pleasure, especially the fathering part.

"No, no!" he called out to the students. "You move like cattle! Lightly! You are supposed to be dancing with your enemy, not crushing his toes under your clumsy feet!"

He kept his face stern, but inwardly he grinned. They would learn. He would see to it.

The last of the advanced class finished cleaning and putting away the kendo gear and left, bowing at the exit. Alone now in the *dojo*, Wu stretched tired muscles as she prepared to practice her *kata*. It had been a late session, to make up for a class missed due to a local holiday. It was past midnight. Sleel was out walking, dragging behind him as always his mountain of self-pity. Sometimes he walked all night, coming in as she was rising. She thought that he tried to exhaust himself so that he could sleep, but she had heard him moaning and thrashing around in his bed. Still, it was not her place to try and treat his wound. If you wanted to heal, you had to do it yourself. She had learned that lesson long ago.

She took her sword from its stand and moved to the center of the floor, callused bare fleet sliding easily over the swept-clean and polished wood. Maybe it had been a mistake to pull Sleel from the wreckage of that flitter, compounded by bringing him back here. It had been what, almost three months, and he was still sunk into his own miseries, to depths she wasn't sure she could reach even if she tried. Still, there was something there.

Wouldn't it be nice if she knew what it was?

Wu assumed *seiza*, placing the sword next to her left leg. She closed her eyes, took a couple of cleansing breaths, and sent the thoughts away, reaching from *zanshin*. Awareness replaced thought, movement followed, and Kildee Wu leaped into the martial dance of hard flesh and harder steel.

Sleel arrived at the *dojo*. Kee had finished her form and was moving to replace her sheathed sword on the rack where it usually lived. She bowed to the weapon, turned, and went to the showers.

Sleel was recognized by the doorcom and admitted. The *dojo* had a pretty good security system; it was programmed to keep strangers out. Kee had told him there had never been a problem with theft, but that certain of her more valuable possessions were protected by coded transmitters. A very good thief could probably bypass the security system, say, but if he attempted to leave carrying a protected item, he would trigger a zap field designed to center on the stolen property. Unpleasant, that experience, and repeated to anyone trying to continue the crime where the unconscious thief left off.

Sleel walked across the *dojo* floor toward Kee's sword, smelling the sweat that laced the air. He hadn't paid much attention to her art; he'd never been particularly interested in esoteric weaponry. Swords seemed fairly impractical in a modern society.

Not so impractical that a man couldn't use one to kill your client, hey, Sleel?

Dammit. He didn't need that thought.

The few times he had seen Kee working out, she had been using either a wooden or a bamboo-slat sword. He had never seen the one inside the white-lacquered sheath. He glanced at the weapon as he came to stand in front of it.

Behind him in the dressing room, the shower came on, the sound of the water obvious in the otherwise quiet building. He looked toward the dressing-room door. Kee was in the shower by now.

Sleel reached out and caught the wooden sheath in his new hand. Maybe there was some kind of protocol about this kind of thing, looking at it required permission or whatever. But he was curious, somewhat surprised at himself for feeling that or any other emotion, and what the fuck, she was in the shower anyway.

He took the sword's grip in his right hand. It was warm to his touch, the wrapping and pattern oddly comfortable in his grip. He had a sudden sense of déjà vu. He did not recall ever handling a weapon exactly like this one, but his thumb found a button that latched the sword into its sheath, pressing the release as though he had done it a thousand times before. Slowly, he began to withdraw the blade from its scabbard. As he looked at the blade, his eyes widened as he realized that the metal was black. As black as the swords of Cierto and his assassins had been.

Black! Why—?

From behind him, a voice said, "What are you doing?"

Sleel spun, whipping the black steel blade all the way out and pointing it toward the sound. The sheath clattered on the floor as he locked his weak hand onto the butt of the sword's handle behind his right hand. The sharp tip of the curved weapon moved as if guided by doppler, coming up—

—to point at Kee Wu's throat.

Naked, she stood in the doorway to the dressing room twelve meters away, dripping water into a small pool welling at her

bare feet. Quite beautiful she was, tight and muscular and wet
that way—

"Gods," she said. "It's you!"

As Wu stood facing Sleel, it was as if she had been struck by
a bolt of energy that welded her to the spot. It didn't matter that
she was naked and dripping from the interrupted shower. What
mattered was the realization that came over her when she saw
Sleel standing there with her sword. It was a combination of
what she saw—the way he handled the weapon, his expression,
his stance—and what she felt, this a sense she could not define
but also could not deny:

Sleel. *Sleel* was her perfect student.

"Gods," she said. "It's you!"

Sleel was shaken, she could see that. As much as she herself
was shaken? Wu did not know. She had finished her shower and
dressed, trying to order her thoughts, but not managing
that very well. Sleel was waiting for her when she emerged. He
had replaced her sword and now stood next to the rack upon
which the *daito* rested.

They spoke at the same instant:

"Why is it black?" he asked.

"Where did you learn that?" she asked.

There was a moment of impasse. Wu broke it. "The
manufacture of black steel is a family secret," she said. "Or
rather, it *was* a family secret. "Brought from Earth by my
great-grandmother's great-grandmother."

"And Cierto . . . ?"

"His ancestors stole the method from mine. Perhaps three
hundred years ago. That sword"—she nodded toward the
wooden stand—"is four hundred years old."

Sleel looked puzzled.

"I think Cierto thinks that his family created the metal. One
of his agents tried to steal this sword. Apparently he has a
reward out for information on such weaponry. He must think
that my family took the secret from his." A short pause, then,
"Why do you think Cierto wanted to kill your client?"

"I don't know."

"I think that I might. Our own legends tell about our theft, only we never knew who the thieves were. Until about fifty years ago. We—it was before I was born, but my grandmother—hired thieves of our own to retrieve our property."

"Jersey Reason."

"I never heard the name, but it could have been him."

Sleel took a big breath and let it out slowly. "He was on that world about then and he did steal something, but he didn't even know what it was." He looked at her. "How can you get back knowledge?"

"The secret might be lost, but the document was reclaimed. I think that was the end of it, for our family. I never knew Cierto's connection to all this until his man showed up here. The old stories were like fairy tales; there weren't names connected to them."

"Shit. That was why you were on Mtu," Sleel said. It was not a question.

"Yes. To settle a very old score."

Sleel shook his head. "From three hundred years past? That doesn't make any sense."

"It has to do with honor," she said. "Surely you know about righting wrongs. Would the passage of time make any difference to you about what Cierto did to you and Jersey Reason?"

"Not to me, no. I wouldn't expect my four-times-great-grandson to lose any sleep over it."

She shrugged. "Karma. One can wait for the cosmos to balance things, or one can help it along, but balance has to happen eventually."

"You sound like Emile. Cosmic justice."

"Mayli believed that, too. Now, my question. Where did you learn to use a sword?"

It was Sleel's turn to shrug. "Outside of the one I took from the guy who attacked us on Earth, I've never owned one. I can't remember even touching one before that. Knives and laser cutters, sure, but swords as such, no. I don't know dick about the things."

A natural swordmaster, she thought. What she had been waiting for these last few years.

"You must learn," she said.

"What?"

"About the sword."

"My hands are enough, thank you. I'm not likely to be shooting anybody else since I parked my spetsdöds, but I can defend myself with the Ninety-seven Steps if need be—"

"This is not about defense, Sleel, it is about art and spirit. Tell me, how did it feel when you were holding the sword?"

"Feel? What do you mean?"

"Was it clumsy? Awkward?"

"Nah. It felt pretty comfortable, you get right down to it. Like I'd done it all my life."

She smiled again, bigger. "It took me three years of daily practice to get to the place where a sword felt 'pretty comfortable' in my hands. You have to train with me, Sleel. You are my student."

"Shit. You've got dozens of students—"

"No, you don't understand. They are just ordinary students. *You* are my perfect student. Every instructor searches until she finds him or her. They are like soulmates; you only get one. There might be others who are faster or more adept or stronger or whatever, but only a single person who is *it*."

"And you think that's me?" Sleel's tone was halfway between amused and scornful.

"I know it. Not here"—she touched her head—"but *here*." She touched her heart with two fingers.

"You've lost your track, fem. Busted a repellor."

"No. It sounds mystical but it isn't. I just *know*."

Sleel stared at her.

He didn't want any more entanglements in his life. Why the hell should he start playing with swords, just because Kee over there had gone geboo on him?

Then again, what else was he going to do with his life? It wasn't as though he had a lot of prospects. As a writer, he had said all he wanted to say. As a matador, he had failed the most important of exams. He hadn't been the son his parents wanted and he certainly didn't want to compound that by fathering children of his own. So, where was he going to go and what was he going to do when he got there? If it didn't matter, if one spot was as good as another, then why not here? If it made Kee Wu happy to show him how to waggle a bar of sharp steel, then why not? Might as well be of some use to somebody, right?

He looked at her again, at her knowing smile. It bothered him to be the focus of someone's hopes and attention. Then again, the alternatives were pretty much null, weren't they?

"Okay," he said. "Why not? I'll stick around and learn fancy carving."

She laughed and actually clapped her hands.

"I knew it!" she said.

"Yeah? What if I'd said space it? What if I had just turned and walked out?"

"But you didn't."

"But what if I had?"

"You wouldn't have. A student needs a teacher. That's part of the equation."

"Ah, Christo, you mystical types always have answers for everything, don't you?"

"More or less. Maybe," she said, "maybe I can help you find some answers, too, Sleel."

EIGHTEEN

FROM HIS TRAINING in sumito, the countless hours practicing the complex patterns of those dances, Sleel knew how to move efficiently. And, since neither he nor Kee were interested in working on *less* efficient ways of moving such as classical kendo, she didn't bother to try to teach that to him. He seemed to know instinctively how to hold a sword. Kee's intent, she said, was to marry Sleel's knowledge of motion to the steel.

They stood in the *dojo*, Sleel drenched in his own sweat, the heavy cotton workout jacket and pants soaked through in places. The warm-ups were done, his muscles were loose and a little sore from swinging the weapon this way and that. Kee stood next to him.

"It's simple," she said. "Where you would punch or chop or kick, we'll substitute the sword."

Simple to say. Not so easy to do. Even though the practice sword only weighed maybe a kilo and a half, having the weapon in his hand threw his timing off. Unlike Kee's sword, the one Sleel now held was a mirror-bright stainless steel, but it was, like hers, sharp enough to shave with from its tip to the hilt. A mistake would mean a deep cut.

Kee told him a story about accidents: "When I was first training, I kept my sword under my bed. It was a replica of a fifteenth-century weapon, there was no catch, the sword was kept in the sheath by friction, a metal plug around the blade at the *tsuba* fitted snugly into the mouth of the scabbard. One morning when I was in a hurry, I reached under the bed and

143

grabbed the end of the sheath instead of the sword. I jerked it out. The sheath slipped off the sword and the sharp edge fell about a third of a meter onto the top of my foot. I was wearing thick socks. The blade was sharp enough to cut through and into my flesh. I was lucky it missed the tendons, but it still took the medic nine staples to close the wound, plus orthostat glue to seal the cut bone."

That hadn't made Sleel feel any more confident. It was not so much the idea of being injured—he had been cut enough over his years—but the thought of looking bad. What's the matter, Sleel, can't hold a knife without slicing yourself with it? Always his curse, that worry.

He shuffled again through the early steps of the sumito dance, waving the shiny blade. When he finished, he shook his head. Despite his ability to feel comfortable just holding the sword, that didn't give him automatic mastery of every movement. And the image of Jersey Reason's head falling had often come back to haunt him in dreams. It was a gruesome way to die, being chopped into pieces, having your head cleaved from your body. He said as much to Kee.

"Like your deaths neat and clean, do you?"

"Excuse me?"

"If you shoot a man across a field or even a room, you don't get the full impact of what you've done. Facing an opponent one-on-one, hand-to-hand or with a sword, you have to accept your personal responsibility. Killing somebody *ought* to be messy. You should be sprayed with his blood, you should be able to hear him scream, catch the death rattle, smell the feces and urine as the bowels and bladder let go. You should have to dispose of the body. So you know exactly what it was you did."

"Gory, aren't you?"

She sighed. "My sister died in a war. She probably never saw the man who killed her. If you are going to deal in death, you should be willing to see the truth of it, not some glorious lie. If I have a battle with another swordplayer, it is between the two of us, our business, our truth. But if you run a planet and you get pissed off at somebody the next orbit over, you each might send a million soldiers to recycling plants. A smart rocket can come from a thousand klicks away to kill you; it doesn't care and it won't be in the least upset that it has blasted you to atomic debris. That's the real horror of modern war, that it is impersonal. Being cut with a sword *hurts*, and if you are close enough to do it, you can't miss the other's pain."

"That's great," Sleel said. "A pacifistic swordfighter."

"Not a pacifist, no." A beat. "You've killed people," she said. "Up close. With your hands."

"Yes. A few."

"Do you remember them?"

Sleel sighed. "Yes."

"Then you understand what I'm talking about. Don't try to play stupid, Sleel. That wall won't hold anymore; I've seen the gate. I can get through. I *know* better."

Sleel turned away from her, tightening his grip on the sword's handle. Would that he could cut that knowledge down. His life had been simple when those around him thought he was the image he worked to project. There had been times, such as when he'd been in prison, when he could almost believe it himself. It was a safe game to play; people didn't expect much from you. Good old Sleel, they would say. Predictable as a rock, never changing, single-minded. Thinks he's the toughest guy in the galaxy, the epitome of maleness, testosterone's own fair-haired boy. Cross me and get stomped. It had been a good place to hide.

"Let's repeat the last sequence," she said.

The information that came to Cierto was momentarily disturbing. The message arrived as he was teaching one of the new students, Rita, the pleasures of anal sex. She was not an eager learner, but he was patient.

His personal com chimed where it lay on the floor next to the bed. Only a few people had his private code, and therefore any calls to it were likely to be important.

Cierto fell full-length upon his partner. She groaned as his weight flattened her, the sound muffled as her face was pressed into the cushions by his chest when he reached over her for the com. He did not withdraw from her as he answered the call.

"Yes?"

"Patrón, you asked to be informed of any changes."

It was Alberto, one of his spies on Koji.

"Sí. What has changed?"

"The woman is teaching the matador."

"Teaching him?"

"The sword. She has given her classes over to her senior students and now works exclusively with the one called Sleel."

For a moment, Cierto felt a stab of worry, a fluttery roil in his belly. Then Rita squirmed beneath him. Her movement was a not-unpleasant sensation; still, control was important. Cierto thrust hard. Rita squeaked and lay still. He grinned. "*Está no importa,*" he said to his spy. "The matador will die when our plan proceeds. Maintain your vigil."

He discommed and dropped the unit back onto the thick carpet. He suddenly imagined that it was Kildee Wu pinned beneath him and the thought flashed and fired in him a hotter desire, a raging lust. The woman's screams were muted by the cushions, but Cierto took pleasure in the sounds as he drove himself to his climax. Yes! Soon it will be Kildee Wu!

Sleel was exhausted. It was as much the newness of the exercises as anything, but after three hours of working out, he was tired and sore. He allowed the hot water thrumming from the shower to pound at him on full flow. In the shower stall next to him, Kee also washed away the sweat of their efforts.

After he was clean and somewhat refreshed, Sleel tapped the blower control. The jets of warm air wrapped themselves around him, drying the moisture. A thick towel finished the process.

He glanced at Kee as she dried herself. Very attractive. Sleel felt the pull, though he resisted it. Thinking with his dick had gotten him into enough trouble over the years, and he found himself reluctant to spoil this relationship, such that it was, by trying to become Kee's lover. Didn't mean he couldn't look and appreciate. It was good that he had the towel, though. He held it carefully.

"Feel better?" she asked.

"Yeah. Hot water is one of the major joys of civilization."

Kee draped her towel over her shoulders, unconcerned that the rest of her was exposed. "You think we're civilized?"

"Well, no, not really. Too close to the days when we bashed each other over the head with some critter's leg bones. Our reflexes are still back in the caves. A loud noise makes you duck, and any real danger makes you want to sprint like hell or smash it flat."

He chuckled. "Dirisha talks about the reptile brain only having a thin overlay. First good thump and the cover comes off, leaving the lizard in charge. Some of us are better than others, but as a species, I figure we still have a way to go."

"Spiritual development," she said. "That's what the arts are about, when you get past the self-defense part."

"So I heard. I guess I haven't gotten that far."

She grinned. "Gives me something useful to do."

There was a short but awkward pause. Sleel looked at her, she at him, and he was really glad he still had the towel. It didn't seem fair that women didn't show lust as easily as men did.

Wu watched Sleel as he dressed. He had a good body, his injuries were healed, at least visibly, and she admired the play of his muscles. Her thrill at having found her student was still vibrating in her. It had been a surprise; she had always thought that she would know the instant she saw him or her. Not so.

No, Sleel was not what she had expected. He was already highly trained, could in fact move better than she could herself. She had quickly discarded thoughts of trying to teach him classical sword forms, knowing they would be too restrictive. The sport forms of fencing were highly stylized and had no place in combat swordplay. There were no rules in a sword-fight, save those the combatants might agree upon, and while you could trust your own honor, trusting the honor of someone who was trying to kill you was hardly wise.

What would Master Ven have thought of Sleel? The matador was physically adept but mentally crippled. Wasn't that her task, then? To elevate his spirit? To help him become one with himself and the sword?

Tricky, she thought, as she slipped into her own clothes. She had always figured that once she found her student the teaching might be difficult, but it would not be particularly complex. So much for that idea. Watching Sleel dance with the sword, she had already had to reconfigure her old thoughts. She had learned new things in the first moments and that had been unexpected. She knew that teaching and learning were intertwined, but such a rapid and graphic demonstration had surprised her.

Desire had surprised her, too. She was normal enough in her drives and it had been some time since she had indulged them, but something in Sleel aroused her more than she would have thought possible. That, however, would not be a good idea, to play with those warm feelings. Lovers were easy enough to come by, you only got the one real student.

No, she would keep it on a teacher-and-student plane. She hadn't looked and waited all these past years to risk losing it to a sexual desire. The spirit was more important than the flesh.

Sleel's life took on a different cast once he started playing with the sword. He spent four or five hours a day working with the blade, trying to dance the sumito patterns.

Sometimes his new hand ached, as did the new eye. When he had lost his foot and had it regrown, he had experienced the same kind of ache. It was a kind of phantom limb pain, the medics had told him then. It was not a missing part but a new one that was not quite the same as the old one that caused it, they'd said. It didn't bother him that much.

In fact, the long days of exercise became his reason for getting up in the morning. True, he still walked at night sometimes, but less frequently and not as far as once he had. The routine became familiar, and was in its way comforting.

Dirisha called to see how he was doing, as did Bork and even Emile. Sleel found, somewhat to his amazement, that he was doing okay. Not great, but better.

So the days and weeks went, blurring past in a mostly

mindless way as he strived to become adept with the sword. It still felt awkward much of the time and he realized he wasn't very good at it, but he was getting better, if only a little. It was something to do. It was better than what he had been doing. It was better than nothing.

NINETEEN _____

NIGHT LAY OVER this part of Thompson's Gazelle like a shroud, speckled with stars but without the light of a moon. The town of Tofaa was smallish, quiet, and mostly asleep. Cierto stood in the shadow of a storage shed, watching the last of his six students move into position. The air had a dusty, manurelike smell, that from the corn-variant grain piled neck-deep inside the shed. An unappetizing odor at best.

The target, a police substation, was directly across the street from where Cierto stood. The three occupants were unsuspecting. There were five cools in Tofaa, the shift change coming up, so that in a matter of minutes all five would be in the station, two coming in from patrol, two more about to leave, the woman on the desk on for the entire night. All were armed with squeezers, compressed gas pellet pistols. Most police agencies were more enlightened than the cools of Tofaa; they carried hand wands or dart pistols or other stun weapons. But the Tofaa force was a throwback to the frontier days, slow to change. The pellets fired by their squeezers could be, properly placed, lethal. These weapons were why Cierto and his students were here.

The test had to be real.

Each of the six students wore a small camera, mounted to record his or her POV, but Cierto would not be satisfied to watch the replay. He would not use his own blade, but he would be close enough to watch the action.

"Patrón," whispered Basilio. "We are in readiness."

"It is your operation," Cierto said.

The student nodded once and hurried across the street. The other five were in place, swords drawn.

The timing was precise. Two minutes later, the patrol flitter arrived, fanned to a stop in its usual parking place, settling to the plastcrete. The doors gull-winged and the two cools alighted. The driver was telling a joke to the other one as they walked toward the front of the station.

"—so the ferry cap says, 'I've never seen anything like that in all my life!' and the woman shrugs and says, 'It's just professional courtesy—' Hello?"

The two cools stopped as Rita and Villas stepped into sight three meters in front of them. The students held their swords ready. Neither of them spoke.

The driver knew trouble when he saw it and he was faster than his partner. He snatched at his holstered weapon.

In a heartbeat Rita covered the space between them and slashed, catching the cool's wrist. The strike was perfect, Cierto noted. The cool's hand fell, severed from the now-panicked man's arm. He screamed.

Villas moved in and skewered the second officer with a simple thrust to the chest. The second man had only begun to draw his weapon. He fell.

Rita snapped her sword back, cocking her hand by her ear, and cut at the still-screaming cool. The blade kissed the man's neck, tore out his throat, and slung blood onto his fallen partner.

Villas crouched by the cool he had taken out and picked up the man's weapon. He stood and pointed it at the door of the substation, then fired the entire magazine. The *whump!* of the gun firing was echoed by the sharp taps of the pellets striking the door. If those inside had not heard the screaming cool, surely they would hear the impacts of the missiles?

Surely they did. The door opened and two cools emerged, still more curious than worried. The man in the lead saw Villas just as the student dropped the handgun. Rita moved to draw his attention, bringing her sword up in a salute, touching the bloody blade to her forehead.

"What the fuck—?"

The second cool bumped into the back of his stopped companion. "Al? What is it?"

Two more students, Burton and Les, emerged from their hiding places to the sides of the door, swords raised. The cools had to know they were in deadly danger by now. Both went for their weapons.

Burton and Les moved in concert. Burton's thrust was to his man's right eye; Les chose a safer target, ramming his sword into the second cool's liver and twisting. The first cool out the door gurgled and collapsed; the second went white and tried to grab the sword that impaled him. He lost a finger when Les jerked the weapon free and repeated the thrust, again piercing the liver. "Ahh!" the cool said. Les withdrew the blade and gave the man yet another thrust.

Meanwhile, Ellenita and Basilio moved in and through the doorway. The station commander would be alone inside.

Cierto hurried across the street to try to see the final assassination. He was but halfway there when the *whump!* of a squeezer from inside told him that the commander had managed to get at least one shot off.

Burton and Les moved aside as their Patrón ran into the station.

The commander was down, her head half-severed from her neck, blood gouting onto the terrazzo floor in a smeary pool. But Basilio was also sprawled on the cool gray floor, a small wound on his chest over the heart also spilling blood.

Against five qualified with projectile weapons, the loss of one was not bad. True, these local cools were hardly the Republic's finest warriors; still, guns against swords, the bearers of the latter with only six months' training, well, that was a fair enough test, no?

Cierto grinned. "*Bueno.*"

The other students had begun to drag the slain and still-dying cools into the station. Once they were all inside, Cierto said, "Bring Basilio."

Ellenita rose from where she had been examining her fallen comrade. "He is dead, Patrón."

"No matter. We do not wish for there to be an extra body here."

"Surely the explosion—?" Villas began.

"—will hide things from local authorities," Cierto finished. "But perhaps this might rate investigation from Republic professionals. They have many machines and much patience. We shall dispose of Basilio in our own way."

Quickly the five remaining students set the explosive charges. Carrying Basilio, they followed Cierto to the stolen hopper and entered it. The vessel had altered identification pulses and registration numbers. By the time anyone could sort those out, Cierto and his students would be offplanet and on their circuitous and separate ways home.

As the hopper lifted and sped away from Tofaa, the star-speckled night was shattered by a series of explosions, so close they sounded as one giant roar. There would be a fifty-meter-wide crater where the substation had been; with luck, no one would ever realize that the sundered bodies of the cools had been sword fodder before the blast.

Cierto leaned back in his seat, feeling pleased. They had behaved well under the pressure of real combat, his students. True, he had lost one, but that was to be expected. Another few months, perhaps three more such training exercises, and they would be ready.

Already he was considering Basilio's replacement. Samuels? Or Gene? Gene. He was a bit slow, but very methodical. He could be improved with work.

Basilio was a loss, but at least Cierto had not had to give up either of his women. Rita and Ellenita were coming along in other ways, as well as being potentially excellent swords-women. Another grin replaced the last one.

Everything moved according to his plan.

Kee Wu watched Sleel dance, the sword seeming to be as much a part of him as his own hands. Amazing. He could do this consciously—what might he accomplish if he could achieve *zanshin*? Truly he was the best student she had ever seen, and she was learning as much from him as he was from her.

Sleel finished the series and stopped. He wiped sweat from

his eyes with the back of one sleeve. Despite the headband he wore, his face was drenched.

"Sorry," he said. "I was off on that last piece."

She said, "It was fine, Sleel."

He shook his head, sweat flying. "No, it was off."

"Let's take a break," she said.

"Okay."

When he had toweled more of the perspiration from his face and neck, they both moved to drink from the water fountain. That done, Sleel said, "I don't think I'm gonna get much better. I can walk the pattern using the sword instead of my hands and feet without falling down. Not much else left, is there?"

"Just the one thing."

He smiled, something he had done more of lately. "Oh, right, the zonked-out trance."

"It's not exactly like that."

"Yeah, sure, but you can't teach me that part."

"No. It can't be taught. Or even learned."

"Mumbo-jumbo time again."

"You'll know it when you get there."

"And how long might that take?"

She shrugged. "Nobody can say." She looked at him more carefully. "Why? You have an appointment somewhere else?"

"Yeah. You might say that."

As he healed from his loss on Mtu, Sleel had become more focused on another thing. "Revenge is a waste of your energy," she said.

He laughed. "This from a woman who went zipping off to find the great-something-grandson of somebody long dead who swiped a formula from her own great-something grandma?"

Wu had the grace to smile.

"Wait, lemme guess," he said. "That's different, right?"

"Well, no. But as a teacher, I want you to do as I say, not as I do."

"Right."

"Besides, you're not ready for Cierto yet," she said.

"Not ready? Shit. I can sure as hell shoot him in the back or clonk him over the head without knowing any more than I knew before I got here."

"But that's not how you want to face him, is it?"

Sleel looked at her. "You do a little mind-reading on the side?"

"You're easy, Sleel. He beat you at what you did best."

"How do you know I'm not ready? You said I was the best student you ever had."

She thought about it for a few seconds, decided to tell him. "Back when I walked the Flex, Cierto and I dueled."

"No shit? Why isn't he dead? Or you, for that?"

She gave him a wry smile. "Because I couldn't think ahead. I beat him. Cut off his foot. I thought that was enough, so I didn't kill him. Personal honor. I didn't know at the time he was related to the thief who stole the family secret. He was down, I had won; killing him would have been . . . superfluous."

"Would you have killed him had you known who he was?"

She repeated the tight smile. "Probably not."

"Opportunity lost. But you did beat him. And you think I couldn't?"

"You might take that Cierto of years ago, as good as you now are. But he has certainly improved. The strike I used was a trick; we were evenly matched. I don't know if I could defeat him today. I can, however, beat you."

Sleel raised an eyebrow, and some of the old cockiness she had seen flash in him now and then came to the surface. "Oh? You said that my sumito coupled with the sword is the best system you've ever seen. And that I'm good at it."

"It is and you are. Your technique is superb. Better in many ways than my own."

"But that doesn't matter."

"No," she said. "It doesn't. It is not about technique."

Sleel laughed.

Wu looked at him, waiting.

"Mayli said that same thing to me once, in front of a class. Only the subject was sex. It's not about technique, she said. It's about love."

"She was wise, my sister. This"—she touched the handle of

her sword—"is about spirit. Technique is only the smallest part of it."

Sleel grinned.

"You don't believe me," she said.

"I didn't say that."

"You don't have to." She sighed. "Go and get two *shinai*," she said.

"Oh, yeah, you got it," he said.

Wu had to smile at him as he hurried to fetch the bamboo practice swords. He was eager to show her how good he was, to prove to her—and to himself—that the past months of practice had been well spent. As indeed they had been. But those lessons were not as important as the one she was about to impart.

She hoped.

Cierto watched his advanced class work with the computer-generated lacs, defending and attacking. There had been some changes in the class, and these were the best of the bunch remaining. Les had lost his nerve, becoming hesitant when required to fight other students with the live blade. Shortly there would be found a good-bye note from him in the house computer, saying that he had left to return to his homeworld. The note would be a forgery, and Les would go no farther than the estate's private recycling plant, at least not in his present form.

Winston, a fire-haired boy of twenty, would move into Les's vacated position.

Villas, alas, would have to suffer a similar fate, since he seemed to have become afflicted with pangs of conscience over those killed in training exercises. Perhaps Jorj could improve enough to replace Villas.

It was about control, Cierto knew, and he was the Patrón.

Jorj. Now there was a name that brought back old memories. His paternal uncle had been named Jorj. The bastard.

The students went through their drills, but Cierto was all of a moment suddenly lost in the past.

Hoja was in his room, studying, when his uncle arrived.

"Good evening, Nephew," Jorj said.

"And to you, Uncle."

"I am sorry that I missed your birthday celebration."

Hoja shrugged. "A thing of no importance, Uncle."

"Ah, but it is. You are now thirteen, and a man."

His uncle moved to sit on Hoja's bed. "Come, sit beside me," he said. He patted the bed lightly.

Obediently, Hoja left his desk and sat next to his uncle. Jorj was only ten years older, but to a boy of thirteen, twenty-three was as far away as the moon.

His uncle put one arm around the boy's shoulders and squeezed lightly. "Your father tells me you are doing well in your studies."

"I try, Uncle."

"You must call me Jorj, for you are a man now."

"Sí, Uncle—I mean, sí, Jorj." The name felt funny in his mouth.

Jorj allowed his encircling arm to relax and he began to rub gently Hoja's neck and upper back. He said, "Well, now that you are a man, there are other lessons you should learn."

Hoja did not understand what his uncle meant.

Jorj leaned over and kissed Hoja full on the mouth. His tongue darted in between the boy's surprised lips.

Hoja jerked his face away. "Uncle!"

"Lessons I mean to teach you, Hoja," Jorj said, as if nothing had happened. "Starting now."

Hoja struggled, but his uncle was stronger. He was taken by force; it had hurt more than he would have thought possible. As he lay naked on his bed, sobbing, Jorj had dressed and left, saying as he exited, "It will be easier next time. You will come to want it, to love it."

The students continued their work with the lacs, but Cierto was there in body only. His memory had claimed him fully and he did not even see them.

Four months passed in the life of Hoja Cierto, four months in which the thirteen-year-old boy was molested by his once-respected uncle almost every night. He had not come to love it, nor to want it, and his shame was great. True, there

were men who preferred other men to women, and this was
well known and accepted. And while Hoja had not yet lain with
a woman, neither did he wish to lie with men, especially his
uncle.

He did not know what to do. Should he tell his father?
Would that make things better? Or worse?

After a particularly painful session, in which Jorj had used
his fists upon him, Hoja decided that he must speak of this to
his father.

The Patrón's private sitting room was halfway around the
main house from Hoja's room. The boy arrived at the room just
in time to see his uncle being admitted.

So much for seeing his father. He could hardly blurt out that
his father's brother had been molesting him for months while
Jorj sat there listening. All his uncle had to do was deny it, and
Hoja knew full well his father would not take the word of his
son over that of his brother.

Still, Hoja did not turn and leave. He padded carefully to the
door and put his ear against it. The muffled laughter of the two
men came through the thick wood, but no words were
understandable.

Of a moment, Hoja felt a burning need to know what Jorj
was saying to the Patrón. He could not hear them through the
door, but there was a way.

His father's private fresher was off the sitting room. The
door from that into the hall was only a few meters away.

Moving with great care, Hoja opened the fresher's door and
slipped inside. The door connecting the fresher to the sitting
room was ajar. He could hear the conversation between his
father and his uncle easily, hunched down next to the bidet and
hidden from sight.

"—yes, at first he fought, but now he accepts me," Jorj said.
"I think he is even beginning to like it."

His father said, "Ah, I had hoped he would show more
spirit."

"Yes, it is sad. To have a son who is a coward, willing to be
used like a woman . . ."

Hoja blinked as the words sank in and he understood them.
His father knew what Jorj was doing!

There was no need to hear any more. Hoja stood and quietly left. His father knew what his uncle did to him, and he thought badly of Hoja for it!

Rage burned in the boy, rage hot enough to sear the shame into ash. Nothing was given for free in the *casa*; you had to earn everything. Very well. Let them see how much spirit he had.

A cruel smile came to life on the face of the Patrón of the House of Black Steel as his students danced, a smile born of the memory of what had happened all those years ago when he had been abused by his uncle. This was the part he liked best.

Hoja was not without imagination and certain skills. He spent all of the next day preparing, knowing he would get one chance only, knowing that to fail might mean punishment so severe he might not survive it.

That night, when his uncle arrived, Hoja was ready.

Jorj overrode the locking mechanism of the sliding door with his keycard as he usually did. Hoja had dimmed the lights, and he lay naked upon the bed, so that his uncle could not miss seeing him there. Before, he had always been dressed and fearful.

The door slid open and Jorj blinked in surprise as Hoja grinned and fondled himself. "Uncle," he said.

Jorj's lust shined through his eyes, twisting his lips into a sneer. Perhaps this was but a test devised by the Patrón, but Hoja had felt his uncle's desire enough to know it was a test he enjoying administering. Jorj all but lunged through the door.

The wire caught him across the shins.

Jorj was, as were all the men of the *casa*, an expert swordsman, but his reflexes were fogged by his desires. He realized something was wrong, and he would have backed out of the room, but he was not quite fast enough.

The metal shelf balanced precisely above the doorway was loaded with almost eighty kilograms of exercise weights. One of the plates hit Jorj squarely on the top of his head, and the man fell, partially buried under the iron.

Hoja leaped from the bed. He grabbed one of the fallen

weights. Jorj was stunned, moaning softly. Hoja lifted the weight—a five-kilo plate—and smashed Jorj's skull, once, twice, three times, until the bone went soft and pulpy, and fluid oozed from the shattered head.

Hoja dropped the weight and stood. He closed the door and began picking up the weights, placing them back into their storage cases against the wall. In a few moments, the shelf and iron plates were in their normal positions. The trip wire and guides were removed. Only his dead uncle—and he surely was dead, not breathing or moving—lay upon the floor.

There was but one other thing remaining before he was done. Hoja pulled his uncle's pants down so that his buttocks were bared. Then for the first time, he did to his uncle what his uncle had for months done to him. His ejaculation was powerful, bringing tears to his eyes.

He pulled his uncle's pants back up when he was done, dressed himself, then touched his com and called his father.

His father arrived with the *casa*'s medic and a guard.

"*Dios!* What has happened here?"

Hoja faced his father, standing as tall as he was able to stand, and looked the Patrón squarely in the eyes. "He fell and hit his head," Hoja said. He hoped all the hatred he felt showed.

There was a long moment of silence. Then the Patrón sighed and nodded, almost as if to himself. "I see."

"I am glad that you do," Hoja said.

His father must have had mixed feelings, Hoja later reflected. To have lost a brother, but to have gained the son he wanted. Or thought he wanted.

Next to the body of Jorj, the medic said, "No fall could do this—"

"You are wrong," Hoja's father said. "My brother has died in an unfortunate accident. A fall."

Hoja understood that Jorj's death would not be spoken of again, save as an accident. And he understood too that the lesson went both ways.

From that day on, Hoja's father would never again turn his back on his son.

TWENTY

As HE STOOD holding his bamboo practice sword and facing Kee, Sleel reminded himself that he was an expert martial artist. True, this was her toy, the sword, but he *was* one of only a few people in the entire galaxy who could dance the Ninety-seven Steps. He'd watched her move often enough, and while she was pretty good, she wasn't *that* good. He could take her. All he had to do was use what he knew. He was bigger, stronger, probably as fast if not faster, and a lot more experienced in hand-to-hand combat, even if she had walked the Flex. He had killed people with his hands, more than once; he wasn't afraid of a little woman with a padded stick.

So, Sleel, if that's true, how come your hands are sweating all over the leather handle of *your* padded stick? Hmm?

Shut up.

Kee stood less than two meters away, the tip of her *shinai* nearly touching the tip of Sleel's, their weapons pointed at each other's eyes.

Relax, Sleel told himself. Loosen up your shoulders. Breathe easy. You've got the reach on her, probably almost half a meter. Just scoot in and tap her and it'll be all over. Don't com your strike, just gather your energy and do it.

As Sleel was about to jump, Kee shifted a few centimeters to her left. The attack he'd planned would fall a hair short now. He slid his feet over a little, keeping his sword held steady. No problem, we'll just adjust our aim a little—

Kee settled a little lower into her stance. Her feet were now

161

hidden beneath the folds of her split skirt. When she moved
back, it was as if she were on wheels, so smooth was her
motion. One second she was *there*, the next, she was a
handspan farther away. Just outside his range.

Okay, okay, bottle that one. Come in from the side and use
a horizontal cut instead. By the time she gets her sword over to
block, it'll be too late—

As if reading his mind, Kee shifted her *shinai*, angling the
springy slats so that a horizontal strike from her left would be
a mistake; she'd be able to stop the cut and he'd be wide open
for the shot to the throat. They weren't wearing *bogu* and she'd
pull the jab, but were she using a real sword, that would
effectively end the fight in her favor.

Sleel considered another attack, something unconventional.
He would throw Laughing Stone. She couldn't be ready for that
one. Even if she could stop the initial strike, the rebound and
reply ought to give him a clean hit on her spine—

Once again Kee wiggled the *shinai*, a compound move that
showed she could negate the first strike and that she *knew*
where the second part of the series would follow.

Her expression was neutral, her eyes seemed unfocused, she
gave nothing away.

Damn. How can she do that?

Fuck it. Enough of all this mystical imaginary thrust-and-
parry crap. Just go for it and outreach her.

Sleel leaped, as fast as he could, extending his sword to the
fullest. It wouldn't be a hard tap, but he would make the
point—

Kee flowed to his left, and time stalled, the tachy-psyche
effect stretching Chronos out like sheet gum under a heatlamp.
Sleel moved in slow motion, unable to increase his speed, and
he saw Kee's sword coming from light years away; it was
taking its fucking time but so was he, and there was no way to
avoid it—

Thwack! He felt the bamboo thump into his ribs under his
still-outstretched arm. If that had been a real sword, he would
be much in need of another spell in a Healy, sure enough. But
before he could react, Kee's *shinai* flicked back and out again,

and the smooth bamboo touched and drew a line across the back of his neck.

Welcome to Jersey Reason's country, Sleel.

Well, *shit*—!

And still mired in the molasses that time had become, Sleel dragged his own weapon around much too late to stop the third strike, a poke to his solar plexus with the padded leather tip.

Three-for-three, Sleel you old fool, any one of which would have put you down and out of it. You really have gotten ancient. What happened to your reflexes?

Time recovered. Sleel finally managed to come back up to normal speed. Too late, of course.

Sleel wanted to spit, to curse and to throw the damned fucking bamboo down and stomp on it. He did none of these things, however. He merely bowed, acknowledging Kee's victory.

To his everlasting relief, she didn't laugh, or even smile, but merely nodded. This was, her expression seemed to say, serious business. Sleel could not help but agree.

"You need a holiday, Sleel," Wu said. "I could use a rest myself."

They were in a restaurant not far from her *dojo*, a place known for its portions more than the complexity of its menu. Still, if you liked basic fare, you got your money's worth and then some. Sleel was halfway through his second plate of stir-fried vegetables and noodles. Since he'd started working out, his appetite had increased, and Wu enjoyed watching him eat. She had nearly finished her own plate of sweet-and-sour wood shrimp, a local freshwater delicacy that came from a reservoir made by flooding what had once been a forest. A couple of hundred years ago, anyhow.

"So, where are you going on your vacation?" he asked.

"I thought we might go up to Carnival Falls."

"Carnival Falls. We?"

"Unless you want to find a place on your own."

He swallowed a mouthful of noodles. "Nope. Sounds aces by me. Any particular reason we want to go there?"

"It's quiet. And restful."

• • •

The sound that the waterfall made as it crashed down into the pool at the base was loud enough to drown a conversation as easily as the cascade itself drowned the glistening purplish boulders and rocks below. The falls dropped a distance of maybe eighty meters, starting out relatively narrow at the top and sheeting wider as the waters sprayed and foamed at the bottom. Rainbows blossomed in the sunshine-lit mists like multicolored flowers. The river resumed its journey at one end of the pool, snaking away in a much quieter meander. From where Sleel and Kee stood on the small arched bridge twenty meters above the river, it was all quite beautiful.

"Peaceful, you said?" Sleel yelled.

"What?"

But she grinned, and Sleel joined her in smiling.

Cierto sat in a rental hopper across the street from the largest kendo school on the planet Mason. The master of the school had just finished his last class and was alone in the *dojo*. Cierto had chosen this target carefully. The instructor inside had walked the Flex, though he had retired a couple of years before Cierto had ever joined it. He had been a minor player, never ranked in the top dozen or so, but he had killed in combat. This was important.

Cierto's six students moved through the well-lit night toward the front of the *dojo*. These were Rita, Burton, Winston, Ellenita, Gene and Jorj. Back on Rift, Raz and Tomas, now his two best students, waited in reserve, in case this man proved to be more adept than Cierto had figured.

Ellenita, wearing next to nothing in the form of short skintights and spray slippers, arrived at the *dojo* first. An attractive woman dressed provocatively tended to allay suspicion that danger threatened. Burton carried her sword as well as his own, both weapons cleverly disguised as part of an old-style powered exowalker Burton wore in his pretense of being a cripple.

The *dojo*'s door was electronically latched, and it would

need to be opened from the inside, unless Cierto wanted to go to the trouble of cracking the lock. It was much simpler to have your enemy admit you unsuspecting.

Ellenita spoke to the query, smiling into the camera's eye. The door opened silently.

Burton, who appeared to be passing by at just that moment, darted into the opening. He moved altogether too fast for somebody depending on an exowalker.

Ellenita leaned against the open door and the other four students hurried into the place.

Cierto alighted from the hopper and strolled across the street.

Inside the *dojo* the master had realized the danger. He stood in the center of the workout area, his sword held like a ball bat next to his right shoulder. He wore *hakima* and a *gi* jacket, both black, and his feet were bare.

Cierto smiled. Good. Perfect. Here was a target who resembled Kildee Wu in a number of respects. Same style sword, same basic art, even the workout clothes were nearly identical. While Cierto's students had spent a fair portion of their training these past months working against kendo simulacrums, there was no substitute for the real thing. If Cierto's test for his son's mother was to be fair, he must not stint on his preparations.

The black-clad swordsman was good enough to recognize that Cierto was more of a danger than the six who drew their blades and moved to encircle him. Cierto shook his head, telling the man that he was not a combatant. The man nodded once in acknowledgment, took a deep breath and expelled half of it.

Cierto observed the master of the *dojo* carefully. He was afraid, but not panicked. Doubtless he had fought multiple-attacker practice matches with padded swords. He had been instructing for a long time, and a good teacher learned more than he taught. As Cierto watched, he saw the man's shoulders relax slightly. Ah. That he was able to do this facing half a dozen opponents spoke well of him. Cierto reluctantly raised his estimation of the man. He was tempted to warn his students, but he did not speak. If they made errors, let them be their own.

The circle, somewhat ragged, finished forming. Burton and Ellenita were behind the victim; this was the most dangerous place to be, because on the face of it, it seemed the safest. He couldn't see them and the tendency would be for them to assume they could strike with little risk. Of course they had been warned against such overconfidence.

The man in the middle knew what this was. In the old days, when warriors routinely carried swords, testing students or masters of one style of martial art against those of another was quite common. A wandering student would challenge a teacher and if the challenger won, he would continue to roam or take over the school. If he lost—and survived—he would often enroll as a student of the man who had beaten him.

Jorj, directly in front of the kendo teacher, lunged in, extending for a quick stab to the heart.

The kendo man swatted Jorj's blade aside easily and snapped his heavier sword out, slicing to the bone with the tip in Jorj's right forearm just below his elbow. Blood welled. Jorj cursed and jerked his weapon back.

The kendo player spun his sword so that the point blurred in an arc to point edge up directly behind him at belly level. He stabbed backward, much as a man paddling a canoe might thrust his paddle into turbulent waters for control.

Ellenita's memory of her lessons and Cierto's warnings of overconfidence must have failed her. She was moving toward the man when she took the samurai sword under the breastbone. Her slayer twisted the sword back and forth once to free it and pulled it back, spinning in a full circle with a one-handed slash to drive his attackers back.

Those able moved quickly to widen the circle.

Burton had removed his fake exowalker and was unencumbered. He screamed and leaped at the kendoist. A fatal mistake. Burton's head was cut from the top of the right ear at an angle, the powerful slice digging all the way to the corner of his mouth.

Rita hopped in as the kendoist pried his weapon from the dying Burton. She slashed, cutting through the man's split skirt

and thigh. From the way her sword stopped, she reached the
bone. She danced away as the man swung wildly at her.

Jorj sought to finish the wounded man, a backhanded cut
with his uninjured left hand that would likely have beheaded
the kendo player had it connected.

The man blocked the slash, dropped his sword's point, and
drove it into Jorj's throat.

The kendoist spent too much time watching Jorj fall,
however. Gene saw his chance and took it. He drove his blade
into the master of the *dojo* from behind, finding a space
between two ribs, skewering him all the way through the left
lung and probably the heart or one of the great vessels.

The kendoist knew he was going down, but he twisted,
pulling the sword from Gene's grasp and raising his own
weapon to cut the startled Gene. Gene froze.

Fortunately for him, Rita stepped in and slashed the kendo
man across the eyes. He tried to turn toward her, uttering a loud
kiai as he did, but she snapped her blade back and thrust it into
his open mouth. The point of her blade snapped off when it hit
the inside of his skull, but that didn't matter because the
kendoist was well on his way to death by then. He fell, landing
on his side, his sword still clenched in his hand, Gene's sword
still piercing him through and through.

Cierto found that he was breathing harder, and he forced
himself to calmness. Three students dead or nearly so. Rita,
Gene and Winston stood here, flushed with fear and exaltation.
Blood smeared Rita's sword, and she had pulled a wipe from
her pocket and was mechanically cleaning it.

Cierto moved to the fallen kendoist. "You died well," he
said. "You were much better than I had guessed." He raised his
fingertips and touched the center of his forehead lightly in a
final salute to the *dojo*'s fallen master. A worthy opponent
always deserved respect. He had taken three of Cierto's best
with him, and while that was irritating on one level, on
another, one had to give credit where it was due. Even the
matador had shown some spine. Between those two Cierto now
had only five blooded students remaining for his plan. Well.
They would have to do. Time was passing and he was not so
patient that he would spend another six or eight months

bringing another student along. Rita and Winston and Gene would be joined by Raz and Tomas.

He had worked for it long enough.

It was time to claim his prize.

TWENTY-ONE _____

THE CATARACT OF Carnival Falls was noisy, but where Kee wanted to go was not precisely the falls themselves. There was a much-used path that hairpinned up the hillside next to the cascade, and it was along this steep switchbacked trail that Kee led Sleel. They wore backpacks with sleeping sacks and enough food for several days. As the falls were several hundred klicks north of the *dojo*, the temperature was somewhat cooler, and the fall air had a crispness to it. Sleel's breath came out in a puffy fog.

They hiked along the narrow path. Kee said, "In the winter the falls sometimes freeze. Ice climbers go straight up it."

Sleel looked at the rushing water. "Not my idea of fun."

Kee stopped. "What *is* your idea of fun?"

That brought him up short. What kind of question was that? For a long moment, Sleel couldn't think of anything to say, nothing. Finally, he said, "Uh, well, the usual things. Good food, good company, good literature, uh . . ."

"That's what I thought," she said. And with that she returned her attention to the climb.

Sleel stared at her back. The synlin pack with the sword carrier strapped to it offered no hint of what its owner meant by her cryptic comments. She carried the sword with her everywhere, something he had remarked upon.

Kee had said, "There is a saying about the ancient earth warriors, the samurai, from whom my art is descended: 'The

169

sword is the soul of the samurai.' One doesn't leave one's soul behind when one travels."

An hour or so later, they arrived at a picnic area next to the river. A cleared spot next to the water was shaded by tall evergreen trees. The path on the other side of the clearing was narrower and less well trod upon.

"Most people stop here," Kee said. "Where we want to go is about three hours past here."

Sleel shrugged. Walking for three hours more didn't bother him, even with the pack. He still spent an hour or two every day roaming about the village, usually at night.

The trail wound its way through dense stands of assorted woods, mostly the same tall evergreens, but occasionally smaller trees whose broad diamond-shaped leaves were yellowing and sometimes falling in the light breeze. Where the path broke out of the cover, there were distant, snowy mountains visible in the clear air. There did not seem to be any other hikers out this far, coming or going. A man could pretend that he was alone on the planet out here, an explorer moving through a new world.

Sleel caught sight of several small creatures in the underbrush, or sometimes he heard the rustle of the dry leaves but didn't see the cause. In a particularly thick section of the forest one of these little beasts, probably startled by the approaching walkers, darted across the trail almost directly in front of them.

It looked like some kind of squirrel, a reddish gray animal about the size of Sleel's forearm, not counting the long bushy tail that streamed behind it—nor counting the fleet flashback of memory that scampered along behind the creature.

The rows of bramble were precisely straight, laid out with computer-augmented perfection, like lines drawn on a drafting screen. As the nervous fourteen-year-old Sleel walked along, holding Melinda's hand in his own sweaty grip, the squirrel dashing across the even ground startled them both. Melinda squeezed his hand and squealed, and though his own heart had leaped as though shocked, Sleel was quick to reassure her.

"Hey, it's only a squirrel, no dib." He hoped his high voice

sounded braver to her than it did to him. Thank whoever was
in charge that it didn't crack, at least.

She smiled down at him. Though they were the same age,
Melinda was a full head taller, and she probably outweighed
him by five kilos. Like him, she wore her school silks, skirt
and shirt, high socks and slippers, all required dress for the
infrequent assemblies held in the actual school building. She
was not fat, Melinda, but she was a full-figured and fully
developed girl who could easily pass for nineteen or twenty.
And she had her implant, though it didn't show. The squiggly
line of the contraceptive tube, not much thicker than a
toothpick, was just under the skin of her left inner thigh, up
near her pubis. Sleel knew, because he had felt it when he had
his hand under her skirt during the communal compulsory
viewing of the history vid.

He was still amazed at himself for that, more for being here
with her.

The old fart Winslow who ran excom ed made them all sit in
a dark room watching an old recording of some war on some
planet Sleel had never heard of and could give a shit about.
They could have just as easily stayed at home and watched it
on edcom, but no, the old fart made them assemble once a
week, march into the communal viewing room and sit on hard
plastic chairs to stare at the big-screen holoproj. Socialization,
he called it.

Well. It turned out to be the best thing that ever happened to
Sleel.

The last time, Melinda, about whom he had heard rumors,
sat next to him and smiled at him.

Smiled at *him*!

The lights dimmed and the screen lit, but it was still pretty
dark in the room. For five minutes, Sleel sweated with fear,
wanting to do it, but afraid. Finally, with a daring he had never
believed of himself, he reached out and tentatively put his hand
on Melinda's knee. He expected her to slap him, or at least
grab his hand and move it as if it were maybe a dog turd, but
no, she had done neither. In the darkness, he had seen her teeth
flash in another smile.

Well, shit! He had his hand on a real live girl's knee! A first.

He felt a thrill that danced back and forth between stark terror and lust.

The war program droned on, a recreation of a battle in which men who dressed funny rode animals—horses?— and shot at each other with rifles. But that wasn't important now. Nothing was important except that it stay dark.

Feeling reckless, Sleel slid his hand up Melinda's leg, actually *under* her thin silk school skirt.

Under his own skirt, his dick strived to mimic a tent pole; his underwear didn't have a prayer of keeping it down.

Melinda shifted slightly, glancing around to see if anybody was watching. Apparently nobody was, for her change in position allowed Sleel's questing hand to move farther into territory he had never explored. She uncrossed her legs and spread them slightly. Her skin was so soft, it didn't feel real, and yet the muscles under the skin were taut, alive, wonderful. She leaned toward him a little, and his fingertips—his hand seemed to have a mind of its own—touched the double-S curve of the implant.

Christo on a pogo board, she had an *implant*! That had to mean she had *done* it! A spike of fear shot though Sleel like a shard of hot ice. A lot of his classmates bragged about getting under this skirt or that, but Sleel had never even kissed another kid his age, boy or girl.

Sleel's questing hand slid past the implant and found a curly mound. Oh, *man*, she wasn't wearing *under*clothes! The hair felt harsh, somehow, thicker and different than his own mostly straight and still thin pubic fuzz. Wow. Another centimeter, two, and—

Oh, Gods in all their kingdoms! he was *touching* it! A girl's *cunt*! Right in the middle of a room full of people, he had his hand on a pussy! Melinda's pussy!

If he had a heart attack and died right here, that would have been fine, for he was a fulfilled human being.

The angle was bad, he thought he might dislocate his shoulder, but he would have happily cut off his arm rather than pull it from under Melinda's skirt. His fingers wiggled this way and that, looking to explore this wet and hot place, the folds of flesh so strange and so inviting. Sure, he had seen the sex edcom, heard the other students talking about what it was like, but that was nothing compared to actually *feeling* it!

Hormone storms raged in Sleel, he felt hot, flushed, his dick throbbed and was so hard it hurt, oh, *man*!

Melinda reached down and caught Sleel's wrist through her skirt. Oh, shit! She wanted him to stop! He would kill himself if she pulled his hand out—

But—no. She began to move Sleel's wrist up and down, pressing his fingers against her. There was a small, harder knot of flesh under his forefinger, and whatever else Sleel was, he was a fast learner. She wanted him to rub that part, must be the whatchamacallit, the clitoris the sex ed teacher had lectured about.

Sleel rubbed, softly, up and down, then back and forth.

Melinda gasped and leaned forward a little.

After a minute, the spot seemed to dry out, so Sleel dipped his fingers lower, between the folds, and moistened them, then went back to touching the part Melinda liked touched.

On the holoproj, one of the animals being ridden by a soldier made a funny noise and leaped forward. Sleel saw the image, but it hardly registered.

Two or three minutes later, Melinda moaned softly and began to quiver in a funny way. Sleel thought he could feel her heart beat under his hand, except that the throbbing was too fast. Then she reached down and grabbed his wrist again and pulled his hand away.

Well, shit. He *had* done something wrong!

"That's enough," she whispered. "Thanks, it was great!"

Sleel had only the vaguest idea of what she was talking about. But she didn't seem upset or mad at him, so that was good.

Then Melinda reached under *his* skirt and grabbed his dick. She squeezed it a couple of times and moved her hand up and down. Sleel stopped breathing. He was afraid his heart would stop, too. Oh, *Gods*—!

Melinda moved her hand up and down again, and that was all it took.

On the holoproj a cannon fired and an explosion followed as the shell hit and burst.

Sleel spasmed, climaxing for the first time with help.

He thought for a second he was going to fall out of the chair. It felt so *good!*

Next to him, Melinda chuckled. She squeezed him one more time, hard, and pulled her hand away. After a moment, she handed him a wipe pulled from her shoulder bag. "Here," she said in a whisper. "Boy, you sure are a gusher." She giggled as she used another wipe to clean her hand. . . .

Sleel, now holding Melinda's hand as they walked in a quiet section of the bramble, smiled at that memory. That was pretty terrific, the high point of his life, but what they were going to do now might be even better.

"Here's the place," Melinda said.

"You've been here before," Sleel said.

"Sure. Lots of times."

There was a pile of leaves gathered at the base of one of the trees. Melinda pulled a film blanket from her bag and shook it open, draping it over the leaves. She sat on the thin sheet, lay back, and pulled her skirt up, revealing once again that she was not wearing anything beneath it.

Sleel dropped to his knees. He knew what to touch, and wasn't it a wonder to actually *see* it? It was quite beautiful and mysterious to look upon.

After a couple of minutes of him stroking her, Melinda said, her voice ragged, "Now, put it in now!"

Sleel didn't need any urging. He slid into her easily—she was so hot and wet!—and she began to buck. It took only three strokes for Sleel's orgasm to start, and Melinda's was already underway, her muscles clamping and releasing him as he spurted.

Oh, wow! Oh, oh, oh, oh, *wow!*

A few minutes later as he was lying next to her, she looked over at him and said, "You're still hard?"

So he was. "I guess so."

She grinned. "Well, then let's do it again."

So they did.

Four more times that afternoon they did it, before Sleel couldn't do it again. Melinda knew all kinds of different things, and when he was too raw to put it in her again, she taught him how to use his lips and tongue, and that was pretty amazing, too.

No question, it was a lot better than the time in the history room. A million times better, easy.

Why hadn't he discovered this years ago?

"Sleel?"

He blinked and saw Kee looking at him. "Huh?"

"You asleep on your feet?"

He laughed. "Nah. Just time-tripping. An old memory."

"Pleasant one, I hope?"

"Oh, yeah. First time I ever had sex."

Her smiled matched his. "This looks like a good place to have lunch. Want to tell me about it?"

"About my first time?"

"Unless it bothers you."

"Bother me? Nah. Sure, why not?"

They found a large and fairly flat rock in the sunshine that was warm despite the air's chill and sat side by side.

As they ate he told her about Melinda.

When he was done, she smiled. "You were lucky," she said. "A lot of people have a not-so-pleasant time of it the first one."

"Voice of experience?"

She took a bite of the hard fruit she'd brought, a kind of pear, and chewed it thoughtfully. "Yep."

"So?"

"My first was an upperclassman at the boarding school I attended. I was thirteen, awkward, still trying to walk and balance the breasts and hips I had sprouted that summer. One moment I was a skinny kid climbing the rocks with the other pre-pubes, tumbling and sexless; the next it seemed I was drawing attention from older kids, male and female, who wanted to flirt and play games about which I had only vaguely heard.

"Felton was sixteen, a sports star, swimmer and shiftball player, muscular, like a big cat. He saw me in the pool doing my laps one afternoon. We usually swam nude or in nofric film for speed and that might as well be nothing for what it hides.

"I was impressed that this hero would stoop to speak to me,

much less find me attractive. Two days after he began working on me, we went to his room. I didn't have a clue about what to do. He laid me on the bed, spread me open, and jammed himself into me. He lasted about forty-five seconds. All I felt was pain. When he was done, he rolled off me, saw the blood from my torn hymen, and said, 'Shit, whyn't you tell me you never did it before?'

"He was mad at me for getting his bedclothes bloody. That was my welcome to lovemaking."

Sleel realized he had put his hand on her shoulder sometime during her recitation. In sympathy. To comfort her. As if apologizing for all men like Felton, or maybe for all the times when he himself had been less caring than he should have been. It surprised him.

She glanced at his hand and smiled. "It's okay, Sleel. I got over it."

He pulled his hand back a little too quickly.

"Hey?"

"Yeah?"

"Thank you anyway."

He felt his stomach roil a little. For some reason her saying that reminded him of the moment when he had first put his hand on Melinda's leg, of that instant of gut-twisting fear all those years ago.

Now why was that?

She put away the remains of her lunch. "I think maybe when we get back we ought to start working on a soul for you," she said.

He blinked, not understanding. "I thought I had one already. Maybe it's buried too deep for you to see."

"Oh, I can see it just fine. I meant an external one." She patted her sword carrier. "I'll explain it as we walk."

TWENTY-TWO

THE PLACE WU had camped twice before was almost as it had been the last time she had seen it. There was a bend in the river, and on the concave side, a thickly wooded plot of land that was nearly surrounded by water. One more good stretch of rain and the isthmus would likely be overcome, making the place an island. The narrow neck of land was already thinner than she recalled from last year.

The trees were tall and cast enough shade so that there was not much undergrowth. Probably there were other campers who came here, thinking the spot was their secret. That didn't matter to Wu. She was willing to share it with them, as long as it wasn't at the same time.

As she and Sleel worked their way toward the clearing near the river where she usually pitched her tent, he stopped, looking alert.

"Something?"

Sleel held up one hand in a gesture for silence. But after a moment, he shook his head. "Nothing. I've had the feeling of being watched a few times along the trail. Can't hear anything, haven't seen anybody. It's something . . . subsensical."

Wu understood the feeling. Like a name not quite remembered, a tickle or pressure inside your mind. She had felt it herself, but dismissed it when there was nothing to back it up. "Stay alert," she said. "The galaxy needs more lerts."

Sleel laughed. "Gods, that's old. Primary ed joke."

"Pre-primary," she said. "At least."

They continued onward.

Cierto sat in his study, poring over input regarding Kildee Wu. The White Radio com alert chimed and he sat back, the custom orthopedia humming to stay with his new position. "Activate com," he said.

The face of his main spy on Koji lit the air and took form. "Patrón," he said.

"Something?"

"The subject has gone to a resort area, hiking some thirteen kilometers along a little-used forest trail to a campsite next to a river."

"So? Some recreation is to be expected, is it not?"

"The man Sleel is with her. There is no one else in the immediate area."

Cierto frowned. He did not require that the woman be a virgin, that would hardly be possible for an adult female with any kind of life; still, he felt a stab of jealousy. "Has she become sexually intimate with this man?"

The spy shrugged. "We cannot say, Patrón. They share a small tent for sleeping and direct observation within is not possible. Getting close enough to see more would risk being detected."

"Hmm. Keep me informed of this."

"Of course."

After he discommed, Cierto steepled his fingers and considered the new information. Well, so what if she was intimate with the matador? He was not a factor about which to worry. True, the man had managed a fair defense of the old thief, but in the end, he had lost. Once you had beaten a man, he was beaten forever. While it bothered Cierto that another might be using what he considered his property without permission, he had not actually laid claim to that property yet. He had taken great pains, in fact, to maintain secrecy thus far. So, he would hold Wu blameless for this. When she knew the situation, it would be different. As for the matador? Well. He was a dead man in any event, and one could not make him more dead for his sins. It was of no importance. He had other things to worry about.

Sleel awoke, feeling somewhat stiff despite the thin air pad under his sleep sack. The open flap of the small dome tent faced the river and there was a sandbar that extended from just beyond the tent well into the water. The white sand glistened in the sunlight, the river's flow was a quiet gurgle. And Kee, naked, stood with the water swirling around her thighs. She was scrubbing herself with a biodegradable cleaner, working up a thick lather of suds. Vapor rose from her into the cool air.

Beautiful, he thought. Would that he had a camera to capture the sight. Sleel lay on his belly and watched her continue to bathe.

After a minute, she turned around, conscious of his gaze, but apparently unconcerned about her nudity. They had seen each other naked often enough in the gym as they showered and dressed after a workout, hadn't they? Why would it be any different here?

"Morning," she called.

Sleel suddenly found that lying on his belly was becoming somewhat . . . uncomfortable. He shifted a little, to relieve the pressure. Just need to pee, he thought.

Kee squatted in the shallow water and allowed the river to rinse her clean. The soapy cleaner would feed natural bacteria in the water. Before the suds drifted a klick or two, they would be almost entirely gone, becoming a part of the environment and harmless. Kee was big on what she called no-impact camping. When they left, the site would look the same as when they had arrived. They even buried their own feces sprinkled with a powdery compound that broke it down to a harmless residue.

"How's the water?" Sleel called.

"Cold," she said.

Not, he knew, cold enough. Sleel reached for his pants. Damned if he was going to climb out of the tent with his dick playing flagpole. It was getting more difficult all the time to think of Kee as a teacher and nothing else. He didn't expect that she felt anything for him that way, and he didn't want to risk, well, screwing things up.

Breakfast was of freeze-dried concentrates plumped with pure water distilled from the river. Fruit, cereal, zip-cooked soypro patties, container-heated bread. Something about the cool fresh air gave Sleel a powerful appetite, and even though none of the food was fresh, it was delicious nonetheless. They sat next to a small pellet stove that gave out more heat than light, but had a little bluish flame that flickered in the faint breeze.

Kee was telling him about her family.

"We have always been matriarchal, the name going with both sons and daughters. And the sword goes to whichever of the children decides to take it up, the oldest getting first choice. Mayli was the oldest, our brother Zam the middle child, I'm the youngest. Mayli started out with the sword but decided to walk another path. Zam wasn't interested, so I inherited the family heirloom."

"What if there aren't any children?"

"There are always children somewhere. If I don't have any, I can try one of Zam's—he's got four. Or Mayli's, if she had any. Or I can adopt one and teach him or her the Way. The link is spiritual, not necessarily genetic."

Sleel nodded. "Mayli, Zam and Kildee. Interesting names."

Kee laughed. "My parents were certainly that, interesting. When I was born they were studying birds, so 'Kildee.' It's a variant of 'killdeer,' which is supposed to be the cry the things make. The ones my parents were observing on the day I was born were mudbirds. The things lived on a lake shore and ate bugs. Glamorous, right?"

Sleel chuckled. He told her the story of how he had chosen his own name.

"What was the name your parents gave you?"

He told her.

"Interesting," she said.

"Yeah. I was named after a plant found on my homeworld."

She smiled. "Well, it's no worse being named after a plant than it is a bird."

"Unless the plant only grows on animal dung."

"Really?"

"Really. A kind of sheep. Apparently the species didn't exist before the sheep started crapping in pastures."

She laughed, and he enjoyed the sound. He found that he very much liked making her laugh.

But that pit-of-the-stomach feeling was there, too, as if there was some danger in being this close to her. Something was there, something he didn't want to think about. Back into the cave, Sleel. The beasts are outside in the dark prowling, and if you don't run and hide they will get you for sure.

The three days went quickly for Wu. She enjoyed the camping as she had before, but it was different sharing it with somebody. On the one hand, she gave up the feeling of total solitude, and the peacefulness of being alone in the wilderness. She always downpowered her com when she came here, so that nobody could break into the quiet.

On the other hand, sometimes a thing shared made it greater and not lesser. So this trip had been. Sleel was relaxing, becoming more open, and while there were times when she would have grabbed him and given in to the desire she felt, she had not allowed herself to do so. It would have stopped something happening in him, she felt, and the immediate pleasure would have perhaps stunted something greater.

She wasn't sure, and she wanted to be sure.

She watched now as Sleel stood in the river, shaking his head and slinging the water from his hair as he came from under the surface. That, she felt, was what was going on. Too much of Sleel was surface. He had depths, but he kept them hidden, from her, and, more importantly, from himself. That was her job as a teacher, to show Sleel how to get to the center of himself.

Well. Nobody had ever told her it would be easy, had they?

Abruptly, she felt a pressure, as if being watched. She scanned the river, looked into the air and woods, but saw nothing. Both she and Sleel had been aware of the sensation almost the entire time they had been here. There had to be something to it. But—what? And—who would be watching them? It made no sense. Why would anybody be interested in them?

Sleel emerged from the water and began to dry himself with one of the thin towels they had brought. Wu looked away. The next step was back in Kyrktorn. Time to go and take it.

TWENTY-THREE _____

"Here is your soul," Kee said.

They sat the in kitchen of her *dojo*, Sleel looking at the little chunks of black metal lying on the table. There were several different kinds, ranging from a bar about the thickness and length of his hand to smaller, rectangular pieces not much bigger than large coins. Maybe a dozen in all.

"A little fragmented, ain't it?" he said.

She said, "Well, yes, we'll do some blending. Here, look." She took a small flatscreen and began to draw on it using a light stylus. Sleel watched the simple design take shape. It took only a few moments. When she was done, she passed the flatscreen to Sleel.

"Looks like the top part of a squared-off exclamation point," he said.

"It's the cross section of a sword, viewed from the end," she said. "The top of the drawing is the back ridge, the bottom the edge. Each of the shaded areas represents a different kind of steel. There are five metals in our family's construction method. The edge is the hardest, the middle the softest, the others somewhere in between. These will be melded together by heat and pounding, folding, blending at the proper time, then reworked until the blade takes shape. When it's finished, you will have a sword that will take and hold a razor edge, but that will be flexible enough so that it will give and not break with hard use."

"Such as chopping off heads?"

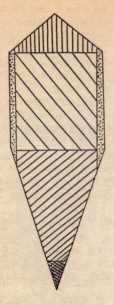

She nodded once. "In the old days, the swords were tested by cutting various objects, bundles of straw, wooden staves, dummies, copper plate and so on. During one period, the testing was done on the bodies of criminals. They would stack the bodies atop one another in a pile—sometimes the victims were still living—and see how many the blade would cut through when swung by a strong arm. The result would then be chiseled onto the tang by the swordmaker."

"How nice."

"A good sword would cut through at least two, sometimes three bodies before stopping."

She was serious, Sleel saw. "Too bad your sword was made after those days," he said, joking. "You'll never know how it rates."

Kee touched the hilt of her weapon where it lay on the table.

"According to my four-times great-grandmother, this is a four-body sword. That's what it says on the tang."

"Jesu Christo," Sleel said. He stared at the pieces of metal on the table.

"The swordsmith who will do most of the work is one of half a dozen in the galaxy who can still make such things," Wu said. She and Sleel were in her flitter, traveling to the far village of Ogami, nine hundred kilometers from her *dojo*. "His name is Miyamoto Bergamo, he was born on Earth and he is about a hundred and fifteen T.S. years old, give or take a few years."

"Shouldn't he be retired?"

"His youngest apprentice is sixty," she said. "There are six of them at his foundry, four men and two women. They make about seven swords a year, I would guess. Sometimes as many as eight."

"As many as that," Sleel said. "They must have other income."

She grinned. "It isn't necessary. A Bergamo blade isn't something you can pick up in the neighborhood market. They run about a hundred and eighty thousand standards each."

"You're kidding."

"Nope. And there is a five-year waiting list, if you qualify to get on it."

"A hundred and eighty thousand stads is a pretty steep qualification," Sleel admitted.

"That's only a minor part of it. He won't make a sword for you unless he thinks you are worthy of it, not for ten times the money. I am given to understand that he once turned down two million stads from a wealthy asteroid miner because the man was impolite."

"Well, I hate to point this out, but I'm not sure I'm up to his qualifications. Not to mention that I might have all of five thousand stads in my account."

She chuckled. "I don't have that kind of money, either. But Bergamo's family and mine have an old arrangment. Goes way back. They, ah, owe us a debt."

Sleel lifted one eyebrow.

"Five or six hundred years ago, the Bergamos ran into some trouble. The Wu family rescued them. They have been working it off since."

"Must have been some fairly major trouble."

"I am given to understand that it was, yes."

"That doesn't help with the other part, though."

"No. But we'll see about that when we get there."

Ogami was hardly a village. As far as Sleel could tell, Bergamo's foundry and living quarters was it, if you didn't count some storage buildings scattered here and there, and some kind of grazing animals that looked like a cross between a goat and a pig. And geese; there were geese waddling back and forth in a flock of about twenty, honking and digging bugs and whatnot from the lawns.

"Big town," he said as she set the flitter down near the foundry. Heat came from a vent on top of the building, fogging the cold air as it rose.

Kee didn't respond to his comment.

She put the flitter down near the largest of the buildings. "He'll be in the foundry," she said. "I've never come here when he wasn't. I think he sleeps there."

The two of them alighted from the vehicle and started for the building. It was only a few meters from the flitter pad, but halfway there, Sleel paused and looked around.

Kee raised one eyebrow.

Nobody was visible, save the geese, who had set up an excited honking at the sight of the new arrivals. Great. Watch-geese.

"I feel somebody watching me," he said.

She nodded. "Me, too. I haven't been able to spot anybody."

"Neither have I. But they're there. Somewhere."

"Who? And why?"

"I dunno. I guess that'll come later."

They continued to the foundry, the geese still scolding them loudly.

At the old-style hinged door, there was a small permanent holoproj installed at eye level. It showed a sword dummy—

Kee had one like it at the *dojo*, made from hardfoam and used to practice cuts and thrusts. This dummy's head lay next to it on the invisible ground, and the body was full of rents and gouges and holes that pierced it all the way through in places. Under the dummy was a thin line of blue lettering. "THIS COULD BE YOU IF YOU ENTER UNINVITED," it said.

Sleel chuckled. "Graphic security. I like it."

But the door was unlocked and opened to Kee's touch on the control. Inside, a short hallway led past a fresher with showers, a kitchen, and two rooms with couches and chairs in them. Another door connected the hall to the foundry proper. Sleel followed Kee through the door.

It was hot, despite a blast of cold air flowing down from the coolers on the high ceiling, and noisy. Somebody was banging on something, steel on steel. The sound had a certain rhythm to it, a hard clank, followed by a pair of softer taps. The place smelled of metal, of something overcooked to the point of being burned, and there was something peppery in the air that made Sleel's eyes water.

"Over there," Kee said.

Sleel looked. A bald old man held a strip of red-hot metal with a long-handled set of tongs or a clamp of some kind, keeping it flat on a giant anvil. In his other hand he had a hammer. A woman of sixty, with long red and gray hair held back with a kind of mesh band, whacked the metal hard with the hammer she held. The bald man tapped the anvil next to the strip twice, and the woman hit the long bar again. That was the source of the almost musical banging. The old man tapped his hammer and moved what Sleel figured was a very rough sword blade, and the woman banged away. The two workers wore firemesh over fabric jumpsuits that might once have been white but were now more of a sooty gray; they also had thick sweatbands around their foreheads.

Behind the two was a furnace, the interior lined with some material that glowed almost blue-white, visible through a sheet of denscris plate about half a meter square.

The old man said something and the woman held her hammer back. He approached the furnace, touched a foot control, and the protective plate slid aside. Sleel could feel the blast of heat from where he stood, a good fifteen meters away.

The old man put the blade into the furnace and turned away. "Two minutes," he said. A voice-actuated timer on the furnace lit and began flashing backward from 2:00 toward zero.

"Ah, Wu-sanita!" the old man said.

Kee bowed as the old man approached, smiling at her.

Sleel observed the old man carefully. Hundred and fifteen, eh? He looked pretty good for that age. Bald as an egg, no hair except for salt-and-pepper eyebrows thick as winter caterpillars, mostly salt and not much pepper. His skin was ruddy, probably from the heat, lined and wrinkled, most of those smile lines, given how they fell into place as he grinned at Kee. His nose was large and sharp, his ears big, and his teeth looked natural and well kept. He wasn't much bigger than Kee, but the forearms that came out of the firemesh and three-quarter-sleeve coveralls were wiry and looked strong enough.

He came to stand in front of them.

"Master Bergamo," she said, bowing again.

He nodded once, a military bow. "Such a pleasure to see you again, Wu-sanita. You honor my house."

He had an accent Sleel couldn't place, something sing-songy in his voice.

"The honor is mine, Miyamoto-san."

The old man looked at Sleel.

"This is Sleel," Kee said. "My student. He needs a sword."

The old man said nothing, watching Sleel. Sleel kept his face impassive. Guy wanted to get into a staring contest? Fine.

"I would furnish the steel," Kee said.

The old man looked away from Sleel at Kee.

"*Zhaverfrayshtol,*" she said.

The old man continued to stare at Kee. His face gave nothing away.

She nodded, once.

The old man nodded in return.

Some kind of fugue going on, Sleel figured, but he couldn't read it.

"Two days," the old man said. "I have nearly gotten that piece of junk"—he waved at the furnace—"ready for tempering and even my incompetent assistants can probably manage that on their own."

The woman who had been hammering on the sword with Bergamo came up behind him and said, "Incompetent assistants? Your skinny little ass! Pay no attention to him, Kildee. His hormones are all stirred up; he hasn't gotten drained since the start of the week. I'll take care of him tonight, he'll be much more pleasant in the morning." With that, she reached over and squeezed the old man's left buttock.

He smiled at her.

The furnace timer whistled at them. "Back to work, foolish woman. Would you let the steel burn up?" He looked at Kee. "Good assistants are hard to find. One has to make do with the dross one is burdened with."

"I'll show you dross, you ancient hulk!"

The old man laughed and ducked away from her pretended punch, hurrying toward the furnace where he retrieved the rough blade, now glowing bright orange.

Kee led Sleel toward the kitchen.

"How old did you say he was?"

"Sex is in the mind, Sleel."

"Must be so."

"The woman is Vivian; she's been Miyamoto's assistant for forty years, his lover for maybe thirty-five. She keeps him in line."

"What did he mean about the two days?"

"It'll take him that long to finish the blade he is working, then he'll start on yours."

"Just like that? No questions? How does he know I'm worthy? Because you vouched for me in that little fugue you two did?"

"He knew the second he saw you. Yes, I vouched for you, but that wouldn't have mattered if he hadn't agreed."

Sleel shook his head, a thing he seemed to do a lot around Kee Wu. "More mystical stuff."

"Whatever you think."

"Patrón," the spy's voice came across the light years, "they have gone to a tiny village called Ogami. There seems to be nothing there—"

"Except Bergamo's foundry," Cierto said.

"You know the place?"

"I know the man's work." Bergamo had refused to make a sword for Cierto, or any of the hired emissaries he had sent to see the old man. Even so, he owned one of Bergamo's blades, bought from the estate of a man who had died after losing the family fortune. By rights he should not have been able to purchase the sword, given that Bergamo had first option to buy it back upon the death of the legal owner. But money sang its song into the right ears at the right time, the weapon was his, and Bergamo did not even know that the owner had died.

Well. That was not important. The House of Black Steel's own family smith was one of two people in all the galaxy who could equal the old man's skills; there was none better.

"What are they doing there?" Perhaps this was a foolish question, since a swordswoman going to see a master sword-maker ought to be easy enough to figure out; still, things were not always as apparent as they seemed.

"We have not been able to determine this yet, Patrón. The place is quite small and therefore difficult to approach without being seen."

"I pay you for results."

"To be sure. We have a man going in sub rosa tomorrow."

"Let me know what happens."

"Do whatever he tells you," Kee said. "Your part in the process is fairly small; you'll mostly be helping with the stretching and folding. Miyamoto will show you what he wants you to do, once. Once the blade is roughed out, the rest will be up to him and his assistants. It'll take a couple of weeks for that part. Other apprentices will be working on the furniture, the *tsuba*, hilt, sheath, like that. A month or six weeks for the whole process."

"When does this start?"

"At dawn in two days."

The geese began squawking the next morning, and Sleel went out to see what had disturbed them. Kee was already up, practicing with her sword behind the foundry, skewering the targets set up there.

A man wearing several thousand stads' worth of carefully tailored clothing alighted from a fancy flitter, attended by two assistants. Armed assistants, Sleel saw, despite their own specially cut coats designed to hide the hand wands. The trio moved to the foundry's door and were admitted by one of the older assistants, a dark-skinned Temboan pushing ninety.

Two minutes later, the trio emerged from the foundry. The rich man looked angry, the bodyguards slightly bored. On the face of it, it appeared that an application for the waiting list had been denied. That would have been cause for a smile, except that something felt wrong about it. Sleel couldn't say what. None of the three men looked at him as they climbed into the flitter and fanned away, tossing up dust and small pebbles in their wake. Out there in the middle of nowhere and they didn't look at him. He would have spared himself a glance or two, had he been them. Something wrong about them ignoring him.

Sleel turned away from the now-distant flitter. Whatever it was, it wasn't his business. He wasn't a matador anymore; he didn't have a client. He was here to do what Kee told him to do, her and that old man in the foundry. Nothing more.

TWENTY-FOUR _____

"TAKE OFF YOUR clothes," Bergamo said.

The local sun had barely managed to lift itself to the horizon and the morning's air was chilly out in the foundry yard. Sleel, who did his best work in the afternoon and evening, was still blinking sleep away. Even the geese wandered about somnambulantly.

Do whatever he says, Kee had told him. Fine.

As Sleel shucked his orthoskins, the old man also began to remove his own jumpsuit. Under his clothing Bergamo was pale, his body not nearly as wrinkled as his face, and in pretty good shape. Sleel hoped he held up as well when he got to be that old. Assuming he didn't freeze to death here first.

The old man stripped to the buff. Sleel matched him.

All right. What now? Some kind of strange sexual ritual? Okay, then, mine is longer—though not by much, Sleel saw. And rapidly getting shorter in the cold, too.

But, no. Vivian came out into the yard where the two naked men now stood. She carried a pan of water, warm vapor rising from it into the morning. Behind her was Sam Sam, the assistant who was probably eighty, and who was also the main polisher. He carried a pan of water, too.

Bergamo accepted the pan from Vivian and nodded at Sleel, who took the second pan from Sam Sam. The container was made of wooden slats fitted closely together and bound with cord. What now? Was he supposed to drink it?

Bergamo said something in a language Sleel didn't understand, looked toward the sky and raised the pan over his head, then poured it onto himself.

"To cleanse the spirit," Sam Sam said, as the water showered down over the old man.

Sure, why not? Sleel lifted his own container as had Bergamo and dumped it onto his head.

The vapor had fooled him. The water was cold.

Another assistant, this one the other woman, Brittan, came out bearing thick towels. Bergamo began to dry himself off and Sleel didn't need a map to figure this part out.

Sam Sam brought Sleel a jumpsuit, freshly cleaned but soot-stained, and a set of coppery firemesh to put on over the clothes. Sleel dressed, adding slippers and a sweatband. Sam Sam also handed him a set of hardfoam earplugs.

Bergamo approached him, bearing a device the size of a small cigar. "Hold out your right arm, like this."

Sleel stuck his arm out at a right angle to his body, fingers extended. The old man pointed the device at him. A tiny red dot flashed and centered on Sleel's chest, then danced out his arm to the tip of his middle finger. Bergamo adjusted the device. Sleel saw the pinhead red dot center on the base of his little finger, then move out to the tip and stop. The old man looked at the device and sing-songed something to Vivian, who nodded and repeated the last part of it back to him.

"Put down your arm." Bergamo turned away and headed toward the foundry, scattering the geese. They protested sleepily.

Vivian said, "The length of your sword. Chest to end of large finger, plus little finger. Go with him."

Kee was inside, next to the furnace, and there was some kind of bowing ceremony going as she presented the chunks of black steel to Bergamo. It didn't take long. Kee allowed Sleel a smile as she left.

The denscris plate slid back on the furnace and the heat reached out and slapped Sleel. The firemesh absorbed most of it, but his face and ears felt as if they had been blasted. Sweat began to run down his face, despite the headband.

Bergamo handed Sleel a long-handled ladle with some, but not all, of the black steel stacked on it in an odd configuration, and nodded at the furnace. Sleel stuck the shovelful of metal into the furnace and stood there. Doubtless there was a more efficient way of doing this, machineries and whatnot, but hand crafting was what this was all about, wasn't it?

After standing there for what seemed years, the old man tapped Sleel on the shoulder and nodded. Sleel removed the glowing pieces of metal and gently deposited them onto the anvil. Bergamo handed Sleel an oddly shaped hammer, one with almost twice as much mass on one side of the long handle as on the other. Vivian moved in to grasp the semi-fused lump of metal with tongs, holding it securely. "Like so," Bergamo said, hitting the metal with his own hammer. "In triple rhythm."

Bergamo tapped the anvil once, twice, and Sleel lifted the heavy hammer and whacked the glowing steel.

"No so hard."

Tap. Tap. Whack.

"Better."

Tap. Tap. Whack.

After several minutes of this, Bergamo nodded. Vivian put the pounded steel back onto the shovel and Sleel inserted it once again into the furnace.

This was repeated until the material became a solid chunk. Sleel lost count of how many times it took.

Later the thinned and flattened metal was bent, using chisels and special pliers, pounded again, then bent and folded, heated, bent and folded yet again.

Wielding the hammer was a lot harder than it looked. Sleel had thought he was in pretty good shape, certainly in better condition than a man old enough to be his great-grandfather, or a woman the same age as his mother. Wrong. Even though he switched grips from time to time, both shoulders, arms, wrists and hands ached with fatigue. What had seemed inanimate chunks of metal now took on a kind of life, flowing liquidly under the hammer. The metal elongated, was folded and stretched again and again. Vivian left and went to another furnace where other assistants worked. She returned with a strip of steel that nearly matched the one Sleel pounded upon. This new piece was sprayed with some chemical and added to

Sleel's, being heated and pounded and folded and stretched some more.

Sleel was finally beginning to get into the rhythm of it all when Vivian touched his arm. The metal was put into a special attachment to the furnace, to "keep it warm," and Vivian led Sleel out of the foundry proper.

"What now?" he asked.

"Piss break," Vivian said. "Also food, if you need it."

Bergamo was down the hall, heading toward the fresher.

Sleel saw a clock in the kitchen. Good gods, it was after noon. They had been thumping away in there for seven hours, easy. Now that he noticed it, he was hungry. He had been drinking from the cooled pitcher of water next to the furnace off and on, so he wasn't thirsty, but his bladder was full.

"Even twenty years ago the old fart would have gone until dark before stopping to pee," Vivian said. "Good thing he's getting up there. I can hold it almost as long as he can now. I snuck off an hour ago, but don't tell him."

Sleel shook his head.

They quit at dark, and Sleel found he hadn't been so tired in years, not since the days at Matador Villa. Who would have thought that swinging a hammer would do that?

Kee was sitting in the small community room outside Sleel's sleeping quarters when he arrived. "Having fun yet?" she said.

"Oh, yeah, loads."

"It is a little taxing."

Sleel regarded her. "Speaking again from experience?"

"Yes. As it happens, the family heirloom here"—she nodded at the sword—"is the proper length for me. Great-grammie-times-four must have been about my size. But I have another sword. Someday it will belong to my daughter, if I ever have one."

Sleel smiled at the sudden vision of a little Kee padding around the *dojo* floor waving a sword.

"Something funny?"

"No, not funny. Poignant. The image of your child came to me."

"Oh? And what did she look like?"

"I saw her at the age of maybe two. Very serious, very beautiful. Following her mother around."

"What color were her eyes?"

Sleel blinked. "Eyes?" He brought back the image of the little girl. "Blue."

"Mine are violet."

"I know. So she takes after her father."

Kee didn't say anything for a moment. Then, "Better get some rest. Dawn will be here before you know it."

"Do I get an outdoor bath again?"

"Nope, one soul-cleansing per blade. You'll work for two or three more days, depending on how it's going. After that, things get more complex and Miyamoto will have to attend to them himself."

"Six weeks, huh?"

"More or less."

After he had gone to his room to shower, Wu sat staring at Sleel's door. Blue eyes, her imaginary daughter?

Sleel's eyes were blue.

In the sanctum of his power, Cierto listened to the spy's report. "My agent has planted a listening device within the foundry, Patrón. Although he was unable to learn much during his short visit, the device has picked up enough conversation for us to determine that the old man is making a sword—"

"I thought as much," Cierto cut in. "Although the one she carries certainly seems to be of good quality."

"Forgive me, Patrón, I have been unclear. The sword is not for the woman, but for the matador."

"What?" Quickly, Cierto clamped down on his surprise and surge of anger. "Are you certain of this?"

"Sí, Patrón. The recordings are quite clear about this."

When the spy had finished, Cierto chewed on this new bit of information. The old swordmaker would craft a blade for this man whom the House of Black Steel had easily beaten, but not for the master of that house? It burned indigestibly in Cierto's belly like a shard of hot metallic ice. Of course it was because the woman had interceded for him; still, it pained him no less.

That she would vouch for this matador meant she cared for him, perhaps more than Cierto knew. He felt a second shard pierce his entrails next to the first, this one of jealousy. How could she feel something for one so inferior? It pained him, truly. For causing it, the woman would also suffer some pain. And the matador would die worse for it, too.

These people did not know what an error it was to cross Hoja Cierto. But they would learn shortly. Another month or so, six weeks perhaps, and it would be done.

At some point during the third day of pounding the long piece of black steel, Sleel found himself imagining once again Kee's daughter, seeing her at the age of maybe twelve, dancing through a *kata*. She looked like Kee, of course, but her hair wasn't that shining jet, it was a lighter brown, and truly her eyes were blue. So seriously did she move that Sleel found himself laughing with avuncular pleasure.

"Too much noise," Bergamo said.

Sleel returned to the present, blinking against the heat at the old man.

"Sorry."

"You have been hammering without thinking."

"Sorry."

The old man grunted and shook his head.

Through the conversation, Bergamo kept tapping his hammer, a faster beat than before, but still double-tapping for each of Sleel's strikes. Sleel had no trouble keeping the rhythm and listening or talking. The sound guided him so that it required no conscious thought as it had on the first day. Tap. Tap. Whack. Now and then the old man would alter the timing, but Sleel was right there with him, keeping the sounds spaced proportionately.

During the break that afternoon, Vivian came to see him, grinning widely. "He *complimented* you!"

"Huh? When? I must have missed it."

"He told you that you were hammering without thinking."

"Yeah, so? That didn't sound like a compliment to me. He sounded irritated."

She laughed. "There have been apprentices who worked

here for months before he bothered to acknowledge them, much less say something not an insult. Hammering without thinking about it is desirable. The old fart would never say it, but you are equal to any we have ever seen with only three days' practice. He will allow you to stay another day."

"That's good, huh?"

"Only twice before has this happened. Kee Wu was one of these."

"Who was the other?"

Vivian smiled. "It was a long time ago, forty years. A young woman of twenty."

"You?"

"So it was."

Sleel chuckled. "I'm honored to be in such company."

"You should be. The old man has been looking for another apprentice for years. He has hopes that Kee Wu will join us here once she ripens. Another twenty years or so."

"Things ripen late around here," Sleel said.

"It is not a young person's art. And now, you."

"Me? Well, I can't see myself beating on little pieces of metal for a living."

"Can you not?"

Sleel thought about it. Well, it did have a certain appeal, to create something from scratch. A kind of simplicity. No matter how complex the metals might be, they couldn't begin to be as complicated as people out there in the real galaxy. "Maybe," he said.

She laughed. "Ah, the old man will dance when he hears this!"

" 'Maybe' isn't much to get excited about."

" 'Yes' and 'no' each close doors as they open others. But anything is possible with 'maybe.' "

Funny, he'd never thought about it like that before.

"Do you intend to waste the entire afternoon in idle chatter?" Bergamo said from behind Sleel. "While your sword waits unformed?"

"You must have owned many slaves in a past incarnation, old man," Vivian said. "And beaten them all without mercy."

"Only when they dragged their heels," Bergamo said. "To work!"

The three of them moved back into the foundry to continue forming Sleel's soul.

TWENTY-FIVE _____

FIVE WEEKS HAD passed since his time at Bergamo's forge; the
call had not yet come telling him the sword was ready. He and
Kee practiced each day, and Sleel found that he much wanted
to do the forms with the blade upon which he had worked.

Kee knew; she laughed at him for it. She had been there, she
told him. Having your soul in another's hands, even the man
who was forging and polishing it, felt strange.

And that was not the only strange feeling Sleel had.
Something about Kee had changed. Or maybe it was him and
not her. He felt drawn to her, like an iron filing to a magnet. He
felt better when she was around. He found himself listening
intently when she spoke. He missed her when she was gone.
They disturbed him, these feelings, and he didn't understand
what they meant. He didn't say anything to her, naturally, and
he was not sure what, if anything, he should *do* about it all.

Now, the night enveloped him like a loose cloak as he
walked, pondering the mystery of Kildee Wu. What, he
wondered, did it all *mean*? He had been a writer once, he'd had
some grasp of emotions, hadn't he? What was it about this
situation that eluded him?

The man with the dog passed him going the other way,
waved, and continued on. Sleel waved back absently.

He was too old for this, Sleel thought. Whatever it was.

Wu was in the *dojo* about to go through Fire Hand when she
heard the noise at the door. The sound of plastic shattering.

Without pausing she took the sword from its stand and turned to face the entrance to the *dojo*.

The threat was not long in arriving. Five of them, one woman and four men, filing slowly into the workout area. They wore swords with long and nearly straight blades, and black fighting tights. None of them spoke as they spread out along the far wall, spacing themselves evenly. These were not Flex players, come to try her after all these years; they would have been children when she walked that path.

Wu stood silent, waiting. This was a challenge and it was their move to outline it. Who—?

It came to her two seconds before he arrived.

Cierto!

Sure enough, he entered behind the five. He wore his sheathed sword and tights to match the others. He nodded at her. "My gift to our son," he said, waving at the five.

She didn't understand what that meant, but she did realize that this was going to be a fight to the death, hers or theirs. She had to narrow her focus. Even so, a thought arose: where was Sleel?

They drew their weapons, five swords whispering against the scabbards as they came into view. All black blades, as was her own. Still Wu did not move.

The man nearest the door edged forward, his weapon held in one hand, aimed at her heart.

Wu took a half step to her left, to tread upon the trigger plate that started the *dojo*'s holocam. Whatever happened to her, Sleel would see it when he returned.

The second man slid forward.

Wu watched them. Her sword snicked out unbidden. She dropped the sheath and moved it away with her foot so that it came to rest against the wall to her left.

The third and fourth opponents moved together.

The fifth one, the woman, yelled, and jumped forward—

Kildee Wu leaped into the Void.

Sleel, lost in thought, felt a pang of something, a cool touch on his spine that made him break his step, almost losing his balance. What—

The man with the dog was behind him, moving faster than normal. That was odd; the man never finished his loop quickly enough to catch up to Sleel before. Why was he in such a hurry?

Ahead of him, a pair of men stepped out of the shadows.

They looked innocuous enough, two friends out on a late-night walk, discussing philosophy or religion, maybe, right? No weapons were visible, there was no reason to think they constituted any kind of threat, but Sleel knew, instantly and without the slightest doubt:

They meant to kill him.

He was puzzled. The man with the dog, coming up behind him in a hurry, he was in on it, too. And looky here, Sleel, there's another one across the street, just leaving the shelter of that doorway, pretending to go toward the flitter five meters ahead of you.

One of the two men on the walk in front of him made an error. Streetlight glinted from a short knife as he moved it next to his leg, trying to keep it hidden.

What the fuck? Some old enemy who had found him and decided to settle things? Sure wasn't a chance mugging, not if the dog-walker was in on it. He had been out here for months, following Sleel—

Never mind that. Worry about it later. Deal with it as it stands.

Despite the danger, Sleel felt a kind of relief. Somebody *had* been watching them. Good to know that sense still worked.

The relief faded as the quick thought behind it rushed in. What about Kee? Were they after her, too?

Jesu Christo! He had to get back to the *dojo*!

Cierto found that he was holding his breath. His camera was recording what he saw, as were the cameras of the five students. Later he would have the recordings cut together to make a total picture, but now, he had to enjoy the reality of it. He had waited a long time for this.

By all the gods, she was magnificent! Absolutely no fear, she was still as a vacuum, solid as the Rock of Spandle, just

waiting. He would love to try her this way. But not tonight.
No, this was for their son.

Rita yelled and went in for the kill.

Wu's sword snapped out—oh, so fast!—and pierced Rita's
heart before the attacker could stop. Rita's face grew puzzled.
What had happened? She was finished and not yet aware of it,
so quickly had Death found and touched her.

Truly wonderful.

Wu spun away, holding her sword in one hand, and in the
twirling of it, removed Gene's head with no more effort than a
man swatting a fly. She leaped, far but low, covering the
ground but not straying far from it. Dead, Gene fell. Both
pieces of him.

Raz stabbed at her back, missed by no more than a hair, and
looked down in sudden shock as his intestines spilled onto his
feet. He looked at Cierto, eyes wide and accusing. You didn't
tell us she was this good, Patrón . . .

These were five of the best students he had ever trained; they
were tested, honed, deadly, and she moved through them as
though they were plants, rooted and immobile, harmless to her
as roses standing in a garden. Yes, they had thorns, but the
only way she would be pricked would be if she blundered into
them.

Cierto felt a thrill akin to ecstasy.

She buried her sword in Tomas's belly, grabbed his hair and
turned him, using the dying man as a shield against Winston.
As Tomas fell, still blocking Winston, she shoved him clear of
the blade and stood facing the last of the five.

Winston leaped.

Wu V-stepped to her left and snapped her weapon out
horizontally, catching him across the throat, drawing the sword
in, slicing through the neck to the spine. Winston's head yawed
back, the new mouth cut under his chin spewing blood,
vomiting up the stuff of his life.

With almost no pause, she turned and ran toward Cierto.

He had never seen anything so beautiful in all his life. His
hand went reflexively to his sword's hilt.

No! Not yet!

He managed to pull the dart pistol from his belt before she covered the floor between them, but only just barely. He shot her three times, the electrostatic-chem flechettes hitting her on the torso and knocking her unconscious almost instantly. Even so, she slid on the mat so that the tip of her weapon almost touched his foot. Half a second slower and she would have made it.

She was awesome. Better than he had expected. What a son they would produce together! And someday, he would show the recording to his son. See what a warrior your mother was? he would say. None could defeat her except your father. I killed her when you were a baby, but you shall see that recording on another day. For now, marvel at the woman who was your mother.

Look, my son, and be proud.

Sleel didn't have time for this. Kee could take care of herself, he knew that, but he still felt fear for her. He had to get back to the *dojo*, only these four were in his way.

The man crossing the street arrived first, a knife held in his hand. Stupid. They should have shot him, but no, they wanted to carve him. Sleel danced from the walk, broke the man's skull, took the knife and buried it in the attacker's back as he fell.

The dog arrived next, snarling, and for a moment Sleel wanted to laugh. But floppy ears and stubby legs or no, the thing had teeth. Sleel booted the dog, the snap kick connecting with the side of its head, knocking it sprawling.

The two now behind him came in, but he twisted and gave them Snake and Spider, breaking bones and sundering cartilage and muscle. As they tumbled, Sleel spun. The man with the dog cursed and dropped his knife, going for a projectile weapon in his jacket. Finally got smart, but too late. Sleel charged, cast Dark Shroud and dropped the man as he fired the air pistol harmlessly into the night. Sleel took the gun away from the man and shot him in the face with it. He turned and snapped off two shots at the man who had eaten the Spider strike, and spun away without waiting to see the man collapse.

It was maybe two klicks to the *dojo* from here, five or six minutes if he ran all the way.

He ran all the way.

Cierto would have liked to take Wu's sword, but his agents had reported that the shielded antitheft system would zap anybody trying to remove it from the building. Since the system was self-powered and hidden, it would take too long to find and disable it. It was a superb weapon, but not what he had come for. He would provide her with one of nearly equal worth when the time came.

He was not worried about the bodies this time. They carried no identification, there was no way to trace them to him, and there would be nobody to make the connection in any event. He had their swords and scabbards. Local authorities would not have a clue. The matador would be dead by now.

Carrying her slung across his shoulder, Cierto moved Wu to his flitter. When he lifted the vehicle into the night, he could not recall ever being quite so happy in all his life.

"Kee!" Sleel yelled. The door to the *dojo* had been shattered. He still had the air gun and he would have shot anybody that moved, only those sprawled on the mats weren't ever going to be moving on their own again. Five of them lay dead. They were unarmed.

"Kee!"

It took only a few moments to discover that he was alone.

What had happened here?

Where was Kee?

Sleel forced the rising panic down. He had been a matador for a long time. He could deal with this. Calm yourself, dammit!

The holocam. If Kee had killed these five, and surely she must have, she did it here. Had she trigged the recorder?

She had. Whoever had come in must not have known about it.

Sleel watched with amazement the recording of the fight. Lord, she had cut them down like somebody harvesting wheat—

Cierto. Standing there on the edge of the mats. She had gone for him—

Sleel cringed as the man shot Kee. Oh, Gods—

Sleel watched as Cierto picked up the swords, removed something small from each of the bodies—what were those things?—as well as the scabbards for the weapons. Finally the man came back and lifted Kee, hoisting her over his shoulder and taking her out of sight.

She was alive. Had to be, otherwise why would he bother? The gun was some kid of stunner, nonlethal darts or pellets. She was alive.

But—Cierto had her.

Why? What was he going to do with her?

What was Sleel going to do about it?

The com chime entered his consciousness. How long had it been ringing? Mechanically, Sleel moved to the com and waved it on.

The image of Bergamo lit the air. He saw Sleel. "Your sword is ready," he said. Then, "There is trouble, isn't there?"

Sleel felt as if he had taken a charge from a hand wand; he was stunned. "Yes. Trouble." He waved at the interior of the *dojo*. "Pan," he ordered the com's pickup.

On the screen, Bergamo sucked in a quick breath. He held up something in the palm of his hand. He ordered his own com pickup to zoom in on the object.

Sleel saw it but couldn't track well enough to understand what he was seeing.

"Some kind of transmitter," Bergamo said. "Vivian found it in the entranceway. We were being spied upon."

Sleel nodded dully. "They have Kee," he said.

"Stay there," Bergamo ordered. "Vivian and I will be there as soon as we can."

Sleel had been breathing deeply and trying to make sense of it all for hours when the old man and woman arrived. It still did not compute in any way he could manage. Would Cierto want revenge for the lost foot after all this time? Why else would he come here? Sleel could understand how the man might want to kill him—he had taken out some of his troops back in The Brambles—but what did he want with Kee?

"Sleel," Bergamo said. "Here."

Sleel took the sword from Bergamo.

"There is usually a formal ceremony that goes with the presentation," Bergamo said, "but we shall skip it this time."

Sleel had no time for games; this sword was not important compared to Kee's kidnapping, and yet, the weapon felt alive in his hand, as much a part of him as his arm. Almost without thinking, he withdrew the blade from the white-lacquered wooden sheath.

It was beautiful. There were whorls and patterns in the steel, and the *dojo*'s lights glinted from the polished black metal almost hypnotically, drawing the gaze deep within itself. Sleel had never touched anything so intrinsically . . . powerful. Gods. It—felt so, so *right*, somehow.

He looked up at Bergamo. It must have shown in his face. The old man nodded. "Yes," he said. "You are welcome." He glanced at the bodies. "What will you do?"

"I'm going after her."

"Of course. Vivian and I will take care of this." He waved at the corpses.

Yes, he would go after her. He would chop Cierto into pieces small enough to feed to baby thumb-birds. He would destroy the man and everything he owned. He would tear the very planet the man lived on apart with his hands—

All by yourself? came his small inner voice.

Goddamned right—!

Sleel stared at the weapon that Kee said would be his soul. Something welled within him, some emotion that would not be denied, rising from his depths, from the murk of his insecurities like a giant bubble. It rose, and burst, and sprayed him with a feeling he could not name, and could not hold in. He sobbed, one ragged indrawn breath.

No. He had always gone it alone, asking nothing from anyone, taking care of himself. But if he went storming after her on his own, without thinking, Sleel against the galaxy as usual, he might lose her. And that's what it comes down to, doesn't it? Your pride versus Kee's life. Which is it to be, Sleel? What is *really* important here?

In that moment he knew that he wasn't the same as he had been. The Sleel who had fancied himself cock of the universe was gone. He wasn't sure what was going to replace the old model, but he knew he couldn't go back.

Damn. You're in deep shit now, boy.

"Sleel?" Vivian said.

"I need help," he said. "I have to call some people," Sleel said. "My family."

Part Three
Let Go the Hilt

TWENTY-SIX _____

Wu SWAM THROUGH waters thick and foul with chemical dregs to reach the shore of consciousness. Had she known where she would arrive, she might have chosen to avoid the effort.

She was lying on her back on a bed, naked, arms and legs spread wide. Her head was turned to the left and she saw a silvery, almost iridescent silk sheet under her. Her arm looked to be unbound, but when she tried to move it, it came up only a few centimeters from the bed before she felt a tug. Her flesh just above the wrist dented, held by some invisible bond. A test of her other limbs revealed that they too were similarly bound by invisible cords at the wrist and ankles. Must be—

"Tight-beam pressor field," said a voice.

Wu was able to turn enough to see Cierto as he entered the room. He wore a green silk gown open down the front, and nothing under it. His penis was semi-erect, interrupting the flow of the gown.

Wu strained, but the field holding her would not give past the four or five centimeters' play. It was like pressing against an unseen brick wall built just above her.

"You are wasting your time and energy," Cierto said. "The field is rated at a thousand kilos per loop. Of course, I expect that you must try."

Wu did try, for another ten seconds. Nope. She wasn't going anywhere.

She wanted to ask him what it was all about, but she didn't want to give him the satisfaction.

"I expect you are wondering why I brought you here," he said, smiling. "It is quite simple, really. I will have a son. You are to be his mother."

She couldn't help herself. "You're crazy."

"Not at all, dear Kildee. My son will have a mother with spirit. Someday, he will see the recording of you as you slew my five students in your *dojo*. You were quite magnificent, you know. I can admit that. You have gotten much better over the years."

"Last time we met I chopped off your foot. Why don't you give me a blade, and let's see if *you* are any better."

He laughed. His robe moved a bit farther away from his crotch. "Ah, that will come, but not yet. First you must carry my son to term."

"Like hell."

"It isn't a request. You will do so. Your matador is dead and no one knows or cares where you are."

She felt a pain in her gut. Sleel, dead? She reached into the Void, past it. Maybe Cierto was lying, to break her spirit. It didn't feel as if Sleel were dead. She would know if he was, somehow. Wouldn't she?

"My medics say that your next egg is still ten days away from arriving where my sperm will meet it. But we can practice in the meantime, no?" He slipped the robe off and it fell to the floor. Certainly his intentions were obvious enough now. All flaccidity was gone.

Wu gathered herself to fight him. Then she saw his expression. That was what he wanted, resistance. Bound as she was, she certainly couldn't stop the rape. But if what he wanted was for her to buck and scream and thus show her fighting spirit—and surely he did, given what he had just said—then she could deny him that.

As he kneeled on the bed between her legs, Wu went limp. And into the Void.

Across the light years the call:
"Dirisha?"
"Yo, deuce. How are you?"
"I got trouble. I need your help."

Dirisha's chocolate face lost its smile. "Geneva!" she yelled. To him, she said, "Where and when, Sleel?"

Sleel felt a rush of emotion but he could not allow it to take him. "Can you get in touch with Bork?"

"Yeah."

"Somebody has kidnapped Kee."

"We'll get her back," Geneva said, coming to stand behind Dirisha. Neither of them had asked who or why. Sleel couldn't believe how relieved that made him feel. No jokes, no questions except "Where," and "When."

"Hey, Dirisha?"

"Yeah?"

"Thanks."

"No problem, Sleel. None at all."

The anger raged in Cierto, burning him into speechlessness. He moved on her, driving, but she lay there, nothing more than a warm and totally unresponsive body. He lifted himself away, still joined to her at the groin, and slapped her face with one hand.

Nothing.

He slapped her again, backhanded. The ring on his middle finger cut her, a small nick over the cheekbone. The scrape oozed a single drop of blood that broke and ran horizontally to the silk sheet.

Still she did nothing else.

He found his voice. "God damn you, you bitch!"

Blood shunted, hormones altered, and his lust dwindled. He shrank, becoming limp, unable to maintain his erection. He shoved hard with his hips, grinding his pubic bones into hers, but his penis bent and slipped out, drooping and defeated.

Dammit!

He shoved himself away from her and jumped from the bed, glaring down at her body. She might as well have been unconscious. Her eyes were open, but they stared into infinity, not acknowledging him.

He stormed out of the room.

Wu knew there might be cameras watching her, so she did not allow the smile she felt to show. But it was there. She had beaten him in the initial encounter. Not a major victory, but one had to take them where one could.

And one battle did not a war make. He would be back.

When Sleel arrived at the port on Rift, he did so under another name. He carried his and Kee's swords in a security-sealed tube, but no other luggage. He took a rental flitter to the port Hilton and checked in.

Somebody tapped lightly at the door to his room. Sleel opened it to see Bork standing there in freight handler's coveralls. Good old Bork, big as a Norse god and twice as strong.

"Sleel. You okay?"

"Better now. Come on in."

Bork moved into the room with a grace befitting a much smaller man. "Dirisha and Geneva are out gathering intel," Bork said. "Superficially the guy's got good security, but it doesn't go back very far. We got the schematics from the guy's house builder, originals are a hundred years old, plus all the additions since. Maps of the grounds, personnel rosters, like that."

Sleel nodded. "Dirisha come up with a plan?"

Bork leaned against a wall. It creaked. "Well, yes and no. She's got some ideas, but she figures the plan ought to be yours."

"Mine? Dirisha is the strategian."

"She says you know the territory better this time around."

Once Sleel would have nodded and smiled and said, "Yeah, I can handle it." Now he wasn't so certain.

"They'll be back in a couple of hours."

Sleel nodded again. "Well. How are things with you, Bork? Still married?"

"Oh, yeah. Veate sends her best."

"You get along okay with your in-laws?"

"Yes. Kinda strange to think of the boss as my father-in-law. He says he and Juete will come if we need them. Dirisha told 'em to sit tight for a while until we checked it out."

Sleel smiled. Emile himself offered to come and help. That's what family was supposed to be about. Damn.

Bork said, "I told 'em I thought that was a good idea, that we didn't need to drag the poor old grandparents out of their dotage yet."

"Grandparents . . . ?"

"Yeah, well, Veate and I, we're gonna have a baby."

Sleel's grin was as big as any he'd had lately. "No shit! Hey, congratulations, Bork! That's great!"

"Yeah, well, I dunno about being a daddy. Course, we'll have you be a designated uncle."

Uncle Sleel. Gods. What a strange thought.

"I'm happy for you, Bork."

"Yeah, I know. You've changed, Sleel."

"I suppose so."

"Don't worry. We'll get her out."

"Yeah."

Wu rubbed at her sore wrists as she paced back and forth in the gym. Cierto had given her a set of workout clothes, blue cotton shirt and pants, and she felt considerably less vulnerable dressed. He was allowing her to exercise, he said, because he wanted her to stay in good shape. The gym had been stripped of possible weapons, however, even wooden practice swords. That was smart on his part. Thinking that she would bear him a child was, on the other hand, pretty stupid. She would kill herself first, and despite whatever medical miracles he might have stashed away, she was pretty sure she could manage it. Master Ven had left his body intentionally, so it could be done. She was pretty sure that if she could move far enough into the Void without making any effort to return, she could shut things down permanently. It would not be her first choice to remedy this situation, but it was there as an option.

So. Given that, what else could she do? She could pretend to give in to him, so that he might get careless that way. If while in the middle of rape her hands were free, she could hurt or maybe kill him. A sword was only an extension of one's own body, after all. Allowing Cierto to think he was enjoying even a moment's pleasure with her, however, had only slightly more appeal than killing herself.

She could fight directly when he or whoever he sent came to

fetch her after her exercise, but that was probably futile in the extreme. If the place wasn't wired for zap, surely her guards would be armed. They could just dart her again and she'd wake up naked and bound again. No, better to stay conscious as much as possible.

None of her solutions so far sounded particularly appealing. Maybe time could give her some other ideas. She hoped so.

Cierto watched her go through a series of warm-ups, the four cameras giving him views of her from that many angles. He had chosen well, he knew. That she had managed to thwart his first assault on her was, in the abstract, admirable. Very clever, the mother of his son-to-be. She had determined what would be the most frustrating for him in the small time before he had entered her body and done it. Once the anger of the moment passed, he had laughed at himself. You did not want it to be too easy, and she is certainly a worthwhile opponent. So much the better. When she is finally brought to heel, it will be that much sweeter.

Yes. Here was a game worth playing, after so long a time of lesser pursuits. She would fight him, but in the end, she would lose. It was only a matter of time. Once she was pregnant, it would become even more complex.

The four holoprojic versions of Kildee Wu danced athletically before him. Such a woman.

He leaned back in his form-chair and sighed deeply. Such a woman.

Dirisha and Geneva hugged Sleel in a long embrace. Like him and Bork, they also wore civilian clothes. He felt warmth fill him. After what seemed a long time, the two women stood away.

"Okay, down to biz," Dirisha said. "Here's what we have. Computer on."

The air danced with the images Dirisha called forth from the computer, and she and Geneva took turns pointing out the information for Sleel.

"—that's the main house," Dirisha said. "Our overfly was in

a commercial liner so we wouldn't spook him. Here's the enhancement . . ."

Sleel watched the pictures and numbers flow past, letting it all sink in and be absorbed. He would view it again, as many times as needed until it became a part of him, memorized to the last detail. For just a moment, the old arrogance flared within him. This Cierto had made a bad mistake. He didn't know who he was fucking with.

The arrogance melted under the memory of Jersey Reason's head bouncing against his leg. But Sleel's determination remained solid. That was a lifetime ago; he had been another man then, a lesser man. Now he was more. And now he wasn't alone.

Hang on, Kee. We're coming for you.

TWENTY-SEVEN

KILDEE WU LAY naked upon Cierto's bed once again, face up. Cierto did not mind that his students saw her that way, and he gestured at her. "Turn her over," he said.

The two hurried to obey.

"Put a pillow under her hips."

They did so.

"Activate the pressor as you leave."

The field reached out and gently caught the nude woman's wrists and ankles, and spread them so that she formed an "X" facedown upon the bed. She moaned softly, still unconscious.

"We will see how strong your resolve is this time," Cierto said.

Sleel considered all the material he had seen and read and the reports from the others. They had all taken elementary precautions, arriving on Rift under false names and registering at different times at different hotels. It was almost impossible that Cierto would or could visually inspect every person who came and went on an entire planet, but even if he did , Bork, Dirisha, Geneva and Sleel had been skinmasked as they arrived, and not wearing their matador gear. So Cierto probably didn't know they were here. They would proceed as if that were the case.

As he lay on the bed in his room, mulling it all around in his mind, he thought about what Dirisha had said earlier. "I'll call it if you want, but I think you ought to do this one."

"Why?"

She shrugged. "You know the players better."

"That's the only reason?"

There was a pause. "You need to do this. I dunno why exactly, but that's what it feels like."

Sleel chewed at his lip. He didn't want to risk Kee's life, he didn't want anything to go wrong, but Dirisha was pretty good when it came to intuition. He'd trusted her too many times not to believe that. Then again, if he fucked it up . . .

"All right," he said. He would take the responsibility.

That had been the choice and he had made it. He hoped to hell it hadn't been the biggest mistake of his life.

Wu awoke. She realized where she was, that she was naked and bound again, her face pressing into the silk-covered cushion, a softer pillow lifting her hips away from the bed. She heard Cierto chuckle behind her. "Awake again?" he said.

Before he could say or do anything else, however, she went back into the Void. If he would play, then he would do it without her.

Cierto stormed into his office. There was a sculpture of a Yuzmekian water ballet on the bookcase next to the door, a lacy thing carved from green crystal from Rangi ya majani Mwezi, the Green Moon in Bibi Arusi. A dozen swimmers seemed to float in the air, held up by nearly invisible strands of the crystal. It had cost a quarter of a million standards and had been a bargain at that price.

Cierto swept his right arm hand in a semicircle and smashed the edge of his hand into the delicate artwork. The rare crystal shattered into thousands of pieces.

He screamed wordlessly. Damn that woman! He would have killed her a dozen times were she not dedicated to bearing his son!

And yet, even in his anger, the Master of the House of Black Steel found a glimmer of admiration for her. In her position, how well would he have fared compared to how she had done?

He sighed and allowed much of his anger to escape with the

used air. Time was on his side, was it not? He had more than nine months to break her, and break her he would.

And after that, she would die.

For three days Sleel and the others studied the material, posed hypothetical solutions and problems to be solved, and worked their way toward the path they would take. Sleel directed the operation.

"Once more," Sleel said. "Communications?"

Bork said, "Scanners on the four main open channels. A com-ferret set to catch the three coded opchans; we've already broken those scramble codes, they're in the comp. He's got two hardwired voice-only lines buried under the ground and both are tapped. If he talks to anybody outside, electronically or vocally, we got him."

"Transportation?"

Geneva said, "He has forty-six registered vehicles, twenty-five of which are stationed at his compound permanently. Sixteen six-passenger flitters, four ten-passenger hoppers, two orbital boxcars, two airbikes and one medical transport, a four-passenger full-ride ambulance. Repairs are done in the compound in his own shop, but repellor harmonic standards inspection must be done yearly at official stations. One of the hoppers and two of the flitters are due to be inspected this month. We have the location outside the compound where the inspections are normally made."

"Defenses?"

Dirisha's turn. "The estate's perimeter fence is electric, four meters tall, and buried two more meters under the ground. Motion sensors set for human-sized masses every fifth post. It's a big fence, so that's not cheap.

"Inside the estate the main buildings are surrounded by another fence, come-see-me zap-rigged, also with sensors. All gates in both fences are manned with human guards backed by deadman dins set to scream and start shooting if the live guard doesn't deactivate them within ten seconds of the gate's opening."

Sleel said. "We have the codes for the dins yet?"

"No."

"Go on."

"They've got doppler spikes for unwanted air traffic, automatic shoot-down if the vehicle doesn't put out the right pulse. Computer, hologram six."

The holoproj flowered with an overhead view of the estate. Dirisha pulled a transponder from her belt and pointed it at the map. "Perimeter missile silos are here, here and here." The pulsing red dot from her transponder lit on the map and caused little purple rockets to strobe to life where she pointed. "There are also four launchers in the inner compound, here, here, here . . . and here."

Sleel and the others nodded.

Dirisha continued. "The main house is protected by door zappers, carbonex doors and full-frame bolts. Windows are class-two denscris where they are externally exposed, except in one place. The walls are ferroconcrete with internal overlapping plates. Computer, hologram eight."

The image altered, fading from that of the estate into an overhead schematic of the main building of the compound. There was a central courtyard, an octagonal design completely surrounded by the house itself. "The windows facing into the courtyard aren't armored; however, there is a rollover roof that can be electrically motored into place to cover the courtyard, from bad weather or attack. The roof is carbonex with denscris skylights."

Sleel looked at the holoproj, then at Dirisha. "So if he hears us coming, he can bottle himself up real tight."

"Like an Aquanian turtle inside its shell. It would take heavy military hardware to dig him out."

And if they threw that kind of weaponry at him, even if they had it, it could easily kill everybody inside.

"Power supplies?"

Bork said, "He's on the 'cast, plus he's got three backup generators, one for the exterior fence, one for the interior fence, one for the house. Missiles and such are all self-powered. You want to see the holo?"

"No, I remember where they are."

So, that was the layout. The bottom drill was plain. They

either went in quiet, so nobody noticed them until it was too
later, or they didn't go in at all. Simple.

Well. Easy to say, anyway. But Sleel had an idea; it had
flown with Dirisha, and it could work. More, there was a
certain amount of irony in it, given that it was only a slight
variation on the way that Cierto had come at Sleel when Jersey
Reason had been killed.

"All right," Sleel said. "We go with my idea for the alpha.
The beta will be what Bork suggested yesterday. Let's lay out
some grids and timings. Give me the interior of the house."

Cierto was calling his art supplier to arrange for a replacement for the sculpture he had shattered. Something grander, he
thought. And more expensive.

A priority beep interrupted the call. Cierto discommed the
art dealer.

"Yes?"

It was one of the men who had been working on Koji to set
up Wu's abduction, but not the head spy. "Patrón," the man
said.

"Where is Verdimez?"

"Dead, Patrón. Killed in the attack on the matador."

Cierto shrugged. So? "Why are you calling me?"

"The assassination of the matador apparently did not go
exactly as planned. We have only just learned of this."

Cierto sat up straighter. "Meaning what?"

"Verdimez and the other three are all dead, Patrón. But the
matador, he—of him there is no sign."

"What? You mean he got away?"

"I cannot say for certain. Only that his body was not among
those the local police found with Verdimez and his team."

"Perhaps you think one of the neighbors came out and stole
the matador's corpse, eh? To use as a garden decoration? Or a
conversation piece for company!"

"Patrón—"

"Idiot! Find him!" Cierto broke the connection.

Damn. It seemed as if the matador had a charmed life. Cierto
would have thought him dead at least three times since they had
met and yet, somehow, he had survived.

He called up the file on the matador. There, there was a good view of him. Cierto put in a com to the Chief of the Planetary Police, an official securely in his pocket.

"Ah, Patrón. How may I assist you?"

"Chief. I am told that an offworld assassin has been hired to kill me. I am hardly worried, but it would probably be wise for an alert for this man to be issued via the Planetary Police force immediately." Cierto touched a control and sent the hologram to the official's computer. "If he makes planetfall, have the port cools detain him. He is to be considered armed, and deadly force is authorized against him."

"Immediately, Patrón," the Chief said.

Cierto sundered the connection and leaned back in his chair. Though the machineries within hummed and tried to soothe him, they did not manage it. This matador was suffused with luck, and such a thing was sometimes better than skill. Perhaps he had been gravely wounded on Koji and had crawled away somewhere to die unseen. Or perhaps he had recognized his mortal danger even if unhurt and fled, knowing he could not prevail against an opponent such as he faced.

Or, perhaps he was at this very moment on his way to assassinate the head of the House of Black Steel as Cierto had told the Chief of the Planetary Police. Worse, perhaps Cierto had underestimated this man. Such mistakes could be fatal, and best if he took steps to correct himself. If this matador showed up knocking at his door, he would soon regret it.

Cierto smiled. Another contest, eh? Break the woman *and* kill her tame matador, two chores instead of the one. Both had proven more formidable than he had expected, but that was fine with him. Better a valiant enemy than not. Victory was much sweeter when the contest required that a man work for it. This victory would be like nectar of the gods to him, the culmination of a life already steeped in winning. A touch of bitterness in that thought. What would a man do for an encore? A question to disturb one, to be sure.

Ah, well. Something would occur to him. It always had.

Geneva said, "Sleel?"

Sleel looked away from the house plans he was studying.

"Looks like Cierto figured out you aren't dead. He's called the local cools and put out an alert for you. Look here."

Sleel glanced at the holoproj over her station.

"Nice picture, Sleel," Bork said from behind him.

Sleel shrugged. "They don't know I'm here yet for sure. I'll stay skinmasked."

"Might make things a little harder. He'll be sharper," Dirisha said.

"So the impossible takes us a little longer," Geneva said. "Right, Sleel?"

"Right," Sleel said. But he felt that cold pit-of-the-stomach rush he got in free-fall. Kee was what was important here. Not Cierto. "Let's keep working, folks. We don't know how much time we have to get this right and—"

Geneva waved Sleel to silence. After a moment of watching her computer and listening to something coming in through her earpiece, she grinned tightly. "That was the transportation chief in Cierto's compound. They're bringing one of the hoppers to the inspection station tomorrow for the repellor check. Tomorrow morning."

Sleel felt his breath catch in his throat, and the coldness in his belly turned to liquid helium. Well. *Now* they knew how much time they had to get ready.

Until tomorrow morning.

TWENTY-EIGHT

THE VEHICLE INSPECTION station was in Riftville, the small town bordering Cierto's estate to the southeast. The place was little more than an open-ended and squarish box full of harmonic scanners and calibration gear. It was in the warehouse district that made up nearly half the town. The building was set back off the road in a large empty patch of paint-lined plastcrete, and there were three lanes leading into the front of the station, all of which also exited from the back. It was fairly busy, with two of the lanes crowded nose-to-tail with maybe eighteen or twenty flitters and a hopper or two; the third lane was blocked by red flashers.

The appearance of Cierto's vehicles here was, as Geneva explained, merely pro forma.

Geneva and Sleel sat in one rental flitter, Bork and Dirisha in the other, both parked so they could watch the inspection station. The blonde said, "Nobody would be so stupid as to offend the richest man on the planet by denying him the codes that say his equipment meets the standards. His mechanics are probably the best for a thousand klicks anyhow, and their equipment is at least as good as anything the government has. What happens is, one of Cierto's drivers brings the flitter or hopper in, one of the inspectors smiles and puts the current magnetic number on the inspection strip. If any of the local enforcement people—a traffic cool or truck regulator—happens to be stupid enough to stop and pull the codes from something registered to Cierto, then it will be found to be in compliance. It wouldn't matter if half the dogs in the city howled their lungs out or the thing shattered windows every time it went by, it would be officially covered."

Sleel just shook his head.

"Hey, power is privilege," Geneva said. "What you want if you're one of the little people is to have some of it run down the walls of the big house where you can lick it off like honey. Maybe if you smile and bow deeply enough it will."

"You think this is gonna work, Geneva?"

She looked at him. "Sure. Why wouldn't it? Because you thought of it and not Dirisha?"

Sleel said nothing.

"You've changed, Sleel. For the better, I think."

"I wish I could be sure of that."

"Whups. Looky here."

The hopper, a late-model ten-passenger Aerodynamatronic Lancer, was gliding into a soft landing in front of the inspection station. The ship had a lot of windows, most of which were photogray thincris and opaqued. Where it wasn't gray it was jet, with a soft gleam that was more like satin than metal or plastic. The vessel was heading for the blocked inspection lane. The lane had been kept so just for Cierto's hopper, according to what Geneva had learned. As the hopper settled, the red flashers went off.

Sleel bit down on the new dentcom lightly. "Bork? Dirisha?"

"We see," Bork said.

This next part was tricky. They couldn't risk jumping the driver where anybody might see it and give a warning. They had to get him out of the hopper and, since he didn't plan to be there any longer than it took for somebody to tap his inspection strip with a magnetic imprinter, he probably did not intend to get out.

"Good luck," Sleel said to Bork.

"Thanks. And to you."

Geneva and Sleel watched as Bork kicked his flitter into the air, made a fairly risky parabola across the street, twisted the craft into a tight turn, and brought it down in the empty lane just as the hopper started to turn in.

The hopper driver hit his warbler and it screeched loud enough to make Sleel's ears ring across the street. Geneva grinned and said, "Man must have been a bird in his last life."

An inspector hurried out of the kiosk to tell the fool driver of the flitter that he could not land there. He leaned against the flitter and said something Sleel could not quite hear on Bork's dentcom. But he heard Bork's reply okay. "Excuse me? You turned the flashers off, so I figured the lane was open."

The inspector mumbled something angrily.

"Okay. I'm gone," Sleel said. He alighted from the flitter and started walking toward Cierto's hopper.

"Yeah, well, I got here first so he can just wait his turn," Bork said.

Rumble mumble mumble.

"No, I don't see how that is."

Rumble mumble.

"Or else what?" Bork said. "Are you threatening me? Step out of the flitter? Why, sure, I'll be happy to."

Sleel saw Bork glide smoothly out of the flitter. He would not wish to be the inspector, suddenly staring up at a man who was nearly two meters tall and wide enough to cause a partial eclipse of the local sun. A long time ago, Sleel had gotten swacked and tried to move Bork. It had cost him a pulled groin muscle and failed utterly.

Behind Bork the driver of Cierto's hopper hit his warbler again. Bork turned and glared at him.

The inspector looked scared, and well he should be. Bork could probably toss him over the line of flitters waiting for inspection without straining himself at all.

The inspector looked at Cierto's driver helplessly.

The people sitting in their flitters took this all in with some amusement. Nobody likes to wait in line, and whatever diversion Bork offered was more interesting than staring at the tail of the flitter in front of you. A couple of the drivers got out for a better look, though none moved closer to Bork. Guy looked like he could pick himself up with one hand and beat you dead with the other. Poor inspector.

Sleel moved closer, keeping the hopper between him and the station.

Bork had not raised his voice but it was apparent that he had no intention of giving up his place in line.

In the flitter, Dirisha played her part. Her voice was high and nasal when she spoke. "Come on, Sim, get back inna flitter and let's go, we don't wanna wind up at the cool station again! Remember that last guy you hit, the one who died?"

Sleel chuckled. Right about now the inspector was probably wishing he had an elephant gun. Or a cloak of invisibility.

The door on the right side of the black hopper slid open and the driver stepped out onto the warm plastcrete. He pulled up his belt and tried to effect a swagger as he walked toward Bork and the pale inspector. Probably he wasn't so stupid as to think he could physically challenge Bork, but he did work for the richest man on the planet, so he could scare him.

This was what Sleel had been waiting for. He moved quickly to the hopper's door and slipped inside. He hurried to one of the seats on the starboard side where the driver wouldn't see him when he returned.

Bork said, "Listen, pal, if you want trouble—who are you, friend?"

The driver's voice was loud enough for Sleel to hear it in his hiding place. "I work for the Patrón! This is his hopper and you are obstructing it!"

Bork played it perfectly. "Cierto? Oh. Oh, well. I . . . didn't know that. Excuse me. I-I-I'll just move my flitter, I don't want any trouble with El Patrón."

Sleel couldn't see it, but he would bet stads to toenail clippers that the driver was grinning as he swaggered back to his vehicle. This is how to get things done; flash the Patrón like a magic wand and poof! trouble go away, right?

Not this time.

Cierto called his chief of security. "Anything unusual?"

"No, Patrón. No one has come or gone without permission. It is as quiet as a tomb."

"Good. See that it stays that way."

Cierto considered things. Perhaps he had made too big a deal about this situation. What could one man do against him? It was wise to be prudent, but there was no point in overreacting.

If the matador ever showed up on his world, he would be dealt with quickly and efficiently. Even luck could only take a man so far.

The hopper's driver was so frightened he was shivering. He had not expected the arm around his throat and the command to land or die. Now he found himself facing four people, including the big man from the inspection station.

"Do you know what this is?" Geneva said. She held up a small glittering object the size of a button. She, like Dirisha and Bork, wore full matador uniforms, including spetsdöds. Sleel was not dressed in the dark gray orthoskins, however. Instead, he wore a pale gray coverall with a cotton sash wound around his waist. Inserted through the sash on his left side were his and Kee's sheathed swords.

"N-n-no."

"It's a microwave-activated popper. Strong enough to blow a man's arm off. Here is the microwave transmitter that will cause it to explode." She waved a tiny rectangle.

The man stared at her.

"Bork, his pants."

Bork grabbed the driver and jerked his pants down. The man was too frightened to struggle.

Geneva approached the man and, as Bork held him still, pulled his underwear to his knees. She bent and stuck the buttonlike device onto the man's scrotum. It clung like a tick where it touched him.

"Skinbond," Geneva said. "Impossible to remove without the proper dissolvant. And if you were willing to give up some of your own skin, it would explode automatically. Dress yourself."

Bork released the driver, who hurriedly pulled his clothing together.

Geneva held up the tiny object in her hand. "I have now squeezed the activator," she said. "If it should slip from my grip . . ."

The already pale man went whiter still.

"Of course, it would not be much of a loss from what I saw," Geneva said, "but surely you would miss them, not to mention the *pain* involved in having one's penis and testicles blown into bloody goo."

"Wh-wh-what do you want of me?"

"Nothing. You are merely to drive back to the estate as you normally would. Only we will be passengers. You will not speak of this to the guards, or you will be . . . less of a man than you are now."

"Th-the P-patrón would kill me for this!"

"Or we can kill you now," Geneva said sweetly. She looked pointedly at the device she still held.

Sleel fought the urge to smile. Geneva looked as if she would not hurt the smallest of insects, which was why she had been given this part to play. Somehow it was more terrifying when a beautiful woman threatened a man. Sleel had agreed to let her convince the driver, and he hadn't known exactly how she planned to do it, trusting Dirisha when she told him not to worry.

"No! I will do as you say!"

As they cruised toward the estate, Sleel, lying hidden next to Geneva, said, "That's an awfully small microwave transmitter you have, lady."

Geneva said, "It's a spetsdöd magazine."

"And the bomb?"

"A button from Bork's dress jacket."

"If Bork was a bird last time, you must have been a cat."

"Dirisha tells me that all the time." She smiled, ever so sweetly.

Sleel was glad she was on his side.

The hope was that they could sail past the gate guards, but there was a backup plan. If the guards grew suspicious, they would take them out. They never had managed to get the din codes, but they would have ten seconds to blow the robots once they got the gates open, which ought to be plenty of time. It might get a little noisy and they would prefer to avoid that, but it was there if needed.

They had lucked out on the weather. Climate control had scheduled a rain shower for the morning and the first drops were pattering the ground and windscreen of the hopper as they approached the estate. The driver brought the vessel down and into the approach lane.

The driver lowered the window next to the guard's kiosk.

"Hola, Bernardo," the driver said nervously.

"Hola, Jose. The Patrón's hopper is inspected?"

"Sí."

"Clear the windows so that I may look inside. We are having an alert, you know."

"I cannot clear them; the stupid fucking control is not working. You will have to leave your dry shack and come look inside yourself."

The rain was coming down harder, enough so that to leave the kiosk and walk around to the hopper's door would involve getting wet.

The guard considered it for a moment. "I don't suppose you have any assassins in there with you?"

Geneva had crawled forward so that the driver could see her lying on the floor next to him. She waved the spetsdöd magazine back and forth. She had been quite specific when giving him his instructions earlier. If the guard should ask anything like that, he was to answer in a certain way.

The driver remembered his lines. He had a lot riding on them; at least he thought he had. "Ah, sí, Bernardo, I have a whole hopper full of them. They are going to blow off my *cojones* if I don't smuggle them inside."

The guard laughed. "You are a funny man, Jose. Go on in."

The rain came down yet harder.

"One to go," Bork said.

Sleel nodded.

Wu faced herself, watching the mirror in the gym. Probably was one-way plastic, she figured. Surely she was being watched. Well. There was nothing to be done about it. And no point in allowing herself to get physically weaker. She practiced her sword forms, holding an imaginary weapon. All of her invisible opponents looked exactly like Cierto. After she had slain him a dozen times, she felt a little better. Not much, but a little.

At the inner gate, the guard said, "Bernardo tells me you have a hopper full of assassins who are going to blow your balls off if I don' let you in. Maybe I would like to see that."

The driver said, "Fuck you, Aaron."

"You wish you were man enough. You will be at the poker game tonight?"

"Sí. I hope so."

"Good. Then I will take more of your wages than I did last time." With that, the guard opened the inner gate.

"Criminal," Dirisha whispered. "Where did he get these guards, from a mental institution? Jesu Damn."

Now to the garage. Once past that, they would be on their own, without the cover of the hopper. Sleel missed his spetsdöds. He would have to trust that the others could shoot well enough to get them into the main house. This trusting other people was a scary business. He didn't much like it. But it was too late to turn back now. Time to dance the dance.

TWENTY-NINE

THE DRIVER LANDED the hopper just outside the larger of the two maintenance buildings, at the end of the row of vehicles already parked there.

Geneva said, "Here, catch."

Before the startled driver could do more than twitch in horror as what supposedly was a microwave transmitter tumbled toward him, Geneva shot him with her spetsdöd. Mercifully, the driver fell unconscious.

"Shame on you, brat," Dirisha said.

Geneva had already turned to the gear bag and was assembling one of the pair of assault rifles. The weapon was a 14mm reactionless carbine. A superhigh-density battery and capacitor would put a few hundred thousand volts into a liquid propellant, transforming it into a plasma that in turn would kick a thumb-sized slug of expended uranium up to a muzzle velocity approaching two thousand meters a second. It might not be able to punch through military-grade denscris armor but it should make such armor ring as loudly as a gone-mad giant with a heavy hammer.

Dirisha began assembling the other carbine. It took the two women all of forty-five seconds to finish, then lock and load.

"We ready?" Sleel said. His voice was tight.

"Thirty by thirty," Dirisha said.

"There're the bikes," Bork said, pointing.

"Timers," Sleel said. "Two minutes from . . . now."

"It's gonna work," Dirisha said, slapping Sleel on the shoulder. "No sweat."

"Listen," Sleel began, "listen, I—you people . . . you're—I—"

"Shut up, Sleel," Geneva said, smiling. "We're on the clock. Tell us afterward."

"All right. Go," Sleel said.

Dirisha and Geneva left the hoppers first, assault carbines slung over their shoulders. They ran for the airbikes Bork had pointed out.

"There's a nice one," Bork said, nodding toward a two-seat sport flitter parked three vehicles down from the hopper.

"Let's do it."

The two alighted from the hopper and ran toward the flitter. Sleel's timer flashed off the seconds, counting from 2:00 toward zero.

Bork reached the flitter first. If there was anybody about, Sleel didn't see them. A little rain was a wonderful thing, if it was timed right. Nice to have climate control on your side, even if they didn't know it.

The big man used the override card they'd bought from a thief. It had worked on several different flitters in practice, but there was a moment of worry as Bork jammed the thin superconductor sandwich into the door slot.

It worked. The master key scrambled the flitter's lock codes in just under four seconds and the doors gull-winged. Bork slid into the driver's seat, Sleel to his left in the passenger's chair. The override card worked on the ignition and power-up as fast as it had on the door locks. The flitter came on line with a throaty rumble.

"Nice machine," Bork said.

"Fifty-seven seconds," Sleel said. He held the two swords in his left hand, feeling the sweat on his palm make the enameled wood of the sheaths yet slicker. Here he was going into a modern attack scenario with weaponry that was nearly the same as a man might have carried four thousand years ago. It was probably as foolish a thing as he had ever done. And absolutely the right thing, as crazy as it seemed.

"We'll just let the repellors mellow out some," Bork said. "No point in trying to lift and getting a stall, is there?"

Thirty of the longest seconds in Sleel's life went by, wallowing like broken-finned fish of iron trying to swim in a sea of mercury.

"Okay. What say we lift?" Bork said.

The sporty flitter bounded into the air.

Wu was in the gym, halfway through her warm-up, when she heard a bone-rattling gong. It was not a sound natural to the house, she knew that immediately, and she could feel the tension in the air following the noise. More, the ringing continued, altering, as if someone were using a hammer on metal. It was at once familiar and yet not quite like anything she had heard before. What—?

She recognized it. It was the sound of a denscris bell, only much larger than the ones the priests in a zendo tapped with their wooden mallets.

Outside the gym somebody yelled, the sound doppdopplering as the speaker ran past.

Trouble.

Wu smiled. Trouble for Cierto was something she minded not at all. What was it? Or, more important, *who* was it?

Wu opened her senses, reaching out, shifting from normal sight and hearing to that elusive state of *zanshin*.

Sleel! She could feel him.

Sleel had come for her.

Sitting in the control room and watching his prisoner on the monitors, Cierto felt the *casa* vibrate with the ringing of the external window armor. He knew immediately what was going on, and he could guess who was responsible. That cursed matador had gotten past his defenses! Dammit!

Cierto activated the vox circuit on his security comp. "Close the courtyard roof!"

The man would play the Devil and all his demons getting into the *casa* once it was zipped up. There were guards out there, a dozen or so of them, plus a score of students in the *casa*. One man, no matter how adept, could not defeat that many on his own.

The outside cameras scanned, looking for the attacker.

An airbike went zipping past, a black woman perched on it dressed in the uniform of the matadors, firing a long gun.

Ah. So the one called Sleel had help. How many?

Cierto activated the house broadcaster. "To arms! We are under attack! All students draw swords!" Then he grabbed his own sword and ran from the control room. He would go and see for himself. He was no backline general to direct his troops from the rear.

"Going to be a little tight," Bork said, as the flitter dropped toward the courtyard. The little vehicle fell like a fat stone in heavy gee toward the narrowing gap. The roof was three-quarters shut and closing quickly as the flitter dived for the opening.

The understruts of the flitter scraped the moving edge of the roof as the little craft skinned through. A few millimeters thicker and they would have been snagged.

Sleel let out his held breath. "Damn, Bork."

"There's a nice window," Bork said. He pulled the flitter up just before it touched the top of a large evergreen topiary ball and headed for a wide expanse of what Sleel hoped was clear plastic or thincris.

"Hang on," Bork said. He killed the power.

The flitter's nose smashed into the window. Plastic. The material shattered and the flitter slid to a halt, knocking over a potted plant and a couch in the room beyond the window, digging a deep furrow in the rug and floor.

"And we'd like to thank you for flying Bork Transportation," the big man said. "Come again real soon."

The two of them scrabbled out of the flitter. "I got the east side," Bork said.

"Call if you see her," Sleel said.

"You got it, boss."

Sleel ran through the hallway toward Cierto's security control. According to the schematic he'd studied, it should be just around the next—ah. Company.

Two young men with swords stood in the hallway. They saw Sleel and turned to face him.

Sleel had stuck his and Kee's swords into his sash. He thumbed the catch on his weapon and suddenly his other hand grew a black razored finger. He wasn't even aware of the draw; one second it was in the sheath, the next it was just *there*.

The first one came at him high. Sleel ducked under the slash and skewered the man's heart, driving his sword's point up under the sternum, then spinning away.

The second one leaped back, but Sleel's twirl brought the edge of his sword across the man's throat in a cut that ran nearly the length of the blade. The startled man dropped his own weapon and clutched at the gaping wound in his neck.

His new sword was blooded.

Sleel darted into the control room.

Kee! On the holoproj screens marked "Gym."

Sleel paused for a second. He put his sword down, picked up the keyboard control and broke it in half, over his right knee. The holoproj images scrammed and turned into balls of swirling blue lint. Sleel picked up a chair and used it as a mallet, smashing everything he could reach. Climate controls, house electronics, com systems, whatever. That ought to give them something to think about.

As he ran toward the gym, he triggered his dentcom.

"Bork?"

Bork's reply was, "Lemme call you back, I'm kinda busy here."

"Dirisha? Geneva? You two okay?"

"Hey, Sleel," Dirisha came back. "It's like swatting drunk flies. I'm surprised these guy can find their dicks to go pee. We've darted nine—"

"—make that ten," Geneva cut in.

"—ten of them," Dirisha said. "You need any help, we can get there; the front door just kicked open."

"Yeah, I killed the security board," Sleel said. "So far we're going okay. Aren't we, Bork?"

"Yeah, sorry I couldn't talk a second ago, there were four guys waving swords at me. I had to shoot pretty fast."

"I'm on my way to the gym; that's where Kee is."

"We'll keep the pot stirred so nothing burns," Dirisha said. "Hurry up, though. We're getting rained on out here."

Sleel ran.

The gym door was still locked and the electronic controls were shorted out, but there was a manual release. Sleel pulled the mechanical handle and the worm gear disengaged, popping the door backward on its track enough so he could shove it open.

Kee was inside crouched defensively. She raised from her stance. "About time," she said.

He pulled her sword from his sash and tossed it to her. "I brought you a present. You forgot it when you left home."

"Thanks."

"And look what our friendly old balloo Bergamo made for me." Sleel waved his own bared sword.

"Nice."

"Let's leave. This party is getting too raucous for my taste." He started for the door. "Oops. Company!"

Sleel backed away from the entrance. People were rushing down the hall from both directions, nine or ten of them. "There another way out?"

"Not that we can use."

Sleel and Kee backed farther away from the gym's exit.

The students began to pour into the room. Nine of them, all bearing swords.

"Don't attack!" came a command from behind the influx of students. Cierto.

He entered the room, his own sword held ready.

"Your luck has just run out, matador. Ready yourself for death."

"Through me first," Kee said, sliding in between Sleel and Cierto.

"Move!" both men said together.

"I don't want to damage you," Cierto said. "Not yet."

"Not your choice," she said. "I have a blade. If you don't kill me, I sure as hell *will* kill you."

Cierto stood still, apparently considering it. "Very well." He pointed his sword at Sleel. "Slay him."

The students had obviously not practiced a mass attack with

this many against one before. They got in each other's way as they jockeyed to move in on Sleel. That there were nine of them in a small space was to Sleel's advantage. He moved to his left and several of them smacked into one another trying to shift to cover him.

Sleel leaped at the crowd.

Wu had time to see Sleel wade into the mob, sword whirling, before Cierto focused on her. Likely he did not call what he did *zanshin*, nor the place where his soul went the Void, but the effect was the same. She barely had time to make the shift herself to meet his charge.

Cierto would not try to play with this woman; he had seen her work, and she was too dangerous to risk anything less than full effort. He became his sword, and all else faded as he went to cut her down. It would be the fight of his lifetime and much as he wanted a son, there were other women who could bear him one. She had chosen to die. So be it.

Sleel felt the stretching of Chronos begin again, but this time he was faster than his opponents. He cut at them as though they were sword dummies put there for him to practice upon. They moved, but were mired in the thick air, and it was his weapon that found its targets and not theirs. Even as he danced through them unharmed, Sleel realized that this was still not the place of no-mind of which Kee had told him. He was aware, but still able to be distracted by the clink of Kee's sword against Cierto's.

He glanced that way, barely avoiding being stabbed as a result, and hastily returned his attention to the task at hand.

Move fast or die, Sleel!

Cierto cut and Wu blocked—
—she riposted with a stab for his face—
—he parried and tried a backhanded sweep—
—but he missed when she scooted back—
—then she thrust for his belly, only—

—he blocked it down and reversed his edge for an uppercut, but—

—she slapped his blade aside with the flat of her own and slashed at his exposed leg—

—missing by a hair when he dodged left and switched hands for a cut at her eyes—

—and she blocked and leaped back as he also hopped away. Five seconds had elapsed since his first cut.

Wu stepped in and faked a cut to his head, turning it into a looping slice for his ankle—

—which he vaulted over, extending his own slightly longer weapon to pierce her throat, but—

—she parried and thrust for his chest, but—

—was met by his stop-thrust, that tangled his guard with her *tsuba* as both leaped to their right, breaking the connection.

Nine seconds had passed.

They both leaped again in—

Six of Sleel's attackers were dead or wounded badly enough to be out of action. The other three had survived by staying away. One turned and ran for the exit as Sleel started for her. The other two split and tried to get behind him, but he twisted in time to jam his sword out low. One of the pair tripped over the extended blade. The other one lunged, but his fallen companion got in his way.

Sleel dropped and chopped down at the one on the ground, catching him across the back of the head. It made a sound like somebody hitting a ship's hawser with a heavy board. Sleel had to pry the sword up from the nearly bisected brainpan.

Sleel jumped over the latest dead man and brought his sword up over his head as if he were going to try a body-splitter stroke. The attacker jerked his sword up in a horizontal block, and Sleel twisted under it and kicked the man in the solar plexus, stealing his breath. The man sagged, and Sleel side-kicked him again, knocking him sprawling.

He turned to see how Kee was doing.

Cierto lunged and tried a five-move combination, cut, cut, slash from the right, stab, lunge from the groin—

—Kee backed away, blocking and parrying, stopping all five strikes, then offering a combination of her own, lunge, high and low extensions, figure-eight slashes, an uppercut rising from the floor—

Cierto dodged or blocked or danced away.

The two of them spun away and stood facing each other across five meters of what had become a very bloody floor, none of it theirs.

"We . . . are . . . evenly matched," Cierto said, amazement in his voice.

"Yes," Wu said, as amazed as her opponent. Though she was still in the Void, it relaxed its hold on her.

"My turn," Sleel said from behind her.

"No," she said. She didn't try to look at him.

"I'm not asking you. Move."

He came to stand next to her, and now she did glance at him. There was a new tone in his voice, something she hadn't heard from him before. It threw her. For a moment, her concentration was broken.

The Void let her go.

Instantly Cierto felt it. He charged.

Wu reached again for *zanshin*, knowing it was too late.

She had lost her Edge, Cierto saw. And the matador, for all his skill, did not have the Edge at all.

Now he would kill them both!

Sleel saw the man coming to hurt the woman he loved.

In that overstretched strand of time, so thin that it was almost beyond measure, Sleel understood that what he felt for Kee was indeed love. A thing for which he had known the words but never the feelings. He had hidden it for months from himself, denied that it existed, pretended to blindness. He had refused to allow it into his soul, but now that he saw it, touched and tasted and smelled and felt it, there was no way he could ever keep it out again. Amazing how one man could harbor so much stupidity, so much ignorance, so much fear. And now it was gone, replaced with a new awareness.

And with the awareness of love came too the awareness of everything else.

Sleel discovered the Void and it embraced him.

Wu prepared for her end, knowing she had less than a second to manage it.

Death came for her—

Sleel blurred past. Razored black steel clashed against an equally keen black steel cousin, and cried like a bell.

Death stopped: his curse rose over the war song of hard metal: "*Dios*—!"

His face very nearly touching Cierto's, Sleel drew himself up suddenly and snapped his blade down with a speed Wu had never seen matched. It was inhumanly quick. The edge of Sleel's sword caught Cierto across the right wrist—and cut through as if the flesh and bone were no more than a thin twig left too long in the sun.

Cierto screamed as his hand, still holding the sword, fell to the floor. He clutched at the spouting stump of his wrist and screamed again, falling to his knees.

Sleel raised his sword and looked at the wounded man.

Eons ran past, entropy enfolded the cosmos, the heat death of the Universe came and went.

Sleel shook his head and lowered his weapon as Cierto fell onto his side, his blood pumping in small spurts onto the gym floor.

Sleel moved toward Kee, turning his back on Cierto.

"You okay?"

She nodded. "Welcome home," she said. "Now you understand."

"Yes."

Cierto came up from the floor, his sword now clutched in his remaining hand, his face contorted in madness.

"Sleel!" she yelled, lunging past him.

The point of Wu's weapon pierced Cierto's left eye, and his momentum carried him forward enough so that the end of the sword exited from the back of his head.

Her warning was unnecessary. Wu looked over to see that Sleel had also spun and driven his blade into Cierto, hard enough so that the *tsuba* pressed against the startled man's breast, most of the sword going through Cierto's torso.

It was a still holograph, a picture frozen motionless, breaths caught and held.

Cierto started to fall, and both Wu and Sleel pulled their swords free.

The man wore a puzzled frown. "You . . ." he began, never to finish. Instead, the Master of the House of Black Steel collapsed for the final time. And died.

THIRTY

"IT'S QUIET OUT here," Dirisha said.

Sleel looked at the bodies on the gym floor, then at Kee. He triggered his dentcom and responded. "In here too," he said.

Bork arrived and looked around inside. "Man," he said.

Sleel looked back at Kee. "Listen," he began, "listen, there's something I need to say."

She looked at him, not speaking.

"I—I love you."

Her smile would have shamed the full moon for brightness. "Oh, I know that."

"You know?"

"Of course. I've known for weeks. It's you who always does things the hard way."

Sleel stared at her.

"I love you, too," she said. "I have all along. I just had to wait for you to get it before I could say anything."

Bork wandered over. "Hello," he said.

"This is Bork," Sleel said.

Bork smiled down upon them. "So, you two going to make it formal?"

Sleel blinked. "Make what formal?"

"A cohab contract. Marriage."

"What makes you think—?"

"Come on, Sleel. You might as well be wearing a big flashing sign. You two look like Veate and I must have looked back when we first met. A blind man could see that."

Sleel started to say something flippant, but stopped. Well. Bork was right, after all. "I think maybe we are." He looked at Kee.

"Of course," she said. "There was never any doubt."

Bergamo and Vivian stood outside the foundry as the flitter landed. Sleel and Kee emerged from the vehicle and walked over to where the other couple stood.

"Your sword has proven itself satisfactory?" Bergamo said.

"Yes," Sleel said.

"I expected no less. It is a passable blade. To what do we owe this visit, then?"

Sleel and Kee glanced at each other, then back at Bergamo. "We're, ah, looking for work," Sleel said.

"Work? Both of you? Here? Doing what?"

Sleel pretended to look grave. "I don't know. We thought maybe you might be able to find something."

The old man could not fully hide his smile, though he tried. "Well. I suppose we might have some chores that nobody else wants to do. Come inside. One doesn't get things done standing around in the sun chatting idly." He turned and walked into the foundry. Behind him, Vivian beamed at Sleel and Kee.

Kee reached over and caught Sleel's hand with hers. "You're sure?"

He squeezed her hand. "Yeah. I'm sure. About everything."

And for the first time in his life, he was.